Standards and Duty

Louise Hazeldine

1

There is nothing more important in your life
than the people you choose to be part of it.

"By the power vested in me, I now pronounce you husband and wife."

With these words from the mouth of the priest at the altar at the head of the church, an echoing coming from the high, hollow ceiling, a rush of emotion ran through her. Pride, happiness, joy, love and a feeling of overwhelming contentment expanded from her heart through her veins to every, last nerve ending she possessed in her body. If it were possible for her to glow with this sense of wonderment, she would have been bright as the sun on a cloudless day. And yet, concurrently, a feeling of sadness, despair and anguish flowed through her. Her emotions were threatening to spill out of her in the form of tears; conspiring to ruin the moment, the day, and reveal her anguish. A smile was spread over her face and indeed within her heart, but a small, yet loud, part of her howled in dismay for the person who was missing - unable to witness this moment of happiness, the start of this journey.

Chapter 1 - Foundations

And so, I stand here, a crossroads before me. A decision needs to be made, and yet I am still cursing the circumstance which brought me to this place.

But, you see, Zara and I had been firm friends since the moment we met; so, what else was I supposed to do?

We had formed an immediate attachment over our favourite rugby players which had put us in the bracket of lifelong friends, with a sisterly bond, the instant we told each other our names. Zara was two years older than me, taller than I was, prettier than I was, and yet I adored her without restraint. Blonde hair and blue eyes, a wide smile and a personality that warmed the coldest of hearts; she was the most brilliant person I had ever met. We met when I was nine years old, she was just turned eleven. Though I was old for my age, she never made me feel like I was harassing her, never made me feel like I was intruding on her ever-growing popularity; and, always made the time to answer my letters or telephone calls. She and I lived very far apart, you see, and to see each other was always our precious time, and oh! how we made the most of it. Our parents knew that we each had sensible heads on our shoulders, and trusted us enough to be without their supervision when we spent time together; times and places seemed much safer back then than they do now, of course. Over the years, Saturday mornings at the shopping centre before the game became a must for us as I gained more independence. We went shopping for makeup, for clothes, for shoes, for handbags, earrings, for everything in between. We posed for photographs in the booths in the shopping centre, each taking two of the strip of four photographs as mementos of our special Saturdays. We spent time together during school holidays; spending days at the theme parks, in the park, at the cinema, going bowling, and having too many sleep-overs at each other's houses to count. We were invited on each other's family holidays: Zara came to Canada with us; I went to Greece with her; and once both sets of families spent a bank holiday weekend at a quaint cottage in Wales near Betws-y-Coed. We both valued our shared time building our bond, cementing the foundation of friendship which would last until one of our deaths in a nursing home, next door to one another. We knew we would be friends forever.

After the first few months of us meeting and swapping information passed, we met two boys of around Zara's age at the rugby: Robert and Michael. The chemistry between Zara and Robert was apparent immediately. They just seemed to fit together; two wonderful halves of an even more perfect whole. They became best friends. Inseparable. It was shocking for two people so young to experience such intensity immediately upon meeting. There was nothing inappropriate at that time, of course, I realise now that some of their other friends had wondered about this as they got older, but no two people have ever been so clearly fated for one another as Zara and Robert were. No two people had ever been so clearly the meaning of each other's lives as they were. He introduced her to everything she had no knowledge of in her life, and vice versa. For Michael and I, the chemistry took a while longer to develop. Shy hellos and awkward conversations, as Robert and Zara indulged themselves in the discovery of all facts about each other, led to Michael and I beginning to do the same. I was so young, of course, and immature by comparison. We had begun tentatively, shy and embarrassed when we spoke, nervous when asking questions about each other's lives and interests except for discussions of rugby where we both showed our passionate sides. Over the course of the next few years, we became a close group of four: Mimi and Michael, Zara and Robert. Robert and Michael became best friends too, despite them not attending the same school. Zara used to dream of the day when we four would be old enough to be married. She knew from the start she and Robert would spend the rest of their lives together, and she hoped for the same for Michael and me. At the time I agreed; my increasing knowledge of him led me to develop feelings for him, and I felt he was almost perfect. Taller than me, blonde hair, brown eyes, kind and caring, considerate yet passionate, he was everything I had ever dreamed of and more.

It was fitting then, that Michael and I began our intimate relationship at a rugby game where, unannounced and unexpected, he kissed me. I had been growing closer to Michael in the previous few months, undertaking activities on our own, without Robert and Zara's company, and this led to an increasing sense of closeness between Michael and I. A few glances lasting just a little too long causing us both to blush yet somehow unable to look away from each other, his arm touching mine every now and then, lingering rather than being instantly withdrawn, led to an unexpected yet pleasant tingling sensation running through my body. Throughout the months, the glances turned into penetrating stares, the touches on the arm developed into a decrease in personal space between us. I had sensed the difference between our previous friendship and the approaching breach of the boundary towards something more, yet I had not expected so soon the crescendo of emotion and physical chemistry to culminate as it did when Michael leaned forward and kissed me. For me, the kiss had been too hard at first, overwhelming even as his hand grabbed the back of my neck too ferociously, the tension between us erupting whilst the opportunity was apparent. When Michael realised I was not refusing his advances, the pressure from his mouth to mine eased slightly, allowing for the tingling, which I had experienced within my body through him touching my arms in the previous months, to begin within my lips and spread down towards my neck and into my spine, creating an extraordinary, unfamiliar sensation deep inside my stomach. My head was whirling with the sensations which were passing through me as his mouth moved against mine, our lips and tongues hungry for each other, the chemistry between us may have taken a long while to develop, yet

11

I was feeling the joy of the momentum we had gathered through the long months before. Breathless and dizzy, I ended the kiss in order to breathe. Looking up into his soft brown eyes, searching for confirmation he had enjoyed kissing me as much as I had enjoyed being kissed, I realised I was holding onto his arms, too tightly, for support. Michael had completely startled me. For not one second had I ever thought what I had heard described was true, yet Michael cemented all the movie legends; he really had made me go weak at the knees. I began to pull him back towards me, and he obliged by leaning down and kissing me again. An eternity seemed to pass and, at that moment, at that most innocent period in my life, I would have spent the same amount of time over again kissing him.

For the next two years or so, Michael and I spent much of our spare time with each other, kissing, mostly, as teenagers are so fond of doing. The relationship had grown from a solid friendship into that of boyfriend and girlfriend. Unlike most people our age, Michael and I were fortunate to have a foundation on which to build our relationship, and with this came complete honesty with one another, trust and respect. Zara and I were closer than ever, almost like sisters. She had been the first person I had told about Michael and I kissing, and as teenage girls we had mulled over every last sensation it had caused throughout my body, just as she had disclosed the same to me when she and Robert had first become an item. I appreciated the gravity of what she had previously told me much more after I had experienced it first-hand for myself. And so, when the question of moving the physical side of our relationship forward between Michael and I arose, as was becoming the teenage fashion of the era, Zara was the person I turned to for advice and guidance. Knowing that Zara and Robert had not yet been fully intimate, and were considering the same, Zara wondered if both she, and especially I, were not too young to be considering the notion of the indulgence. Zara, Robert and Michael were all Catholic, I was not. They had been taught a stronger sense of morals, boundaries and consequences than my less strict upbringing. Whereas, of course, my parents had guided me to believe waiting was the correct action, and that I should not feel pressured into doing anything with which I was not comfortable, and to be safe and use precautions, I did not fear the internal sense of dread and consequence which had been established in my boyfriend, my best friend and her boyfriend. Apprehensive yet impatient, I had pursued the notion of intimacy with Michael some months after he and I had first become an item. He had said that out of his respect for me, he had wanted to wait till I had felt ready. He had said he was nervous, and hesitant, yet he indicated his desire whenever we spoke about it. He and I had gone through the uncomfortable and embarrassing practicalities, been to the clinics to gain all the advice each of us needed, and were prepared. He and I just had to find the right time. Zara was very traditional and hoped that she may be able to wait until she and Robert had married, yet she had said that being with Robert caused the traditional side of her personality to be pushed to the back of her mind; the physical instincts foregrounding any conscious thought whenever she was in such proximity with Robert. She had told me that she felt she was willing to give in to every physical urge whenever he kissed her for a sustained period of time. I was able to completely understand what she had described to me, as I too had felt this whenever Michael and I were alone together, and finally after two years of being his girlfriend, I could not wait any longer.

The day Michael and I took each other's virginity had begun like any other day we spent together. He had met me at the station and we had taken the bus to town, had an indulgent lunch at a sandwich shop, complete with chocolate cake afterwards, and spent a couple of hours window shopping, comparing imaginary purchases. We had always enjoyed imagining what we would buy when we were older, and we had careers and an income of our own. For Michael, a lot of music was on the list, my list contained more clothing and shoes. Occasionally, we used to look inside the jeweller's window and Michael used to murmur in my ear that one day he would be able to buy me a ring and we would be happy for the rest of our lives. It was days like that which made me joyful and I am sure that I used to walk around with a beaming smile across my face, looking deranged. But it was not every girl who had the boy of her young dreams to herself, feeling the same way as I did, imagining a future together. After we had been window shopping, Michael and I had gone to his house, which we often did, before dinner, only to find it empty. His parents had left him a note stuck onto the refrigerator by a magnet bought on a holiday they had been on, to Brazil: his brother and sister had gone out for the day with them and would not be back until late. There were instructions from his mother on what was to be eaten for dinner, she had made some shepherd's pie to be reheated for us, and a list of emergency telephone numbers were at the bottom, should he need to contact anybody for help. There was a reminder of his grandparents' telephone number, lest he forget, the local chemist and his parents' best friends, just in case.

With the house to ourselves, Michael and I began to watch a film on the television, but it was not long before we were distracted, and his hands had begun to wrap around my waist, pulling me closer to him on the dark brown Chesterfield. For half a moment, the feeling was uncomfortable as my sit-upon met with cold leather; a shock in comparison with the spot I had warmed for myself. I gazed up at him and, as his mouth hungrily met mine, I thought I knew that it was the right time. My body felt like it could not wait any longer and neither, it seemed, could he. The delicious feeling of his mouth moving down my neck sent a moan from my throat, the likes of which had never occurred before. Michael stopped kissing me and looked up; I tilted my head and smiled at him, whilst my heart shook with nerves, reassuring him he had not hurt me, my gaze assuring him I wanted him to continue. He smiled back at me, his soft brown eyes glistening, and nodded slightly to show he understood that the sound which had escaped my lips was one of apparent desire and pleasure, and he resumed his attentions upon my neck. My hands tentatively moved over his smooth muscular arms, making me appreciate the effect his rugby training had had upon his physique within the last eighteen months. As his hands slid down my legs, moving to the inside of my thighs, I stiffened, my breath stuck in my lungs unable to escape. Michael stopped again, looked down at me and suggested moving to the bedroom. I agreed, eager to be in a more private place for this moment which would certainly change our lives and our relationship forever, hoping it would subdue my unease. As he led me upstairs by the hand, my breath became rapid and shallow, shaking as it escaped my nose. My feet would not work properly, becoming unusually uncoordinated as they caused me to miss one step and trip up another rendering me unsteady as I ascended to the first floor. My mind was racing too much to cope with the basic motor skills of moving myself forwards and upwards concurrently, resulting in a flush of blood to my face as embarrassment enveloped me. I was worried about the mechanics of what Michael and I were about to undertake; I had long wondered if and how we would know what to do. I had also agonised over Michael and I being naked in front of each other – a nagging doubt had always been in the back of my mind that this was something I was not supposed to be doing – perhaps it was my age playing on my conscience, I suppose I was too young to tell; and yet, at that moment, I could not stop myself from wanting to be with him. As we entered his bedroom, he turned to look at me. Feeling my cheeks flush once more, for a different reason, I knew that they had turned an uncomfortable shade of red under his gaze; I fought my embarrassment, letting my desire for physical intimacy and relief claim victory over my feeling of awkwardness. I reached out for him with a trembling hand and moved myself into his body, burying my head in the hollow of his neck, a place where my head seemed to fit almost perfectly, just so that he would not be able to read the emotions so plainly displayed on my face. The sweet smell of his skin combined with his hand touching my lower back caused something deep inside me to

15

somersault. "Mimi, I love you" he whispered, and I was shocked by his sincerity. His voice was so pure, true and loving, I knew at that moment Michael and I would be connected forever.

As he undressed me, he took time to pay attention to what felt like every last inch of my body, clearly enjoying the experience. I tried to put out of my mind the feeling of unease, discomfort, at being separated from my clothes. Slowly and steadily, he awakened every nerve inside me, allowing me no respite between the waves of pleasure which were beginning to lap at my extremities. As I took my turn to remove his shirt, and then his trousers, with hands whose tremble had increased to a distinct shake, I flushed at the sight of him. I had never appreciated the male form in all its glory before this moment, and I was extremely self-conscious to know he was watching, and studying, my reaction to him. Despite this, I could not help but want to press every part of myself against him. Hurriedly, we toppled onto the bed, side by side, using our hands and eyes and mouths to explore one another. The sensations pulsing through my body were unlike any I had ever experienced before. As he pressed himself against me, I felt the somersaults inside me deepen in intensity and quicken in pace in reaction to the firmness I felt against my lower stomach. It was such an odd feeling to have something so much warmer than my own, unsheathed, skin being forced to try to find a place to settle between him and me. Eventually, his hands parted my legs, and at that moment I wanted nothing more than to let him inside me, the hollow pooling feeling almost made me plead for his presence within me, yet Michael, passionate and caring, considerate and kind moved down away from me. Just as I was about to ask him where he was going, he caused the most intense feeling to run through my body as he moved his tongue between my legs. Slowly he ran his tongue from my knee up my inner thigh to the top and then paused. He did not pepper my skin with kisses, rather licked my skin in a manner akin to trying to prevent melting ice-cream from dripping down its cone and escaping. It was not the most pleasant action, but the larger sensation it caused was something which I could not ignore. He repeated the same motion on the other leg, making me realise I had never before known my inner thighs were so sensitive. For the briefest of moments, wonderment washed through me as I questioned how on earth he had ever learned to do this, how he had become aware of what to do to make me relish him so much so soon. I had always heard that boys read about these things in magazines, and shared information with each other from generation to generation, but until that moment I never really believed that they did. These thoughts quickly left my mind as he used his thumbs to part me, and slowly ran his tongue around the outside of my most sensitive area. I gasped, revelling in the delicious feeling, hoping for it to continue endlessly, yet wanting more, desiring a greater feeling. His speed increased just slightly as Michael began to use his tongue in a lapping motion between my legs; long, firm strokes of his tongue caused me to squeeze my eyes shut as I half squealed in joy and excitement, and half screamed because I just wanted more. At that point, it did not matter that I had felt that what I was doing was wrong. It did not matter that I had been so uncomfortable. I relented to teenage hormonal desires. As he moved upwards, towards my most sensitive spot, the anticipation was almost as strong as the sensations he was causing me to feel. And then he connected with my source of pleasure. Despite the anticipation and yearning, nothing could have prepared me for the intensity of his tongue, the pressure, the texture, and the frequency as he rubbed and licked between my legs. The feeling made my body buck in reaction to the electricity which was flowing through me. A guttural scream from deep inside me escaped my mouth, and this only served to intensify the concentration of attention Michael paid to my pleasure. Combining his fingers with his tongue he caused me to writhe about on the bed, thrashing my head in between the pillows trying to muffle my screams. Gasping for breath, I became unable to differentiate between up and down, left and right, consciousness and unconsciousness. For what seemed like an eternity I struggled to breathe, unable to do anything but be overwhelmed and consumed by the furious forces of pure pleasure running through every part of my body. For just a second, the world went black as I reached the climax, my first climax, of my physical reaction to Michael all too quickly, then before I could remember where I was, his face was suddenly in front of mine, and I felt what I had been longing for; I felt his presence inside me. Stinging a lot, at first, causing me to take hissing breaths between my teeth, I eventually felt myself relax around him as my body shifted to accommodate his length and girth, and as I lifted my head up to kiss him he whispered, "I love you, Mimi." As our mouths began to move against one another, I felt him move within me, slowly and shallowly at first, then with more and more momentum until I was clutching at his arms, his back, running my hands over his chest, and somehow, able to wind my legs around his to draw him in deeper inside me. I suddenly realised this was the cure for the hollow feeling which overcame me each time he and I were in close proximity to each other. I stared at his face as he reached the climax of his physical reaction to being inside me and I knew he had not regretted what he and I had done, and that he had enjoyed it as much as I had.

For a long while afterward, Michael and I lay in each other's arms, I was exhausted; and yet every nerve in my body felt more alive than ever before. It was only when I felt the aftermath of his enjoyment leave me, as the cold air smothered my skin, lowering my body temperature to an uncomfortable level, and I realised how sore I had become because of Michael's endeavours, that the impact of what he and I had just done dawned on me as a sense of dread flowed from my brain to my heart; and I realised if anyone were to know what had just taken place, Michael could be in serious trouble.

I was under the age of consent.

He was not.

Chapter 2 – A Problem Shared

My mind whirled, my heart raced; I thought about the implications for Michael's potential career: he had just begun taking Law at A-Level and intended to become a solicitor. One of my first thoughts as I had been relaxing, recovering, after the incredible experience which had just enabled my passage from girl to woman to be completed had been to share with Zara what had occurred between Michael and I, and yet these thoughts of repercussions had flown through my head with incredible speed in a panic. The fear for what would happen to the boy I loved should anyone find out we had just spent time enjoying the most intimate of activities with each other, prevented me from enjoying the aftermath of our first experience of indulgence. I worried that if I told Zara, her morals and standards might make her feel like she had a duty to tell someone about what Michael and I had done. My parents, whilst less strict than Michael's, would most certainly have been angered to the point of making a complaint to the police; they did not, after all, truly know how close Michael and I had become. If they discovered their underage daughter had been intimate with him, they would have felt compelled to reprimand Michael – they believed in long term consequences for actions people should know better than to undertake – thus abruptly halting my happiness at the time. Zara was of much the same mindset, and would have almost certainly, in my mind at the time, have had to have told them.

Standards and duty: two words that were at the forefront of Zara's approach to life. Zara was an achiever. Not only was she one of the prettiest girls in her class at school, certainly the prettiest girl I had ever met, she was clever, too. Although she was naturally gifted, she constantly challenged herself academically. Learning as much as she could about everything; she had begged her parents for an encyclopaedia set for her seventh birthday, and as they had no real reason to refuse, her birthday present had become her pride and joy. She had spent hours delving into the pages, searching for information to expand her growing knowledge of everything and she absorbed and retained the contents as though she were a sponge. By the time I met her, she had read through the entire collection, twice. Her mother used to joke that when she was older Zara would be a very popular member of the pub quiz team; but at such a young age Zara did not comprehend what her mother was saying to her. As her knowledge and approach to learning grew, the marks she gained in school soared. The teachers were very pleased with her, and so she began to expect top marks of herself all the time, putting great stress and pressure on herself to achieve and be the top of the class. Zara was honest to the last. She found it very difficult to tell lies. Not because she blushed, flushed or became flustered, but because she felt such a strong feeling of guilt when she lied. Her morals, her standards, prevented her from lying. Whilst she was my best friend, it was for this reason I agonised over whether or not to tell Zara about Michael and I. For two weeks after Michael and I had first been intimate, I deliberated with myself. Although I felt I knew Zara better than any of my other friends, and better than some of hers, I was not completely sure of her ability to keep a secret. Whilst not divulging the information regarding Michael to anyone else would not be lying, it would be withholding the truth and yet at the same time, I felt guilty because I was keeping the secret from her. At the time I did not realise that it really was none of anyone else's business. Zara was my most precious friend; she was completely mine because apart from Robert and Michael, I did not have to share her with any of my other friends. Selfish, possibly, but for me it just elevated her to a status I felt she deserved. Unique, undiluted and untouchable. When I considered this, I eventually decided to tell her, but I made a bargain with myself. I would ask her not to say anything to get her friend, my boyfriend, into trouble. And so, one Saturday before the rugby, we had a rare moment to ourselves without the company of Michael or Robert.

We were in the shopping centre food court surrounded by an unpleasant smell of reheated sausage rolls, baked beans and jacket potatoes, alongside pizza and spicy chicken, from all the different restaurant outlets on offer. There was a children's birthday party going on in the corner of the seated section, a large furry mascot being grabbed and hugged by miniature humans who made more noise than should be possible. A pile of shoes inhabited the steps outside the ball pit palace, a new addition to the shopping centre which was proving extremely popular with small children and their parents alike, each parent looking distraught and exhausted as they tried to quickly swallow whichever caffeinated drink they felt they needed, before wrestling their child out of the ball pit in order to continue their shopping trip. Whenever we visited, it always seemed to be overflowing with children. Zara and I were partaking in our latest phase of fruit smoothies from the smoothie bar. From the way Zara looked at me, as we sat opposite each other at the plastic table whilst sitting on plastic chairs with slats that trapped skin and were too uncomfortable for a long visit, I knew she knew I had something to say. And so, with a deep breath, looking at her inquisitive face, I began to tell her.

I asked her to promise not to repeat what I was about to say. Curiously she looked at me, under already frowning eyebrows. I requested again her secrecy and she nodded just once in agreement. And so, with careful and deliberate words, I told her that Michael and I had moved our relationship forward to the next physical step. Panic flooded through me as I regarded her first reaction: a gasp. My head whirled as I wondered if, after all, I was right to consider withholding this information which best friends of our age usually shared so openly. Without realising it, I was worrying that this may affect our friendship, and the thought that I might lose Zara as a friend caused my heart to hurt. For just a brief second the hollowness this thought triggered in my chest caused tears to spring to my eyes, stinging them, and as she looked at me intently; a frown on my face, my lips forced together, jaw clenched tightly to forbid any sound which may betray me escaping, and I saw the recognition of my difficult decision to tell her begin to spread over her delicate, perfect features as she began to realise this had been difficult for me. It was as if in an instant she had realised the problem, and understood what it had taken for me to tell her. She asked me when Michael and I had been together, and I tried to remain calm as I told her it was a fortnight or so ago; it had actually been sixteen days, not that I was counting – honestly! Her second reaction was to question why I had not told her sooner, but from the look on my face she understood. I watched her carefully as she took a slow and steady breath in through her nose, and then sighed deeply, looking down at her carrot and satsuma smoothie as though there was something very interesting contained within the plastic walls of the tall cup which could help find some answer to the issue with which she had now been presented. I told her I was afraid that she might feel compelled to say something to someone due to the age gap between Michael and I; his legal status and my underage. She nodded slowly, and her mouth twisted in thought, her eyebrows knitting together creasing her forehead and causing a shadow to cross her face. For me, the silence was awkward, painful even. I began to babble, stress permeating my speech, my rambling increasing speed with each and every word telling Zara how I did not want Michael to get into trouble and how much I had agonised over telling her about him and I, and I was just about to draw a breath and beg her not to tell anyone when she placed her hand on mine causing me to look into her perfect, perfectly composed face.

"Mimi, I love you" she said. Apprehension filled me. I was sure there was a "but" coming, and yet, concurrently, I was relieved that my actions had not caused her to hate me. Time seemed to pass very slowly, her next word taking forever to part from her lips. I looked at her face, she seemed to be mulling over questions in her mind. She asked me if I had been pressured, and I said no. She asked me if I had enjoyed it, and I could not help my face turning into a broad, embarrassed, smile when I said yes. She asked me if Michael and I would be intimate again, and I answered yes, with trepidation. Not trepidation over the thought of repeating with Michael what had been the most perfect event in my life to date, I was anticipatory of that, impatient even; the trepidation resulted from the possibility Zara may not be quite so understanding if we continued to be intimate. Not that she was necessarily understanding now, she had not said anything to affirm that she approved since I had replied to her last question of whether Michael and I would be repeating our intimacy. My head spun even more than before, regret tinged the edges of my mind, regret for telling Zara, and just for a fleeting moment, regret for having anything to tell her at all. I quickly banished this thought from my mind, defiant that I had nothing to regret, and internally deciding that if Zara did not understand, then I would deal with that. It pained me though, she was my *best* friend; she was supposed to understand and stand by me, and my decisions, and support me through my life, just as I did with her. She was my most favourite person. I felt as though I should not have had to summon this inner defiant strength and prepare to direct it towards my best friend. However, there was not a "but" from Zara; there was a "well". She continued to say that she could see I was worried, and I nodded my agreement, that she could tell I had tormented myself for two weeks over how to tell her, and that no matter what had happened, she did not hold me to the same levels of standards and morals as she aimed for herself. I can barely describe the immense feeling of relief which washed over me as her last sentence ended. Relief that I would not have to find the strength to forsake the relationship I had with Michael, and also a feeling of confirmation. I had known in the instant I had met Zara that we would be lifelong friends, and now we were older, this internal assurance of mine stood firm, knowing that no matter what, Zara and I would share our experiences for as long as we both lived. The feeling of defiance began to melt away, calm residing within my heart once more. To help lighten the mood, she offered me an Opal Fruit, and rolled her eyes when I told her that they were called Starburst now and that she should learn to embrace the change and the development of everything through time. Giggling, we left the shopping centre.

As we began walking towards the rugby ground, after the atmosphere had lifted, I asked Zara whether she was considering the same with Robert, as she had mentioned a while before that she had been struggling with the decision. I knew her internal standards were preventing her from giving into her physical urges and indulging in some intimate time with Robert, and I asked about her morals and why it was she believed in them so very much. I told her I was not questioning her beliefs, or judging, or indeed saying they were wrong. I was curious. Things like this I did not understand because I had not been brought up to embrace the Catholic religion, and Michael and I had never really discussed his faith and beliefs in depth. I was eager to understand more, to understand my friends more, and to understand Michael's way of life more. Zara told me that she had always known that God was with her in everything she had ever done. She knew that she had a constant companion watching over her. She knew she could always go to church to pray, to talk to God, and go to confession to confess her sins and receive her penance in order to make up for her wrongdoings against God. She said that over the years, her wrongdoings were different, evolved as she had matured from childhood, through adolescence, and into young adulthood. Her worries now were larger, her sins more complex. God for her now was different than when she had gone through her confirmation. Zara told me that the consequences she faced as an adult were much more acute than when she had been a child, which reflected on the strict choices she made in her life. She told me that whilst God was still beside her in everything she did, she realise that her responsibility to serve Him had increased, and that, in turn, affected her decisions in her life. The lessons which Zara, Robert and Michael had been in receipt of as youngsters, framed the lessons of life which she had to learn from as an adult. Zara told me that she realised that this description she offered sounded very severe and constrained, but that actually, it was reassuring. She told me that she felt reassured that God was always by her side, and that He had been by everyone's side since the Catholic Church was first created by the first Pope. She enjoyed the tradition of the church, knowing that it was the same worldwide. She also told me that to have the ability to go and confess her sins enabled her to purge her conscience and learn from her mistakes on a frequent basis. It was this in particular which she found beneficial, she told me, because it offered her an opportunity to reflect on her growth and development as a person at regular intervals. She also appreciated the guidance of an adult other than her parents; her priest had known her since she was born but provided an external view of the issues and matters she discussed with him in confession. Nurturing and caring, yet distanced from direct involvement, Zara likened confession to the new trend of having a therapist which was gripping society at that time. Zara asked me if I had ever consider converting to Catholicism. I told her, with a slight wry smile, that the thought had briefly crossed my mind when Michael had hinted at the possibility of future events, and her face lit up with excitement. I did not want to tempt fate, but as we walked the rest of the journey to the rugby ground, we giggled and imagined planning and what life would be like should we both marry, in a few years of course, when we were older. Zara even suggested at one point a double wedding, half the arrangements to make, half the price to pay, but double the fun and celebration.

And then a happy thought struck me.

A problem shared...

Chapter 3 – Progress and Developments

Time passed and over the next couple of years, Zara and Robert and Michael took their A-Level exams and passed with flying colours. I took my GCSE exams and passed with good grades too, enrolled at college and began my own A-Level courses. Robert and Zara were both accepted to their local university and decided not to stay in halls, but to house share instead. I had teased Zara about the situation being a practice run for when they were married, and she had tried to, unsuccessfully, turn my attention away from their growing closeness. I did mention to her that in all seriousness it was perhaps a good thing that she and Robert were house sharing, real-life experience being so fundamentally useful to people of our ages when it came to kick-starting and developing our careers and aiming to achieve a work-life balance. However, eventually I relented and gave up teasing Zara, instead asking about the details of the process of applying to university since it would be my turn soon.

At the beginning of their third year of university, and my first, Michael and I had gone to stay for the weekend at Zara and Robert's house. We were celebrating Robert's twenty-first birthday with a nice dinner at a restaurant and an evening seeing a show at their local theatre on the Friday evening. It was a wonderfully relaxed weekend, stress free and fun, filled with laughter as we made jokes over the smallest things. We laughed about everything from Zara's parking ability, or lack thereof, to Michael's choice of socks. They were, I have to admit, bizarre. Not your usual novelty socks, with Homer Simpson on them. Oh no. Michael's socks were more luminous than that. So much so Robert used to suggest that Michael never had to pay for electricity in his house because they were so bright. Oddly enough, Michael never denied this, which just made us laugh even more. Robert had originally wanted to have a barbeque for his birthday, but due to the typical British autumnal weather, namely rain, we had enacted our reserve plan to go to a restaurant instead. The meal was lovely, Zara even allowing herself a glass of white wine which was exceptional for her; usually she did not drink. In fact, the only time I saw her drink alcohol was at a mutual friend's wedding, and I assumed other than that she only drank the wine at Mass on a Sunday. The theatre was wonderful, Robert's choice had been to see *Twelfth Night* and we all howled with laughter at the comedy in the garden scene. As the play ended, I could not help but hope that, without the confusion of course, Robert and Zara would be as happy as Orsino and Viola and that Michael and I would be as happy as Olivia and Sebastian, if each couple were to be able to put in the dedication needed for our respective relationships to work.

On the Saturday morning, I was awake before everyone else in the house, and after twenty minutes of lying in bed trying to go back to sleep, I decided I was awake for the day and it might be an idea to get up. I crept out of bed, so I did not wake Michael; he had had a long drive to get us to Zara and Robert's house the day before, and deserved to rest. He had passed his driving test a few months earlier, and was keen to be able to provide the transport, but this had been his first long journey and so it had taken its toll on him. Downstairs in the kitchen I found the bread, margarine and apricot jam and the plates and began to make some toast. As I was eating my two slices of multigrain wholemeal toast, the latest thing to be seen in the local supermarkets, I heard the soft padding of feet coming downstairs; I pulled my dressing gown around me just as I turned to see Robert coming into the kitchen, yawning and running a hand through his hair ruffling it up. He looked handsome, dishevelled and adorable, all at once. I asked if Zara was still asleep, she was. He asked the same about Michael and I reminded him that a long drive made Michael tired. Assembling his breakfast of cereal and milk, with some chopped strawberries from the container Zara had prepared the previous night, he took sharp breaths and paused repeatedly, as though he wanted to ask me something but did not quite know how. I watched him carefully, as he concentrated on his breakfast, and I realised that he and Zara were very much alike. When she was pondering over an issue, running something through her mind, she focused on something unimportant as though it might offer some answer. Robert looked up at me, and asked me if I would be willing to do him a favour. For a brief second, I wondered what was wrong, but I said that I would of course help him if I could. From the seriousness of his tone, I knew he was not going to ask me to pop to the shop and fetch some milk, or something along those lines. And then, blurting out his request, tripping over his words, Robert asked me something which both shocked and thrilled me. Robert and I had always been friends, and over the last couple of years since he and Zara had begun university we had grown closer, but I knew that this would help deepen our bond. I was thrilled and honoured he had asked me to help, and of course I was to keep the secret; even from Michael. I thought this would be the most difficult. Although I never kept any secrets from Zara, just like sisters we shared everything, but Michael and I barely had any secrets. Our relationship brought trust and complete honesty; the only thing he ever kept from me was what was to be my birthday or Christmas present. And for the most part I did not mind that. I was not overly keen on surprises, yet I always appreciated the effort Michael had put into the gifts, and the lengths he went to, to keep the surprise. Robert and Michael, I knew, often traded gift ideas and so I was puzzled that Robert had not asked Michael for his opinion, I was baffled as to why Robert was not asking Michael to help with this favour, but I did not mention this to Robert. I gladly and eagerly confirmed I would help Robert in his task for that day, and promised I would not tell a soul what he had asked me to help him do.

Robert had asked me if I would go and help him choose a ring.

Smiling, incessantly, I dashed up the stairs as quietly and quickly as possible, hopped into the bathroom for the quickest shower I had ever had in my life, hair washed and put up into a bun, and dressed in flat shoes, chinos and a blouse. Grabbing my bag and my mobile telephone, I scribbled a note for Michael to let him know Robert and I had gone shopping and would be back soon. I assumed Robert wrote a similar note for Zara as he was waiting for me when I reached the bottom of the stairs. As we drove into town, Robert at the wheel, I could not help but keep looking over at him. He was a tall man, slender but strong, with sandy blonde hair and sparkling blue eyes, a smile which put everyone at ease in an instant and a demeanour of friendliness. I had always known what Zara saw in him; he was a lovely person, his heart made of gold, and he was easy to be around. The fact that he was good looking, too, did not hurt. They were a perfect match and he was going to ask her to marry him. I was overjoyed; in fact, I do not think I could have been happier if I was to be asked the question myself. I was happy for Zara, I was happy for Robert, and I was happy for both of them as a couple and their lives being merged into a unit with which to take on anything the world could throw at them. Robert caught me looking over at him, with an insane grin on my face, and smiled back. I knew he knew I was elated. He asked me if I knew Zara's ring size, and I told him with a happy encouragement that I did not need to, we had the same size fingers and wondered why it was that men never noticed that women shared clothing and accessories all the time. Men! Sometimes I wondered how on earth they got through the day being such unobservant creatures.

We parked on the multi-storey car park, and walked to the jewellers in the centre of town. Robert said that we should start at this shop and if there was nothing suitable, then we should go to the one on the outskirts of town. He had said that he would have liked to give Zara an heirloom from his family, but since there was nothing which had been passed down to his generation, he was going to have to buy something with which she could begin the tradition for the next generations. I always knew, because Zara had insisted, that Robert and Zara would marry, but the thought of them having children had not occurred to me before. I supposed this was the disadvantage to being two years younger than Robert, Zara and Michael. The thought of Michael and I having children, or even me singularly, had never crossed my mind. I had not thought that far ahead, not planned for the event. Of course, Michael and I had been taking precautions to prevent it for a considerable amount of time, but the thought that Robert had considered the time in the future where he and Zara would plan to have children, pleased yet almost overwhelmed me. Selfishly, for just a fleeting second, I wondered if Zara and I would still be as close as we were if she had children, or if I would lose her to the duty of motherhood. Then, suddenly, my sense returned, and I realised I was being ludicrous: I would be an Aunt! If anything, if she were to have children, Zara and I would be closer than ever. Robert and I arrived at the jewellery shop just as it was opening, and the short, stout man behind the counter asked if he could help us. Robert told him that he was looking for an engagement ring for his girlfriend and that I would be helping with the sizes as we both had the same size fingers. The man nodded and began to ask questions: gold, silver, white gold or platinum? Traditional diamond or another stone? An engraved message or none? Would Robert like to buy the matching wedding rings now, or would he and his soon-to-be fiancé be returning to choose those together? After letting me indulge myself just ever so slightly trying on rings for the sake of it, Robert and I eventually decided on a 18 carat white gold ring, with a cluster of four princess solitaire diamonds in an invisible setting, completed with diamonds running down the shoulders of the band. It was beautiful, breath-taking, and of course, Zara would love it.

In the car on the way back to their house, I asked Robert when he planned to propose. He told me that he had planned to ask her that night, because if she said yes, it would be the best twenty-first birthday present anyone could hope to have. I asked him if he was going to take care of her, because she was my best friend, my sister practically, and I wanted to make sure that he was never going to hurt her or let her down. As her best friend, it was my duty to double check. He assured me he would do his utmost to make sure she had everything she wanted in life, and he would love her till his dying day. He thanked me for helping choose the ring, and he thanked me for being such a good friend to Zara and to him. And then he thanked me for making Michael happy, and I was astonished. I knew that Robert and Michael were best friends, but I did not realise just how deeply they cared about each other. I had not realised they had had such a bond which resulted in them being happy the other was happy in their relationships. And then, Robert grabbed my hand, and brought the back of it to his lips and kissed my hand in a thank you gesture and said, "I love you, Mimi" as we turned into the drive of the house. I smiled at him, my eyes prickling with happy tears, my heart warming in the knowledge that Robert and I had a bond that would never be broken.

That evening, in front of Michael and I, and a room full of people as we were out for dinner at the pub, Robert got down onto his left knee, presented Zara with the ring in its box, and asked her to make him the happiest man on earth, to give him the best twenty-first birthday present anyone had ever had, and agree to marry him.

I was in floods of tears as the whole room erupted in applause as she said an excited, yes.

Chapter 4 – Planning, Pronouncement and Pregnancy

After their third and final year of university had ended, and Robert, Zara and Michael had graduated, I had just ended my first year of university when the wedding plans which had started slowly, with general outlines and vague details and ideas, suddenly burst into action. Zara and I, along with Zara's Mum went shopping for her dress and the dresses for me and the other bridesmaids. When she had asked me to be her chief bridesmaid I was thrilled and immediately accepted. The venue for the reception was chosen, the table decorations selected, the menu tried, tasted and confirmed. Robert and Michael had been to the tailors to have their suits made, Michael was to be Best Man and the flowers and button holes had been ordered. The cake had been designed and the vows and service had been discussed with the priest. Robert and Zara had decided upon the traditional service. The invitations had been printed and sent out, and the R.S.V.Ps were arriving on Zara's Mother's doorstep thick and fast, all saying yes and sending congratulations to the happy couple. The music had been selected, the entertainment booked, and final fittings were taking place. I had called some of Zara's other friends, and between us, we had arranged for her hen night to be immense. A friend I knew from university, an art student, had printed up some t-shirts for the hen night, and one of Zara's friends, Claire, had arranged for a stripper. Zara was mortified at first, but laughed and screamed along with the rest of the hens as the evening progressed. Everything had been arranged, and all the arrangements were perfect.

A week later, and the big day had finally arrived. I was up early that morning, double checking all the arrangements for the day. I made sure Zara had a good breakfast, making a Full English for her so that she might not be hungry, or tipsy on champagne, throughout the day. While she ate her breakfast, and opened cards of good luck and congratulations, I spent the time taking care of my hair, makeup and dress well in advance, so that I could then help Zara with hers. Zara looked stunning, absolutely radiant, when she was dressed. She looked like a beautiful princess, the very image fairy tales are made of. Her blue garter around her thigh was a present from the bridesmaids, being her something blue. A necklace I had bought her, with a garnet pendant, her birthstone, being her something new. A matching pair of earrings from her Mother being something borrowed and the clip which held her hair and veil in place, the something old. It had been her great-grandmother's on her wedding day who had passed it down to her grandma, and she, in turn, had passed it down to Zara's Mum when she married Zara's Dad, who was passing it down to Zara on her wedding day. Everyone was thrilled to see Zara so very happy, and as she floated effortlessly down the aisle, she looked like an angel. Her blonde hair and perfect features glowing as she walked towards Robert, who looked dashing in his morning suit. I glanced over at Michael, and he was swallowing hard, happy for his friends who were starting their lives together.

"By the power vested in me, I now pronounce you husband and wife." With these words from the mouth of the priest at the altar at the head of the church, an echoing coming from the high, hollow ceiling, a rush of emotion ran through me. Pride, happiness, joy, love and a feeling of overwhelming contentment expanded from my heart through my veins to every last nerve ending I possessed in my body. If it were possible for me to glow with this sense of wonderment, I would have been as bright as the sun on a cloudless day. My two best friends were married, a unit recognised by law and the entire world. In front of the congregation of their friends and families, they had become one. And in that moment, I could not wait to do the same myself.

As Michael and I danced at the reception after the meal and the speeches were over, and Zara and Robert had had their first dance, I gazed at him and hoped that one day, Michael and I would be as happy as Zara and Robert. And then, at the end of the evening as Robert took Zara to a honeymoon destination about which only he knew, a terrible thought struck me. Zara had known instantly that she and Robert were going to be married and together forever. Why had I not known the same about Michael and I? Why was I not as sure as she had been?

A month or so after the wedding, Zara and I met up for lunch, she wanted to show me her honeymoon pictures she had taken with her new digital camera. She would have had to spend a fortune on it, if she had bought it when they were the new thing to have, she told me. I took note of her different approach towards technology and change. I recalled the many times, through the years before, when I had told her she had to embrace change and the development of everything through time and she had rolled her eyes at me. Slowly, she was admitting that technology was not all that bad. Robert, on the other hand, was all about progress. He was clearly a good influence on Zara, albeit a slow one. After we had placed our orders, Zara started showing me her photographs. The beach looked amazing, white sands, turquoise water, and empty. Heaven on earth. I could not wait till I was finished with my degree so I could go on a holiday to somewhere like that. She described with enthusiasm how much she had enjoyed the honeymoon, and how much relief she now felt not having anything to arrange. She described her days walking along the beach, exploring the local town and souvenir shopping, and finding quaint local ornaments for the house that she and Robert now owned. She told me that now the house had been bought, and the wedding was over, all they had to do was decorate and that would be that. I smiled at her, so pleased her life was happy. For just a second, as my mind was wandering wondering when I would get to see what she brought back, I could have sworn I heard her mention something about turning the smallest bedroom into a nursery. I had to do a double take and ask her to repeat what she had just said, thinking that if I had heard her correctly, she was being just slightly pre-emptive, making plans that far in advance. Then I saw her face, as it broadened into a smile and I knew that it was not too soon and I had heard her correctly. My jaw fell open, as I comprehended what she was confirming. I was shocked and surprised, happy yet apprehensive. My mind filled with questions, each vying for the opportunity to be the first to be asked: What about her career? Was she happy? Was Robert happy? How far along was she? Did she realise what she was taking on at such a young age? I took a deep breath and asked if she was happy, she told me she was overjoyed. I asked about Robert's feelings, she replied that he was shocked but happy. She told me she was only three or four weeks along, so I must not tell anyone, not even her parents, and I promised I would not. I asked if I could tell Michael and she asked me to refrain from doing so for a short time, just until it was safer to do so. Then I asked about her career. Her forehead creased with contemplation as her eyebrows closed further together in a frown, her mouth closing firmly and twisting in thought. She told me that honestly, she had not planned on having a child so early after getting married, but, now that she was pregnant, she would not have things any other way. She said that she would solve the issue of developing her career after she had had some advice from her parents. She had clearly considered the possibility of giving up her job, but she did tell me, reassuring me almost, that if the worst came to the worst she could always go and work at her parent's firm full time. She had worked there part time through university, and she was sure that they had wanted her to remain there, but she had wanted to prove herself in the world, and thought that she should live up to their standards of making-it-on-your-own, and do her duty to understand more about the non-sheltered working life most people led, and be a productive member of society. I could see that she had not quite settled on a plan of action, but that she was happy, and so I was happy for her.

I was also over the moon for myself.

I was going to be an Aunt!

Chapter 5 – Only in the Movies

As Zara progressed through her pregnancy, she did remarkably well. After the initial morning sickness had passed, she obtained the healthy glow women benefit from when pregnant. It was then her cravings began. She had some weird and wonderful wantings: everything from fried bread with ice cream, to celery and raspberry jam. In her fourth month of pregnancy, it was around Christmas time and Michael and I had arranged to meet up with them to swap presents and go for a meal which would be our Christmas. Michael and I were intending to have our first Christmas with each other alone, no family visits, just he and I together. He had wanted to take me away, but because I had essays for university due in after the Christmas break, we had to make do with time at his house, celebrating in front of the fire, albeit gas not log, and watching the traditional Christmas movies on the television. Things between Michael and I were wonderful, comfortable, relaxed, natural, despite not seeing each other for weeks at a time because of university, first him and then afterwards me. But when we had the chance, we spent the most incredible days together; window shopping as we always had, and the nights we had we spent in complete indulgence of one another. It was like we had never been apart when we were reunited. After years of developing our relationship, we knew every millimetre of each other, we knew exactly how to create ecstasy for one another, our passion never wavering, never decreasing, only maturing and strengthening the connection between us. And I was happy. Contented. I thought things were perfect.

As we sat at the table, our perfect foursome of friendship and love warmed the room around us. The waitress came to take our orders for drinks and our meals. As we were waiting for our meals to be cooked and brought to our table, we swapped gifts. Zara and Robert had decided on small gifts, since they were saving up every penny they could to ensure they had every gadget they would need for the baby; Robert's idea, not Zara's. She was of the opinion that if millions of women for thousands of years had managed with the basic necessities alone, then she would too. But Robert insisted, wanting the best for his child. Robert received a new briefcase from Zara, and a Filofax and an engraved pen from Michael and I. Zara and I had co-ordinated with each other in order to make sure that Robert's gifts were not only nice, but useful also. Robert gave Zara a diamond necklace, much the same in appearance as her engagement ring. I was surprised he had not asked for my help to choose the jewellery since I had helped to choose the ring, until I glanced at Michael and saw he and Robert share a smile of co-conspirators. Zara feigned outrage at the expense, but delighted at her gift, a small gasp and huge smile and a long, deep, passionate kiss for Robert as a thank you. I gave Michael the newest Rugby shirt and tie for our team, and Robert and Zara gave me a CD compilation set I had wanted. And then it was my turn to receive my gift from Michael. He placed a small pale blue bag, with white handles on the table in front of me, and I peeked inside and then glanced up. Around the table, expectant faces looked intently at me, Robert relaxed in his chair, his arm behind his wife, Zara's hand placed on his knee and her head tilted slightly into his shoulder, and then Michael, leaning forward, his head resting on the top of his folded hands, his arms propping up his head, elbows on the edge of the table. A small square box was inside the bag, and as I took it out, I wondered what style of earrings Michael had bought for me. I opened the box, slowly in anticipation, yet what greeted me left me speechless. An oval amethyst surrounded by small diamonds sat on top of a white gold band.

I looked up to find Michael's seat empty, he was kneeling in front of me. "Mimi, I love you. will you marry me?" A tear sprang to my eye, and my throat was caught in a knot as I tried to answer him. I nodded, and a huge smile spread across my face. I leant down and kissed him passionately, happier than I had ever been, all the while hearing the faint sound of applause from the tables in the restaurant surrounding us. The only thought which ran through my head was one of hope. I hoped this would be the best thing I ever did. Looking up, I knew that Michael and Robert had been shopping for both Zara's necklace and my ring, because I had actually taken a little peak at a ring very similar when I had gone to choose Zara's ring with Robert. I suppose I always knew he would have told Michael I had been looking at rings for myself. Just in case. Michael and I had not even talked about being engaged, other than when we were very young, and he used to say one day he would be able to buy me a ring. We talked about everything, plans for the future, holidays, trips, arrangements, when to go and what to see at the cinema, everything. But never this. I was so surprised.

Two months later, I was still walking on cloud nine. I had not seen Michael in three weeks, and although I missed him, I knew it would not be long until we were able to spend the summer together. I had bought a few bridal magazines, but found myself only half-heartedly looking through them for inspiration for a dress. I think the word to describe my mood then, is lacklustre. I found myself wondering whether this was because the excitement of planning a wedding had been slightly dulled for me, since I had had such a part to play in Zara's. I assumed that when Michael and I had decided on a date, and after the stress of university had ended for me, that I might become more interested. Not that I was not happy, but I still could not envision the wedding in the same way Zara had seemed to have been able to. I was thrilled to be engaged, to know that my relationship with Michael was progressing, developing, and moving forward, that it was not pointless; but, when I tried to see in my mind the day of the wedding, I just could not. It was as though there were something in my mind which just prevented me conjuring up the vision of my future with Michael.

Eight weeks before Zara was due to have the baby, a month before my second year of university ended, the reason why I could not imagine my wedding day with Michael hit me. I had taken a Drama module at the end of my second year, to broaden my horizons. It is almost a rite of passage to take some drama at university, surely? The small lecture group was full of people whom I had seen in attendance at university, a few in the same lectures as me, but they were not part of the inner circle of friends I had made since I began my degree. I was enjoying the module, we studied *Oedipus the King* by Sophocles, and this enhanced my appreciation and understanding of psychology and what little I had learnt about Freud. I had glanced through a psychology book to include some of the theory in one of my essays, and whilst this, thankfully, did not cause me to analyse every activity of my daily life, I began to see that some of the theories of psychology could apply to various aspects of my life, and the life of those around me. I found it intrigued me. During one of the seminars for my Drama module, the lecturer was inviting us to debate whether it was psychology which had caused the actions in the play, or if Sophocles had resigned the play to be about the fate which Oedipus had succumbed to.

Fate. That was not a word I had necessarily believed in. In all honesty, I do not think that at such a young age I had really considered the difference between choice and fate. I do not think that anything had ever caused me to consider the topic. That was until that day in Drama, four weeks before the end of my second year of university when, nonchalantly, I had glanced up from my work and my eyes met a pair of intensely blue, sparkling eyes, looking back at me. My heart stopped. My breath caught in my chest. And in that moment, everything fell into place. In that moment I fell in love. It hit me. I knew that these eyes which were looking back at me were the eyes I was supposed to look into every day for the rest of my life. I cannot explain the feeling which overwhelmed me; not in a bad way, in an uncontrollable, enthralling, electric way. I felt warm, my heart began beating again, but not beating just to keep my body alive; it was beating for him. It felt as though it was beating at double the strength it had been just seconds before, the intensity both increased and relieved by gazing into his dazzling, crystal blue eyes; because now my heart was beating for him. Everything in the room fell away into the background, numbed, hushed, and insignificant in comparison with what I was feeling. I had never experienced this all-consuming sensation before. In that second, when my eyes met his, I saw my life in front of me. I saw our wedding, him in a gold waistcoat, black morning suit, a red rose in his lapel. My wedding dress was white, intricate designs in gold silk decorating the front panel; my bouquet was made of white and red roses with green leaves. I saw Zara in a dress which was the same cut as mine, but the colours reversed. I saw us taking our vows, promising to love honour and respect each other till death do us part. I saw our house, a three-bedroomed semi-detached with a driveway and a car, a long sitting room, a kitchen diner and a utility room. I saw our children: four. Two boys, two girls, all blonde haired blue eyed like him. I saw our life; chaotic but blissfully happy. I felt complete. He was what I had been missing. I had not known it until that moment, but I knew then. My existence had been empty, until that instant. Everything I had done before was insignificant, except that it had led me there. I had only ever heard of things like this in the movies and in books; the only thing as powerful as this to which I could even compare the feelings pulsing through my heart was the description of imprinting in *Twilight* which was a recent popular book everyone was talking about, and I had succumbed to, or Romeo and Juliet's instant, compelling love in Shakespeare's most famous love story. And even those two things fell short of matching the feeling enveloping me at that moment. My heart knew in that instant we would have a happy ending. I was not sure if I knew anyone who had felt this before. Perhaps Zara and Robert. It was only now I knew how she had known she would spend the rest of her life with him immediately. It was as though my entire life was created for this moment; to be sitting opposite

41

him, to be looking into his eyes right now and to see our future together. I looked at the rest of his face; handsome, pale, dimples in his cheeks, exaggerated if he smiled, blonde hair giving a boyish charm to his slightly rugged countenance. His mouth was slightly parted, and he was staring at me intently, much as I was staring at him, and I knew he was feeling the same thing. We were as one. Everything else in my life faded away, nothing was as important as him. His name was Will; I knew that because I had heard people say his name. I wondered why I had never taken the time to look at him before this, or at any of the other members of the cohort. But then I expelled the thought from my head; it did not matter. I did not care. What mattered now was that I had looked at him, seen him, and he had looked at me, seen me, our eyes had met, and we had fallen instantly, wholly and completely in love. It was an unspoken bond, an unbreakable magnetic attraction, a welded connection, an almost magical occurrence, we did not need to say anything; but we would. As the class ended, he waited for me outside the room and asked me to go for a coffee. I nodded readily amazed at the formality of him asking, I would have followed him anywhere without him uttering a single syllable to me, and we walked towards the café on campus.

Without warning, in the most natural feeling of motions Will took my hand.

I looked down at it and suddenly it was as heavy as lead.

My engagement ring from Michael was on the hand that my future husband was holding.

Chapter 6 – Explanations

It was then that I had started to panic. The enormity of the task which lay ahead of me hit me like a ton of bricks. I realised in an instant that the reason I had not been able to picture my life with Michael the way Zara had seen her and Robert's life was because I was not supposed to be with Michael. I realised that the reason I had never referred to Michael and I as 'we' rather than 'Michael and I' was because I knew that we were not a unit. We were not supposed to last. It was not going to happen. It had been a choice, not fate. I was resigned to what had to happen next, but the thought of it hurt my heart. I loved Michael; he was such a large part of my life. He had been my first; my only. He had been mine. And I had been his, and I had been happy. I told Will that I was engaged, and he nodded slowly. He knew I had to explain things to Michael before we could go any further, but that it would be worth the wait. He knew as well as I did that our life was with each other now; he would wait until things had been put right and then we could be together. It was ridiculous in a way, we had only had one conversation, held hands once, not even kissed yet, and already we knew we would be married as soon as we could save up for the wedding. Our lives had the direction now which they, unknowingly, lacked before, and we had an ability to communicate which was unspoken. We knew that everything would turn out, no matter what, and that we would be able to build our lives together as soon as possible.

It seemed bizarre, alien, uncomfortable even, to have to swap phone numbers with Will. It was odd to have to ask him for something as small and insignificant as his email address. He was just as uncomfortable as I was when we had to ask where each other lived. It seemed that this information was superficial, yet regrettably, it was necessary. We felt awkward that we did not already know the basic details about each other's lives, because we already knew we were a unit. Our souls knew each other, but our physical bodies and our lives had not yet become as one. It was so odd. As we sat over drinks, we took it in turns to divulge every last morsel of information about our lives until that moment. I told him about my passion for rugby, and surprisingly, he enjoyed it too. I told him about Zara and Robert and the baby, and again he shocked me by saying he already knew. He had heard me talking with pride about my best friend, her husband, the wedding arrangements, and how I was going to be an Aunt to my friends at university. I was shocked; I had not been aware that Will had even noticed me before today. Suddenly, I felt selfish, and, also, abruptly aware that the world happened from the perspective of other people as well as my own point of view. It had not occurred to me that Will may have known who I was before today, never mind that he had known much more about me than I had about him. I asked him if he had felt before what he had felt today, and he said no. Relief flowed through me when he answered, and I was puzzled by his reaction. Curiously, I believe I was happy he had not felt before what he felt now, relieved I had not missed out on this perfect feeling, nor deprived him of it. He said he had seen me in the lectures and seminars, but had not really looked at me till today. From the tone of his voice, I could tell he was as bewildered as I was about the power, passion and magnetism between us. From the look in his eyes I knew he was being honest; he had been studying me constantly, and I him, since our eyes had met, gladly soaking up any and every new facial display, memorising each which we were able to behold before us. Will told me all about his family; he was really close to his elder brother, and his parents were quite progressive. During his teenage years, his brother and he had not been subjected to many boundaries and rules, rather being asked their opinions regarding behaviour, social standards and etiquette. It was this, he told me, which allowed his brother and himself to choose the manner in which they behaved and presented themselves. His parents were academics: his mother a clinical psychiatrist, his father a lawyer; and yet, somehow, they had allowed their children the freedom to develop with guidance

44

rather than dictating to them. Will told me that this filled him with ease and, that from a very early age, he found himself being able to take a step back from situations and apply logic and try and look at the abstract, the bigger picture and decide what was for the best.

The more I heard about Will and his upbringing, the more I fell in love with him. I had not known that was possible. I loved his mind, I loved his giggle, I loved his sense of humour, I loved his diverse interests and his passion and enthusiasm for each of them. It was as if everything he was, every aspect of him and his life, was the exact opposite of Michael and seemed to fit so much more with what I felt and believed. Well, of course it did; he and I were meant to be together. And I did not hate Michael for being opposite; I loved him very much. Eventually, as the evening drew to a close, Will and I parted company. I resigned myself to the daunting task which lay ahead of me, and as Will leant in to kiss me goodnight, I pulled away from him. As much as I loved him, with all my heart and soul, I loved Michael too much to do anything which could be seen as being unfaithful. I told Will I had more respect for Michael, and I did not think that he and I should consummate our relationship in any manner until I had told Michael I could no longer be with him.

As I wandered home, my mind wandered with me. What would Michael say? Would he understand? No. Would he hate me? Possibly. Would he forgive me? Probably not. Would he shout and scream at me? I did not think so; he never had raised his voice in my presence before. I hoped he would not, but I would understand if he did. Before I was half way home I felt the first tears stinging my eyes. As I reached my house, I was quietly sobbing. I felt horrendous inside, yet I knew I was doing the right thing. I knew that for myself I had to do this, and that I could never be truly happy unless I was with Will. My thoughts meandered and for a split second, I thought that this was better for Michael too. I thought about looking at things from the abstract, using logic, and stupidly a small "ha" burst from my lips as I realised Will had had an immediate effect on my outlook. But, in truth, I knew I was just trying to deceive myself into thinking that hurting Michael was for the best. It was not for the best. Not for him, not for me, not for Will, not for anyone. I lay on my bed and cried myself to sleep.

The next morning, it was a Saturday, I called Michael and told him I needed to see him as soon as possible. I journeyed by train to his house and he met me at the front door with a smile, which quickly faded when he saw the serious look on my face. He let me into the house, and we sat down in the lounge on his Chesterfield sofa, which was just like his parents' sofa. A brief flash of a memory of the first time Michael and I had been intimate crossed my mind. That had started on a sofa just like this. And now, our relationship was to end on this sofa. I could not stop myself from crying. I felt ashamed. Not ashamed that I was in love with Will and we were going to be together, but ashamed because I was crying. I had no right. I knew Michael would already be worrying what was wrong, it was not often I cried, and certainly not in front of anyone else, and he would soon be vowing to amend whatever problem or issue had upset me. He was such a good person, really, he was. The salt of the earth, the pick of the crop; and I was about to break his heart. I took a deep breath and tried to steady my nerve. I allowed myself one last gaze into his deep, warm brown eyes. The love I saw there overwhelmed me. I asked him to hear me out before he said anything. He nodded agreement. And then I began. I told him I had not planned it, I had not known anything about it till it hit me, I told him that I never ever would have wanted to hurt him, and that I was so very sorry I was doing that now. I told him that I could not stop it, and that I did not really want to. I told him I had no choice. His eyebrows knitted together in a frown as he was trying to decipher what I was saying to him. I told him that I did not know how to say what I needed to say in any way other than coming straight out with it. I told him that there was no way

46

I could ease him into this news, there was no way for me to put this information in a delicate manner so as to avoid causing hurt and damage. I told him that although I loved him, and had loved him with all my heart, I had not known there was a different type of love. I told him that yesterday I had fallen *in* love. I stared down at my shoes as I told him that I had felt what so many people describe and yet many never believe. I heard him take a sharp breath. I told him that Will and I somehow knew each other's hearts immediately, and that we were meant to be together. I told him that it had hit both of us as a complete surprise. I told him that before yesterday I had not known who Will was, and that he had not known who I was, really. I told Michael that somehow, this felt right to us. We could not help it, it had just happened. Neither of us had chosen it, or asked for it, or even wished for it. I told Michael that I had chosen him, and that I would not take back our time together, but I would take back this hurt that I was causing him if I were able. For that, I told him I was sorry. Because I *was* sorry. Sorry with all my being. I would have given anything to have not hurt Michael, and yet, selfishly, if I could have turned back time, I still would have chosen to be with him. I told him I loved him. Because I *did* love him, truly I did. I was at a complete loss to explain myself with any sort of sagacity. Explanations evaded me.

And then I heard the words I did not deserve to hear ever again.

"But Mimi, I love you."

I took the ring off my finger, placed it in his hand and curled his fingers around it.

Chapter 7 – Remorse and Repercussions

I felt awful. I cried all the way home on the train. But I was not crying for me; I was crying for Michael. I was crying because my friend had been hurt. Friend. That was what he was now. He had been relegated. I hated that I was the one to cause that hurt. I loved him; he had been my rock, my absolute, he had been my only concern for so long, my first, my only and my centre. I adored him as much as I adored Zara, merely in a different way due to the nature of our relationship. I had worshiped him. Michael's face had been contorted into such agonising pain when he realised that our relationship was now ending; I swear I felt it stab at my heart. He had asked me why. I had replied that I did not know, nor did I understand why it had happened, why it was Will, why it was now. He asked me if I was unhappy with him. I replied with complete honesty that no, I was not unhappy with him; when he had asked me to marry him, my heart had soared. I told him I had been genuinely happy, happier than I had ever been before, happier than all my life's moments culminated in comparison. And then, he said that it did not matter. I could not be sure if he was asking me a question, or if he was stating a fact. I told him that it had chosen me, that I would never have chosen to hurt him and that he meant too much to me to even contemplate doing that. I had felt selfish, even as the words left my mouth. How could I be focusing on what he meant to me rather than on what I was doing to him? I felt bad. There was no other word for it. I simply felt bad. Rotten. To the core.

As I reached my house, I found a message on my answer machine. Zara. She wanted to talk to me. I deduced from the serious tone in her voice that Michael had called Robert and told him he was now single. I hit one on the speed dial, and as I waited for my call to be answered, I wondered what Zara would say to me. Robert answered the telephone and after the usual, hellos and how are yous? I asked to speak to Zara. I waited for what seemed like an eternity; she was taking longer and longer to get to places as her pregnancy progressed and her size increased. She had joked, as most women do, about feeling like a beached whale but that there was a reason whales do not walk. I had laughed at the mental image which had formed in my mind, but now, even that, failed to cease the hurt. Zara was out of breath when she finally said hello to me. I replied with a dejected greeting. She asked me what was wrong. I was astonished; perhaps Michael had not called Robert to tell him the news. I took a deep breath and told her Michael and I were no longer together. The silence on the other end of the telephone was deafening. I could have heard a pin drop. For the longest time, Zara did not reply. Finally, she stuttered and asked me what? Why? What happened? What went wrong? What did he do? And with the last question, I burst into uncontrollable sobs. My chest hurt, my lungs, my heart; it hurt to breathe. I could not stop the wailing which ensued as I tried to explain it was not Michael's fault. I was to blame. He had not done anything wrong, but at the same time, I did not feel I had done anything wrong. I knew I had, but to me, being with Will felt right. I could not and would not apologise or change that. Zara struggled to make sense of what I was saying and told me to stay at home, to not go anywhere and she was going to be at my house in an hour.

The hour took an age to pass. I felt I should do something, make myself productive. Do something positive to make up for the huge negative which I had inflicted upon one of the kindest human beings on earth. Yet I drew a blank for ideas about how to possibly make up for my wrongdoings. So I sat, in silence, trying to block out the thoughts in my head. I wondered if I should text Will, to tell him the news. But I decided against it. I thought I would be better prepared for the next phase of our relationship to develop if I had had some time to recover and justify to myself with more logic, there was that word again, what

I had done to Michael. In amidst all my thoughts of logic and pitiful self-loathing, the sharp rap of the heavy brass knocker against the thick wood of my front door disturbed my stream of thought. Bracing myself, trying to stem my now silent tears which had not ceased to fall from my stinging red eyes, I opened the door to see Zara's concerned face and open arms. I had to fight against all my worth not to fall into her offer of comfort and embrace, telling myself I did not deserve to be comforted. I led Zara into the lounge, and she sat facing me on the sofa. I took a deep breath and told her what had happened. I really did try not to plead my case, I tried not to ask her to see my point of view, I felt I did not deserve her understanding, support or comfort. And that was just as well. Because twenty minutes after I had finished describing what passionate power and magnetism now existed between Will and I, and how this had impacted on the relationship I had had with Michael, it was apparent from her countenance I would not receive her understanding, support or comfort.

Zara's jaw hung slightly open; her face frozen with a shocked expression. Her eyes offered no depth, no insight as to what she might have been thinking or feeling with regards to me or the situation I had just described to her. Zara just sat and stared at me, motionless, wordless and beautifully statuesque; aghast at what I had just told her. Looking back, I do not think the severity of what I had said over the telephone had been appreciated by Zara; I do not think that she was able to make sense of what I was saying. Yet now, she understood fully. I watched her perfect face, her delicate features for any indication of what was to come. And then, finally, I saw her blink, once, twice, three times, and her eyebrows knitted together as her mouth drew closed. The muscles in her cheeks rippled beneath her skin as her jaw tightened and clenched. She was taking long, slow, controlled breaths through her nose, her shoulders rising and falling in line with her chest and I could see the tension building in her. Questions ran through my mind. Was she angry? Was she

50

upset? Was she feeling defensive towards her friend, my now ex-boyfriend? That was something I never thought I would say. The answer was probably yes to all of these questions, I thought, and quite rightly so. For the first time in my life, I tried to imagine myself in her shoes. It was not often in my short years that I had really looked at another person's point of view. It was not until Will had told me that he had known who I was and knew more details about my life than I had about his, that the thought had ever really struck me that the world happens from billions of perspectives and not just mine. I realised that, without meaning to be, I was a very selfish, self-focused person. I had realised that I was at the centre of my own universe and that I had never realised that the world did not revolve around my point of view. I wondered if I was the only one, or if more people were the same. Perhaps that was what was wrong with society now: the perspective had changed from the community, to focusing on the individual. It was right then that I vowed to myself that I would change my ways; that I would think of others and take their feelings into consideration more than I usually did. I was not mean to people, far from it, I tried to be as kind and caring as I could, especially to my friends. But to put others first, that would be my new goal. Just as I was making this internal pledge, my train of thought was brought to a swift halt as Zara began to speak. She asked me if she had heard me correctly. I said yes, everything she thought I had said had been indeed, said. She paused to take in a breath. Then she started to shout. Her questions and accusations were no less than I deserved, and they were hurled at me with abundance: how could I do this? Her arms moved with rapid short motions, punctuating the words of her question. What was I thinking? Her hand knocked against the side of her head, then quickly pointed in my direction; a silent question asking about the state of my brain. Did I not know what I was throwing away? Another arm gesture, accentuating how angry and disappointed she was. How could I do this to Michael? Her hands, clasping at her chest over her heart as if to help stem the flow of the pain I was causing there. What on earth was I doing with my life? How could I hurt her friend? How could I hurt her? How could I ruin her plans? The last four questions had been reinforced by her not removing her hands from her chest. Yet the visible tension in her arms and shoulders increased with each of these questions she enquired of me as I could see her pressing her hands against her chest harder, to the point where the physical discomfort may have rivalled her emotional pain.

It was this last question which completely threw me. I had no idea what she meant, and I asked, with trepidation, what plans of hers had I ruined? I tried so hard to make sure my tone was not argumentative: I had no right to defend my position; nor did I wish to claim it. All I wanted was to understand what Zara had meant. Thankfully, my tone must have inferred this wish, as it was then she delivered the most bewildering news to me. The message on the answering machine which she had left for me was not with regards to Will and I, or my ending my relationship with Michael. What she had wanted to ask me was much more important to her. She wanted to ask if Michael and I would consider being Godparents to her baby. Now, she said she was not so sure she could trust me enough to ask.

Silent tears surged down my face as I realised my love with Will might end my friendship with Zara.

My life was in ruins.

Chapter 8 – Comfort and Progress

It was then I began to react. I could not maintain my tone of trepidation. My friendship with Zara was far too important to me to be mindful of the way I was saying things. At least she would know, I thought briefly, that I loved her enough to fight for our friendship. And so, with urgency in my voice, I begged Zara to consider things from my point of view. I told her that I had not had a choice; that I had not chosen for this to happen, that I had never been unfaithful to Michael, I loved and respected him too much for that. She scoffed when I said I loved Michael, as though she did not believe it were true. I told her that I had not meant to hurt him and that I had not been looking for this. I took a deep breath and told her that I would not apologise for it though. I was categorical in this, and amazed myself that my voice was able to hold to reflect how immovable I was regarding Will. He was already my *everything*, and I told her that what Will and I had was what she had felt with Robert from the second they met. Unexplainable, unwavering and everlasting. She looked at me, a dubious look of doubt on her face, but she must have seen the sincerity in my eyes because her demeanour softened slightly. And that was when I knew; I knew that no matter what, Zara would be my friend for the rest of our lives, that we would be next to each other in the nursing home, after all. That, although she might not like what had happened, and it might take a while for her to grow accustomed to the notion that all she had dreamt of when she was a girl may not happen, but she would. There would be no happily ever after, just the four of us; Robert and Zara, Michael and Mimi, but she would understand and eventually forgive me. I saw this in her face before she had even opened her mouth to say she did not realise it was the same with Will and I as it was with Robert and herself. I nodded solemnly. I told her how my heart had stopped the minute our eyes had met, and how now it beat not just to keep my body alive, but it beat for him, and that we were together, and we were going to build our lives as a unit. And then she said something which told me she understood, something which would stay inside my head for my entire life: you do not choose who your heart follows but follow who your heart chooses.

Relief flooded through me.

I gently asked her if she wanted to meet Will, or if it was too soon. She hesitated before she replied. She told me she was of two minds; she did not know whether sooner would be better so she could get it over and done with, so to speak, or wait until he and I had had the chance to be together. After all, he did not know I had ended my relationship with Michael, and she said she was not sure if I should have the opportunity to do that first. I said I would send him a text, something with which she was now comfortable doing for herself after Robert insisted she have a mobile telephone in case there were any problems with the baby while she was away from him. I was searching my brain for ways to further ease the discontent between us and speed up the process of her accepting the situation. So I asked her for advice on how to ask Will to come over and meet her, and tell him that things had been dealt with so we might now be together freely. She helped me word the text message; not surprisingly, she suggested the exact words I would have sent to Will. It still amused me at how similar Zara and I were sometimes; as though we were sisters brought up in the same household with the same parental influence shaping our development. Will replied immediately, saying he would be able to arrive at my house within half an hour.

Half an hour alone with Zara during this time of apprehension worried me. I felt a shiver go down my spine as I sat next to her on the sofa, wondering if I should say anything. I eventually arose and decided to make a smoothie for us each. Zara followed me into the kitchen, reaching for the ice as she passed the freezer. I heard her sigh behind me as I turned my attention to the blender and my chopping board and fruit basket. "Mimi?" she asked, in a voice quieter than I had ever heard her. I turned and gazed at her face, her perfect face, beautiful and full of grace. "I love you, Mimi" she told me. And with that I opened my arms, and rushed towards her. We stood in the middle of the kitchen just hugging. Silence being our method of communication. I knew our friendship would survive; it had to. I knew that we had such a solid foundation that we would survive anything. Then she spoke against my shoulder, and told me that she had not meant what she had said, and she did want Michael and I to be the Godparents to her baby. I could not help but smile. I was overjoyed. I told her that I would do my best, I would be the greatest Godmother on earth; that I would find a way to make things right with Michael so we might still be friends, and that I would make sure her child was the happiest child there ever was. My head was already filling with ideas about birthday and Christmas presents, trips out when he or she was older and all the paraphernalia I could buy from our rugby club to help decorate the nursery. As I told her all this, her head started shaking and she began to laugh at me. She told me, just as I was asking which would be better, a silver money box or a silver spoon for the Christening gift, that she was sure she had made the right choice, and that if anything happened to Robert or herself, that I would do a very good job of making sure their child had all the love and support and care in the world. Then she shocked me even further. She asked me the biggest favour I had ever been asked, or have ever been asked in my life. She asked me that if something were to happen to her and Robert, if Michael and I would be the legal guardians to the baby. I did not hesitate. I did not consider the implications of what she had asked of me. I said yes immediately. And I meant it.

Before I could ask any questions, or even tell her that I hoped circumstances never dictated I had to complete my promise, the sharp rap of the heavy brass knocker against the thick wood of my front door startled us both. Zara remained in the kitchen, busying herself with making the smoothies we had never started. I rushed to the door, checking my reflection in the hallway mirror as I hurried past. I did not look my best, my eyes were still red and slightly puffy from crying, and my face was very blotchy. I opened the front door and there, standing in front of me, was my *everything*. As I looked up into his sparkling blue eyes, my heart stuttered, its rhythmic beating interrupted as the shock of electricity flowed through me again. He asked me if I was all right, I said that, yes, I was all right now he was there. I told him that things had been dealt with. A broad grin erupted over his face as he walked through the doorway into the hall. He wrapped an arm around my back and pressed me against the wall, lowered his head, and kissed me. As his lips met mine my knees almost gave way. My breath caught short in my throat and I had to resist the urge to moan in pure glory. It was delicious. Our first kiss. I would remember this forever; the way I had been devoured by his mouth, his body pressed into mine; both with complete and total true love and tenderness but with raw passion and need also. I felt as though I was floating; tingles and shivers ran up and down my spine. Somewhere in my lower stomach, I felt my insides melting, and beckoning for him. I could have stayed there forever. Somewhere from the dulled background noise I heard the sound of a blender, and I was soon brought back to earth. I pulled away from him, with what strength I do not know because at that moment I had none. I glanced at the kitchen door and told Will that Zara was in the kitchen making smoothies. He stared into my eyes, and I returned the gaze, once again becoming lost in them. I saw them grow smaller for just a second, a question; was it all right for them to meet? A smile played around my mouth, and I nodded. I took his hand from around my waist and led him down the short hallway and into the kitchen. I took a deep breath as Zara turned to face us, and introduced them.

The next half an hour passed with much more ease than I anticipated. I had expected Zara to be a reluctant participator of conversation, yet she was open, friendly and accommodating with Will. I was grateful and thrilled he tried to make such a big effort; asking about the baby, when Zara was due to give birth, asking what her husband did for a living, asking about the wedding, asking how married life was treating them both. He asked about Robert's hobbies and interests, and I was overjoyed he was trying to gain so much knowledge. For me, this displayed that Will wanted to be part of my life even more than I already thought he did. The fact that he was trying to get to know something about my friends, whom he clearly knew meant the world to me, meant the world to me. Finally, Zara said she was getting tired and she had better start the drive home; she had an early start for Church in the morning. I walked to the car with Zara, wanting to see her in safely, and as she opened the car door, she turned to face me. She told me that she knew Will and I were meant to be, that she understood that I had not chosen this but that it was what would make me happy and complete. She told me it would take some getting used to, but that she would try. I hugged her and said thank you. I thanked her for trying to see things my way; I thanked her for giving Will a chance. And I thanked her for being my friend. I waved her off as she drove away down the lane and wandered back to the house.

Waiting for me at the front door, Will was leaning against the staircase banister. A long slow breath escaped me; relief that the introduction had gone well coupled with the amazement of him standing before me. My eyes ran up and down him, his dark blue faded jeans hung loose around his legs, masking the shape of his thighs from my vision. His checked shirt, navy and white, tucked in at the waist, reminded me of a cowboy; the sleeves rolled up, were straining against the bulge of his upper arm muscles as he flexed his arm. The shape of his shoulders, strong and wide made my insides quiver with anticipation. I hoped we would spend the evening together and allow our love to progress and incorporate the physical. I did not have to hope for long.

Will offered me his hand, and pulled me into the tightest, most comforting embrace I had ever known.

I led him to my bedroom and as he kissed me, I swooned.

Chapter 9 – Discovery

Will did not stop kissing me for what felt like an hour. Not that I was complaining. His fingers brushed against my spine where his hands rested against my lower back and I shuddered. The sensation shot through each and every nerve in my body, with an intensity unlike anything I had ever felt before. It amazed me, such a tiny movement, such a slight touch, and I felt alive. More alive than I had ever been, more in tune with my body than I had ever realised was possible; and all because his fingertips had grazed against my lower back. Before I realised it, a moan of pleasure had escaped from my mouth and I pressed my lips harder against his, my body moving closer and firmly against his without any conscious effort; an involuntary and necessary reaction to him. We were lying side by side on my double bed, fully clothed. There was an internal incessant urge within both of us, I felt his need as he kissed me as I felt my own need within the depth of my body, yet we did not feel the need to rush. We were taking our time, exploring each other's body; we had the rest of our lives to do this. I had placed my hands on his wide, muscular chest, appreciating his form, teasing the material of his shirt between my fingers. His hand slid to my waist and lingered for a while, pulling me gently into him. Then he ran his hand slowly down, over my hips to my thighs, pulling me towards him harder, wrapping my leg around his. He slipped his tongue into my mouth and I moaned at the delicious feeling it caused. Before I knew it, my impulses had taken over and I was tugging at his clothes and undoing his shirt buttons. I had so very much wanted to make this last, savour each and every second of our discovery of one another, and yet, I could not help myself. My soul ached because I was not as physically connected to him as I could be, and the physical reaction my body displayed as a result of this was impossible to ignore. Will rolled onto his back, hooking my leg with his hand so I went with him and became astride his legs, balancing on my knees. I reached down and undid his belt, his button and his zip on his jeans. With his chest bare, his jeans undone, the only things which were left between us were my clothes and his boxer shorts. I began to try to remove my blouse, but Will seized my wrist, preventing me from moving. He shook his head slowly as I looked at the devilish look on his face; full of passion, desire, naughtiness and wanting. I understood; he wanted to discover what was under my clothing for himself, in his own time and at his own pace. The realisation caused my face to display a reassured smile.

Slowly, deliberately, he propped himself up on his elbows and tilted his head to look up at me. I ran my hand over his neck up to his jaw line and leant forward to kiss him. His weight shifted beneath me as he sat up fully, moving me upright, his hands snaking behind my back, tugging my blouse loose from my skirt. I felt his skin briefly meet mine as he pulled the last of the material from its confines and I shivered. He moved his attention to the buttons and slowly began undoing them, from the bottom up. As he undid the last, he did not pull the material to either side to reveal to him what was underneath; instead he let his mouth trail down from the small kiss he planted at the base of my jaw, down my neck, over my décolletage; moving the material with his teeth to reveal my lace covered breasts below. Paying each the attention it so deeply craved, I moaned with increasing excitement, exhilaration, tension and desperation for more; more pressure, speed and more exploration. His tongue flickered back and forth, causing my visible response to him become even more prominent than before. The aching I felt in my chest deepened, accompanying that in the pit of my stomach. Before I knew what was happening, I realise he had undone the zip to my skirt, and was pushing it up, over my waist. As his hands brushed the very top of the back of my thighs, I pressed myself down against him and felt just how much he desired me, too. Dispersing the last layer which lay between us, we were ready to become truly as one. I had no qualms; I was not worried, I knew that this would be magical, and so, as I kissed him one last time, I sank down and felt the long, filling presence of him deep within me. My heart glowed. I felt warm with his love, with our love, and complete. My pooling need caused a moan to rise from his throat, into my mouth and I responded by increasing my intensity of kissing him. Slowly, I began to rock and he matched my rhythm perfectly, as if we had been doing this with each other, together, all our lives. My head emptied of thoughts; my emotions usurped all rhyme and reason. The warmth which my heart felt as a result of being as physically close with the man who was my *everything* expanded into every last fibre of my being. I felt true love with every movement, pure acceptance from each of us ebbed and flowed as we moved and joined our bodies together. I was so absolutely happy, the feeling of completeness overwhelming me. And I wanted more. Our hands were everywhere, and after a while, our breathing became so rapid and hard that our kissing reflected it. His fingers traced the outline of my breast, his hand ran up the outside of the back of my thigh, causing my movements to jerk, triggering him to twitch inside me. As our moans and groans of physical and emotional ecstasy grew; louder and more frequent, more passionate and demanding, we reached the climax of our intimacy together. I was awash with him; our love overflowing from one another, to one another. I did not want him to leave. For a long time we stayed very still, gazing at each other, kissing softly, murmuring incomprehensible words and sounds. And then, he told me softly, "Mimi, I love you." My heart beamed. I had never been so happy in my life. I had never felt so complete, so wanted, so needed, and so attuned to someone as I did with Will. We had been made for this moment, for each other; we had been made to be together. And then, for the first time in my life, I reciprocated the sentiment. "Will, I love you too."

We had gradually drifted off to sleep. His arms had wrapped around me; my head had nestled into the hollow of his shoulder so perfectly, I felt as though it was my home. I knew I would always be welcome there, and that there was where I was supposed to be. We fit together so well, so easily, so comfortably. It was bliss: heaven on earth. I was happy, contented, and I *knew* Will was too. Without having to ask, I knew from his demeanour he was contented. We were complete, happy and complete with each other. The last thing I remember that night before succumbing to the depths of sleep were his arms tightening around me, holding me closer to him, as though I were too far away by being just next to him rather than pressed against him and enfolded and embraced within his reach. Halfway through the night, I was disrupted from my dreamless sleep by the gentlest feeling nudging at my lower back, followed by a kiss on the back of my neck. The feeling filled me with delight as I knew what was in store, once more, for us. I smiled and turned over.

The next morning, I woke up to an empty bed. For a brief, confusing moment, I wondered if I had dreamt far too much, but my feelings of unease and discontent were soon evaporated when from downstairs I heard the faint noises of cupboard doors being opened and closed in the kitchen. Glancing at the clock and seeing that it was past nine o'clock, I was grateful Will had let me sleep in. Our activities through the night had exhausted me considerably more than I had anticipated. Before long, I heard footsteps softly padding up the stairs and as the door opened slowly, the divine face of Will peered around the gap it created, his hair ruffled in a manner that made my heart melt, his eyes sparkling and inquisitive. Seeing I was awake, he pushed the door open with what sounded like his knee from the bang it made, and as he complained under his breath I saw he had brought a tray upstairs; he had made me breakfast in bed. A single red rose, from my garden I assumed, lay alongside the plate of toast and bowl of cereal. I smiled at him and told him that I had not known he was romantic. He said that he had not known he was either, but that he wanted to do something nice for me, because he knew that I had had an emotional day the previous day. Immediately I knew he saw the pain the memory brought to my face. He asked me if what I had had with Michael was the same as what we had. I said no, it was not, and that I supposed on some level I always knew that it was not, but that did not mean that I was not happy with Michael, because I had been, and that I loved him very much, and probably always would. Will nodded slowly, and told me that he understood. He asked me if I thought Michael and I would be able to be friends in time. I sighed and told him that I hoped so, but that there was no guarantee. I had not been able to think about how to build bridges with Michael yet. I had promised Zara I would do everything within my power to make sure that we were friends and got along, for the sake of the baby, our soon to be Godchild. Now I just had to find a way to do that.

And as I finished my breakfast Will suggested, with a twinkle in his eye, that we take a shower.

I readily jumped out of bed to join him, eager to discover what he looked like wet.

Chapter 10 – Routines and Welcomes

Six weeks had passed since the day Will and I had fallen in love and we had become an item. It was strange, at first, trying to become accustomed to each other's lives and schedules. His lectures, my lectures, our work, our free time, his sports within and outside of university, my study sessions with the friends I had made there, and most importantly, Will had learned quickly that Monday nights were off limits as Zara and I spent up to two hours, or sometimes more, on the telephone having a 'catch up'. This was, of course, whether we had spent the weekend seeing each other or not. Will and Robert were easing towards the step of friendship. I could tell Robert was not very happy with what had taken place, perhaps even edging towards being angry and hurt about it; Michael was his best friend and no doubt he was reporting back to him, but from the way he behaved, almost too polite at first, I was sure that Zara had spoken to Robert to remind him to be on his best behaviour because Will and I, we were the real thing. We had gladly taken the opportunity to visit them two weeks after Zara and Will had first met. Zara suggested we spend the evening in their local pub, a public setting perhaps being a more inviting and relaxed atmosphere than the confines and solitude of their home. Thankfully, Zara's bladder, being pressured by the baby, monopolised most of her evening, and we had plenty of opportunities to pop to the bathroom to discuss how we thought the chaps were getting along.

It had been a slow beginning, the usual guy talk about sports, rugby, politics, which beer was better to drink and why, which female celebrity had more fake parts to her than another and of course, when Zara and I had re-joined the conversation at that particular point, in how many ways they each preferred their partners! Rolling our eyes at them, Zara and I had giggled, and I was elated that Robert was making the effort he was not obliged to make to get to know Will. I was grateful beyond expressive capabilities, although I did try to convey how appreciative I was; as I had sat down, I reached for Robert's hand and gave it a squeeze of thanks. So then, six weeks after we had fallen in love, it was Will who had a telephone call from Robert. I was in a lecture, Will was not, and so Robert had called Will to ask him to meet me at the end of my lecture to tell me that Zara had gone into labour. It was two weeks early, but they were not concerned, Robert had told Will. And so, at the end of my lecture, I had been greeted by my *everything*, with a serious but happy face. He told me the news and I could not help gasp with surprise and happiness. Will and I rushed back to my house to fetch clothes, the congratulations present and card I had bought a few weeks earlier, and supplies for the hospital should we be there for a long time. Will carried the bag and we got into his car hurriedly. I was as excited as a child in a sweet shop on the way down the motorway to the hospital. Zara and Robert had chosen not to find out if they were having a son or a daughter, and it had infuriated me during the early stages of her pregnancy. Yet now, I saw the reasoning behind their decision. Through all the pain and suffering, Zara would get a happy surprise at the end, rather than a foregone conclusion with little to look forward to and discover.

We arrived at the hospital and found a parking space on a side road to avoid the car park charges. Will said he was amazed that a place with an Accident and Emergency Unit could possibly charge people for parking. He wondered how they would have the time to find loose change to put into the machine and put the sticky ticket into their windows if they were in agonising pain and needed medical transportation but had driven to get help. I agreed with him, but pointed out that, as a lot of other things in society now, money was the root behind everything. We shook our heads in bewilderment and dismay and walked towards the building when I suddenly stopped frozen on the spot: Michael. I had not thought he would be there; the thought had not crossed my mind. I had not expected to see him, but I do not know why I had not expected to see him; of course he would be there. I was confused by my reaction to his presence, I did not know what to think; I had not even spoken to him, properly, since I had ended our relationship. I had tried to email him, to see how he was, to see what was new with his life, to see if he was willing to try to be friends, not that I could blame him if he could not, but I had had nothing in return but short, rushed, yet polite, replies. I could not blame him, of course, I could only blame myself. Will paused a few steps in front of where I remained rooted to the ground, unable to move. He asked me what was wrong, and stared intently at my face. I had felt the colour drain from my features as my eyes had met Michael's as he stood, equally frozen, at the doors of the hospital. Will followed my gaze and as his eyes rested upon Michael, he understood my countenance as Michael's name escaped my lips in a shocked, breathless whisper.

I do not know why, but panic flooded through me. I could not at that time make any sense of the emotions which followed the panic as they surged through me. Fear, panic, worry, apprehension, trepidation and dismay were rushing through me in all directions. Thoughts and questions whirled incomprehensively through my mind. What would happen? Would Michael cause a scene? If he did, I would have no defence to make. Would Will be under any threat of danger? I did not think that Michael would become violent, I hoped he would not, and the thought that something, however insignificant may happen to my *everything* made me feel like I was about to faint. I knew it was ridiculous; Will could take care of himself, and the fact that I thought they might fight over me, struck me as selfish, something which I had made a resolution to try and avoid. Why would Michael even care? But I knew he did, I just did not know how much. I had not moved, I had barely breathed; my world was spinning in the wrong direction, and then my salvation presented itself before me. Will stepped in front of me, breaking my eye contact with Michael, Will's crystal blue eyes brought me back to my centre, my *everything* grounded me. He held my shoulders firmly, told me to breathe and my lungs responded without needing much conscious encouragement. My mind was whirling still, but my world was grounded by Will. My breath was shaky, and my eyes were stinging at the prospect of newly forming tears. Suddenly, warmth overcame me; Will's arms provided a blanket of comfort for me against the world. I was safe. Happy. Contented. I knew nothing could hurt me here, and that I could remain here for as long as I wanted, in his arms, and that he would be happy to hold me. We fit together perfectly, the contours of our bodies matching our personalities, matching our hearts. We were a unit, and we would deal with whatever faced us together. Will was my rock, my strength and my salvation. I exhaled deeply and nodded once against his chest. His hand found mine and we walked towards the hospital doors. Michael was still standing there; he had been watching everything.

My heart was crying. Even though I knew that nothing could break it, it still wept for my friend. Michael meant so much to me, and it hurt me to know that he was hurting because of what I had done. Michael and I exchanged polite, somewhat stifled, greetings as we approached the hospital doors where he was standing. I saw his eyes scan over Will, questions written all over his face. He was quick to cover them with an aura of politeness, the way his parents had brought him up; but for a split second, I had seen the looks of doubt, wondering, jealousy, even, flicker over his face. In the lift on the way up to the maternity floor, without being able to look directly into Will's eyes and feel the rush of calm flowing through me, anxiety again began to tingle at the edges of my being. I felt torn. I desperately wanted to be held by Will, or hold his hand, I wanted us to bask in the warmth of each other, revel in the safety and contentment; yet I wanted to link my arm through Michael's and offer him some relief from the tension which was so clearly visible by his clenched jaw and pulsing temple vein.

I felt it was the longest time I had ever spent in a lift. I had never truly understood the use of the phrase, 'felt like an eternity', until that moment. I felt like a traitor for wanting to comfort Michael, and wondered what Will would think with regards to my empathy and concern for Michael. Part of me was startled to find I still had such strong feelings for Michael, that my love for him was always based around friendship, and that, somehow, I did not feel guilty towards Will for having this love for Michael still in my heart. Finally, our metallic confinement came to an end, and we all reached the maternity floor. Michael and I approached the nurse's desk as Will stood slightly behind me. I understood that Will would not be next to me where Zara was concerned; it was as though he understood that the four of us, Robert, Zara, Michael and I had a tight, and almost exclusive, contained friendship. The feeling of being torn returned to me, I desperately wanted Will to be as much a part of the group as I was, and yet I understood that it was just not possible. My heart sunk slightly as this realisation was confirmed for me in Will's choice of standing place. We asked where Zara was and were pointed in the direction down the corridor and to the left. Excitement overcame me as I realised what and whom I was about to see and an uncharacteristic bounce resulted, as my body expressed my inner joy by itself. I felt a small squeeze of my hand and as I turned to look at Will we exchanged smiles, our eyes connecting once more, communicating without words that one day, not too far into the future, we knew we would be in Zara and Robert's position, beginning our own family. I glanced over at Michael, and for the time being, he and I seemed to be feeling the same emotions, anticipation and excitement at our Godchild being just the other side of the double doors leading to the bay in which Zara's bed was.

The three of us walked through the doors to see a radiant Zara filled with smiles and admiration at the wriggling bundle in her arms. As I looked down, Robert turned to Michael and I and introduced us to the child: we had a Goddaughter. They had named her Tara. I bit my lip as I watched Zara's seemingly expert handling of the baby in her arms, and as she looked up at me and asked me if I would like to hold my niece, words escaped me; all I could do was nod in confirmation. As I held my arms out to hold the baby, I knew my world was about to change forever. Immediately, as she settled into my arms, I felt fiercely protective; as though it was my job to make sure this beautiful baby girl would never go without love, support and happiness, as though I was *charged* to do this. Logic told me that I would never have to, but I knew I would give my life for her. Tara opened her beautiful blue eyes, and as I gazed at them, speechless – for I had not yet been able to utter a single word - my heart jumped in my chest as it grew to immediately love her as much as I loved Will. I was not just gazing at a new baby; I was looking at an additional centre for my universe to orbit. I was astounded how something so small could wield so much power over a fully-grown woman like myself, and I could only imagine that if this was the strength of my feelings, how overwhelming and totally enveloping Zara's feelings, emotions and heart must be, reacting to Tara's arrival.

I do not know how much time had elapsed as my vision was focused, almost hypnotically, gazing at Tara; trying to memorise each contour of her face, mesmerised at her long eyelashes, her rosebud mouth making me smile even more as it moved so slightly, and when her hand clasped my finger I felt as though I could stay in awe of her for my entire life. She looked exactly like Zara: a miniature version of my most treasured and best friend. I was astounded by her pure beauty. My gaze was finally interrupted by Michael, who had moved to my side and was asking to hold Tara. Reluctantly, I passed her over to him, and watched as she wielded her magic over him as well as she had with me. I turned to Zara and told her that I was amazed at just how beautiful her daughter was, and I hugged her tightly, fighting back tears of joy and happiness for myself and for Zara. I moved across the room and hugged Robert, giving him a kiss on the cheek and saying congratulations, and warning him that he had better take the greatest care of my niece, or he would have me to answer to. Naturally, I moved back to Will's side, without even realising I had moved and without realising I had chosen my destination. I felt Will's arm around my shoulders, and I leaned my head into him, and my eyes settled onto Michael and Tara. I was vaguely aware that Zara had opened the card and present we had bought for her and Robert, and that Will had congratulated them both, shook hands and slapped Robert on the back, and kissed Zara on the cheek, whilst I had been holding Tara, and even afterwards, as I stood with my head resting on Will, his arm around me, I could not pay full attention to the conversation in the room; my focus was dictated by the baby's location in the room. My eyes flickered to and from Tara and Michael and for a slight instant, my gaze was greeted by those so familiar chocolate brown eyes I had once loved.

And as Michael's eyes met mine, an unspoken agreement was made between us; I knew we would do anything for her.

We had discovered a new kind of love.

Chapter 11 – Settling in

Relations between Michael and I had become somewhat easier, more relaxed, since Tara's birth. Communication between us was centralised around the baby, but I took solace in the fact that at least it was occurring. Michael had sent numerous pictures via email and mobile telephone whenever he had visited Robert, Zara and Tara so that I could see her development, and when Will and I went to see them, I sent pictures to Michael of our visits too. Will and I were happier than ever, and we spent hours conversing on the subject of our future together. We were so very relaxed around each other; we could talk about anything, openly and honestly, without reservation or restraint, and without discomfort or awkwardness. We had only been an item for two months and, although we had naturally fallen into a routine around our schedules, we still had a lot of the mundane things to discover about each other; and yet, it was all so exciting to me. We discussed everything from holidays to favourite foods, sport to politics, religious beliefs to clothing, childhoods to hair styles, music to books, shopping to gardening. I was elated; talking with Will was so easy, it was like talking to myself. We finished our degrees shortly after Tara was born, and graduation was a big success. We had a wonderful day, with lots of preceding parties in the days and weeks before graduation, and on the night of the day of the ceremony, our entire class attended the graduation ball. It was a night I shall never forget. We all dressed up in formal attire, hired a limousine to take us all to and from the big venue, and I had never seen Will look so dashing. He was handsome wearing nothing of course, but he looked enchanting in his tuxedo. I felt like a princess in my floor length ball gown, with the necklace Will had bought me as a congratulations present resting around my neck, the pendent sitting on my décolletage. I had purchased a pair of gold cufflinks with his initials engraved into them as a graduation gift. The night was spent saying goodbye to friends, celebrating good results, thanking our lecturers, and never leaving Will's side. Our hands barely parted all night; only returning to our own bodies when it was time to eat, toast the class, or take photographs. The string quartet during dinner played the most melodic music I had ever heard, although unfortunately the pieces they played were not any I was familiar with. As the evening progressed, the music became more modern, and the D.J. easily enabled our group to transcend into a party atmosphere, celebrating by dancing to convey our happiness at our journey through university, and the friendships which we had made, made all of us sure they would last forever.

We were both extremely lucky to gain jobs immediately after graduating, especially considering the economic climate of the time, and Will and I put down a deposit on a small apartment to rent while we were saving for our future. It was not a palace, and by no means was it anything special, or fancy, but it was our home, and we loved it. We spent a week decorating it before we moved in, although Will was resigned to do most of the painting as I was not very handy with a brush or a roller; most of the mocha brown found its way onto my clothes and into my hair. I busied myself cleaning the apartment from top to bottom, and arranging what little decorative ornaments and furniture we had into the best, friendliest, welcoming, homely arrangement I could manage. The chores fell naturally between us after we moved into our first home together: cooking, dish washing, laundry, vacuuming, all seemed to be split easily between us without any division having to be decided. We were settling in to life as a proper couple. I felt almost like a proper grown up adult. Our days were spent at work; our evenings spent talking over our dinner about jobs, life, gossip, and plans for our future. Our nights were spent in awe of each other. Every night we were just so happy to be falling asleep next to one another, tangled up in each other's skin in sheer bliss. Our weekends were spent relaxing and enjoying each other's company, getting to know even more about one another, and visiting Zara and Robert.

We had fallen into a pattern of fortnightly visits to Zara's house, each time Tara had changed and developed so much. Robert and Zara seemed to be coping very well with parenthood, although they did have dark circles under their eyes from the sleepless nights. Tara was not the most peaceful baby, waking her parents up two or three times a night to respond to her needs. Zara told me that although she was tired, and although the workload was much more than she would ever be paid a five figure salary for, she would not swap the job of being a mother for the entire world. She told me that one day she had not done an ounce of housework because Tara had first laughed, and Zara proceeded to spend the rest of the day attempting to recreate the event. Robert had been filming Tara almost continuously, to which Zara still occasionally rolled her eyes when he produced the digital video camera. During the first few months of fortnightly visits, I tried to do as much for Zara around the house, and minding the baby, as I could; once I sent Robert and Will to the pub to have a break from the house, and I sent Zara to the bathroom to enjoy a long relaxing soak in the bath tub whilst I took care of the baby and made dinner for us all. I knew I could not make any grand gestures, but I tried to do as much as I could. I was finding it easier to fulfil my personal vow of being less selfish, and I almost did not have to think about it where Tara was concerned. Almost - because I did have to remember, occasionally, to return her to her parents before I left to go home with Will. Will usually smiled and shook his head at me during these instances, and jokingly apologised to Zara and Robert for almost kidnapping their daughter.

Soon, it was time for Tara's christening. Michael and I were to be the God parents, and I was so excited about the ceremony, I was almost bursting. I asked Will to make sure he took plenty of photographs of everyone at the ceremony, the church, and all the guests, so that when Tara was older and came to stay at our house, the house I saw in my head that we would buy as soon as we had saved for our wedding (a three bedroomed semi-detached with a driveway and a garage, a long sitting room, a kitchen diner and a utility room), we could show Tara the photographs of the beginning of the important days of her life. He had had an odd look in his eyes as he agreed, and I did not understand at the time what could have been the matter. Will looked dashing in his suit; I had splashed out on a nice skirt and jacket, a new blouse, a hat suitable for church, and new shoes which were glorious, but uncomfortable. We arrived at the church amongst a throng of Robert's friends and family, Zara's family were already inside, and I introduced Will to Zara's parents for the first time as we sat next to them in the pew. Michael, I saw, was already seated in the row opposite the nave, and I smiled across to him, and was awarded a friendly smile in return. I asked him if he was nervous, and he told me that he had been trying to remember what we had to say when the priest asked us our questions. I told him I was relying on the Order of Service to guide me through, as I was far too excited to concentrate. A small giggle escaped his mouth, and hope tingled within me that Michael was able to forgive me enough to laugh at my silliness. As the time came to move to the front of the church and hold Tara as we promised to fulfil our duties as God parents, I knew that Michael and I would do anything for the child I held in my arms. As we posed for photographs after Tara had been baptised and welcomed into the family of the Catholic Church, I understood that Tara would grow up knowing she had two people in her life, other than her parents, who loved her unconditionally, because they wanted to, because they could, and because they felt it was their duty.

I also knew, and despaired, that Tara would see Uncle Michael and Aunt Mimi as a unit.

It saddened me; where would Uncle Will fit in?

Chapter 12 – Adjustments and Requests

As Tara grew older, my life and plans took on some adjustments. I was enjoying my job, working hard enough to feel rewarded but not too much so I felt drained for no reason. Our savings were building up, enough to take a few mid-week trips together to Hayle Bay on the south coast in springtime and during the summer to enjoy the golden beach and beautiful scenery and blissful peace it offered; the wedding planning was moving slowly but smoothly. I had always known, since the moment Will and I fell in love, what our wedding would look like: Will in a gold waistcoat, black morning suit, a red rose in his lapel, my wedding dress; white, intricate designs in gold silk decorating the front panel, my bouquet was made of white and red roses with green leaves, Zara in a dress which was the same cut as mine, but the colours reversed, us taking our vows, promising to love honour and respect each other as long as we both shall live. It was this scene, which had, automatically, so long been nested in my mind's eye, I was working towards organising. I had asked Will what he thought about waiting until Tara was old enough to be a flower girl at our wedding to get married, and the smile on his face made my heart sing. He told me that he had just one condition regarding her being part of our wedding ceremony; that he would get to ask her to be a flower girl. I agreed immediately. I had been plagued with worry that Tara would not love and accept Will as much as she would Michael, because he was not her Godfather as Michael was. I believed she would think of Michael and I as a unit; her Godparents being self-contained and exclusive. It worried me because I did not want to be a traitor to anyone, or disappoint Tara. Silly, I know, yet these fears afflicted my mind on a regular basis and at that time in her life I had no proof to support or reject my fears.

Another adjustment I had to make, less pleasurable than waiting for Tara to age, was to lose every second weekend with Will to his career. He had to undertake a training course for twelve months, in order to be eligible for a promotion at work. It was an unexpected opportunity since he had not long since begun to work at his job. The company he worked for divided the candidates for promotion into two groups; fast track and steady climbers. The fast track people were offered the course intensively; relocating to an isolated village in rural England so as to avoid distraction for their month-long course. The steady climbers were required to spend every other weekend undertaking the course, allowing for time in between, to work on their presentations and research in order to prepare for the interview and role they were aiming for. Will was offered the fast track option, but felt that he could not spend a month away from me, and I knew I certainly would not be able to bear not having him at home for that amount of time. So he immediately turned down the fast track option, preferring to take his time and thoroughly learn and prepare for the interview for the promotion. I was so thankful we knew each other so well; he had not even telephoned me to ask if I wanted him to turn down the fast track option, he had turned it down and opted for the steady climber option automatically. Despite knowing that losing Will for every second weekend was the least-worst option, it still did not sit well with me because of him missing time with Tara. A lot of my visits to Zara's house coincided with Michael's, and so my fears were being reinforced every weekend Will was missing. A significant part of me hoped Tara was too young to comprehend the dynamics between Michael and I.

On the positive side, Michael and I were able to build on the ease that had begun to grow between us. I tried hard to avoid talking about Will in front of Michael, instead trying to focus on building a friendship with him. I was sure Michael knew I was trying to avoid talking about how happy I was now that Will was my life, and I was certain he felt as though he was infringing upon my natural happiness. I felt terrible because I did not think he should feel any worse because of my actions. It surprised me how difficult it was to avoid saying 'we' instead of 'I' whenever I was describing the events of the week. So much of my life included and depended on Will being with me during any event other than work, that it was difficult to separate myself from him throughout daily life. This was the major difference between my relationship with Michael and my life with Will. Michael and I had not been able to spend as much time together, but the drive to be in each other's company consistently had not been present between us. Now we had to adjust to seeing each other more than we did when we were in a relationship, but as tentative friends hopefully moving towards a solid friendship; something we had not had for many years.

One weekend when Tara was nine months old, Zara and I left Tara with Robert and Michael at their house and went into town to go shopping as we had done every weekend before our rugby matches when we were youngsters. It brought back so many memories of smoothies, and girl talk, sharing and secrets, and we spent a considerable amount of that morning reminiscing about our youth. I appreciated the chance to reminisce about our, what felt like lost, youth, yet with our rare time together without company, I had hoped to discuss wedding plans with her. Over lunch, I broached the subject of my wedding delicately, asking her advice on where to buy reasonably priced, yet good quality, card to make the invitations with. She gave me a list of suggestions, and I took my diary out of my bag and started to write down the wealth of information she was sharing from the storage compartment in her mind labelled 'Wedding.' I asked about flowers, and balloons, table decorations and comfortable shoes. After the pain my feet had been in for two weeks after Tara's christening, I had decided I needed comfortable wedding shoes or I may have to resort to wearing trainers under my floor length dress. It was then I informed Zara of Will's request to ask Tara to be a flower girl for our wedding. It was the first, and last, time I had ever seen her speechless. A smile began to spread over her face, and tears welled up in her eyes, and she told me that she had not realised I would want to include her daughter in my wedding. I told her not to be so silly, and that of course if I was going to have her as my Maid of Honour, I would want my Goddaughter as my flower girl. I told Zara that we had discussed the matter, and we wanted to wait until Tara was old enough to be our flower girl to marry. She said she could not believe we would put our marriage back just for the sake of Tara being a part of it. I told her that I would not have it any other way, and neither would Will. Will and I were not Catholic like Zara and Robert, we did not feel the pressure to marry before we lived together as they had, we knew in our hearts our commitment to each other was as solid as any diamond in a ring on my hand could be, without having to have the ceremony and a piece of paper to confirm it. We wanted to marry, because we wanted to celebrate our love and lay equal claim to each other for the rest of our lives, but it was not a prerequisite to cement our commitment. I wanted his last name, he wanted to be able to use the term wife when describing me, and I wanted nothing more than to call him my husband, but our devotion did not depend on being married. I made Zara promise me that she would never mention to Tara the prospect of being our flower girl as she was growing up, and she agreed readily, smiling, saying that she would not even tell Robert that Will wanted to be the one to ask Tara to do the honours. I smiled and giggled slightly as I told her that it was all right to spill the beans to her husband.

As we drove back to Zara's house, I contemplated the adjustments in our lives.

Everything seemed to be going swimmingly.

Chapter 13 – Moving

Because we had decided to put the wedding back for a few years till Tara was old enough to be our flower girl, our wedding savings were able to be amalgamated with our house savings, and before we knew it, we were viewing more houses than our estate agents had in their professional lives. Our mortgage broker was very impressed that we did not require a one hundred per cent mortgage like the majority of his clients. He mentioned to us that it was a very rare thing to find young people, couples, such as us who had saved and prepared for the future. He was approaching retirement he told us, and in his many years as a financier he had noticed a steady decline in the number of people using his service who had investigated what was necessary to purchase their homes. He told us that most couples our age were nowhere near in a position to be able to think about buying a house, and that most of his appointments for the under 25s were for rental properties. We told him it was a combination of being taught by our parents, by asking questions of those older than us at work, and by generally paying attention to the news and current affairs on the television and the Internet regarding all the different housing and interest rates. A raised eyebrow and a slow nod of approval was our reward for being prepared.

Finally, after much searching and second opinions from Robert and Zara of the short list, we had found our perfect home; a three bedroomed semi-detached with a driveway large enough for both our cars, a long sitting room, a kitchen diner and a utility room. The en-suite shower room was lovely, and the main bathroom was huge. We were lucky because there was an extra room downstairs which we had not put onto our wish list, which would serve nicely as a study in which both of us would be able to work. Will was very happy with the garage at the top of the driveway; it was a good size, so we could keep one of the cars in there along with the lawn mower, which he promised to use each weekend to keep the garden in pristine condition. Somewhere in my head I imagined he would stretch that out to a fortnightly rota, especially if the weather continued to be wintry and the rainfall did not desist enough to dry out the lawn in order to mow it. Will and I had often stood at the window of our apartment in the months which had constituted summer of the previous year, shaking our heads at the hail stones which fell angrily from the sky. The house did not need much in the way of improvements or DIY and it was modern enough so that the electric wiring did not need to be replaced, yet old enough that it had some character to it. We even liked the colour scheme and were not planning on decorating for at least twelve months. It was perfect.

Zara had asked if we wanted any help moving in, and we readily accepted the offer. Tara spent the day at her grandparent's house, Robert's mother desperate to spend some time spoiling and playing with her granddaughter. While the men did all the heavy lifting, Zara and I started to unpack, gossiping and giggling as we did. We had arranged for all our furniture to be delivered on the day of moving into our house, and as the boys waited for the sofas, the beds, the utility room machines, various cabinets and a new vacuum, ours had broken the weekend before moving, Zara and I went food shopping to restock our now almost empty fridge-freezer. Will and I had made sure we had not bought any food for a month to ensure when we moved over our fridge-freezer to the new house; the food would not spoil, or fall out, during transport. After a long day of unpacking boxes, hanging up my hundreds of items of clothing, trying to organise my shoes, cleaning up the mess that we had made getting everything into the correct rooms, we sat in the lounge - the television on low, exhausted yet deliriously happy. Zara and Robert sat on the new sofa, his arm around her and her head on his shoulder, looking thoroughly worn out but happy; for us I presumed. We were sitting on the floor, Will behind me with his arms wrapped round me, my right hand on his forearm and my other on his left knee. I remember sighing with contentment as I glanced around at the walls of our lounge. Our first home. I was in a state of bliss. When Zara and Robert had recovered some of their energy, they said their goodnights and went to fetch Tara from her Grandmother's house. Waving them off from the front door I smiled, my mind planning for dinner parties years in advance, possibly even hosting a Christmas here.

My hopes for the future were briefly interrupted as Will reminded me that we had to go and see the solicitor in a few weeks' time to write our wills. Since we were not married yet, we had to specifically leave our halves of the house to the other should anything happen to us. I did not want to think about it. It caused me great pain. It was a terrible predicament. I did not want to live without Will, I knew I would never be able to cope if something should happen to him, and yet I did not want to be the one to die first, knowing how heartbroken he would be without me. The thought of either event coming to pass made my skin turn ice cold and the colour drain from my face. Will saw my physical reaction to the dreadful thoughts running through my mind, and the emotions they caused, and held me tightly. I remember his whisper in my ear, the instruction to not even think about it, that it would never come to pass until we were old, and I prayed that his reassurances would come to fruition.

Within seconds the thoughts of our mortalities were banished to the back of my mind as more pressing matters came to the forefront of our consciousness. Hearing Will inhale deeply by my ear was a private signal to my innermost muscles that he had spent too much time away from me; with that intake of breath, I had known that my most favourite event was approaching. In his most seductive and suggestive voice he whispered the notion that we 'christen' the house. I asked which room he wanted to christen, and he told me that he had been assuming that we would christen all of them. A delighted squeal erupted from my lips as he lifted me up and took me into the bedroom.

81

Over the next two weeks, we found favourite spots to indulge in each other all over our new house. Will very naughtily suggested we employ the back garden as a spot for our intimacy, although I declined suggesting to him that we at least wait until the conifers were at a height to provide enough privacy from the neighbour's windows. As we grew older, our tastes were developing and an experimental edge was occasionally included in our love making. We were not bored, not in the slightest. The smallest kiss could bring shockwaves to my entire body if I had been without his company for more than a few hours. Our relationship had developed to a point where we were so at ease and comfortable with each other, that if ever we saw inspiration from a film, or television programme, or read about anything, we could openly and easily suggest, debate, and experiment and test new things out to discover if we enjoyed them. One of my favourite things Will had introduced into our passionate lives was spending time together in the shower. We found it very sensual to wash each other and make love surrounded by water whose heat matched our fervent desire for one another.

Then suddenly, without realising where time had gone, it was time to go and see the solicitor.

And all of our love making could not numb the nagging thoughts at the back of my mind.

Chapter 14 – Devastation

Four years later, we were settled into our home, our life and we were completely happy. My friendship with Michael had reached a point where we were able to take Tara out for the day on our own without any bad feeling between us whatsoever. Similarly, Will was falling in love with her more and more each time she came to stay at our house. We had a nice routine in place. Every last weekend of the month, Tara, Michael and I would spend Saturday together, at the park or going swimming, and then she would stay with her Aunt Mimi and Uncle Will. I was thrilled, and just ever so slightly broody. Will and I had often affirmed to each other we wanted to have children, yet the unspoken consensus was that we would wait until after we were married. We had strong opinions regarding having children. We did not want to rush into it. We wanted the time to be right for us, for our careers, and above all, we wanted to be financially stable and prepared for anything. We were not rich by any stretch of the imagination, but we were comfortable. We had a holiday each year to the Maldives; two weeks of sun, sea and relaxation. We worked hard in our jobs and deserved our time away. But we wanted to be in a position where we had enough saved up for a rainy day in case we should ever need it after we had children. We wanted to ensure we had children for the right reasons; not for the sake of having them. We wanted to ensure we gave them everything we could, and that they would never be in a situation where their upbringing suffered because we had not been responsible enough to plan for their future and put their needs first. The wedding fund, which had gone into the buying a house fund, was re-accumulating nicely and we had enough to pay for almost everything. In another eight months we would have enough in the bank to pay for our entire wedding, and so we were aiming to be married in a year's time.

Then my world ended.

I remember it like it was yesterday, it was an autumn afternoon which was practically evening; it was fast approaching winter. The sun was blanketed by the thick, heavy clouds full of rain, darkness betraying the hands of the clock; the wind took pleasure in stinging the cheeks of those who dared to walk in its presence. I was at work, and my work friends were asking about my wedding plans when the telephone on my desk rang. I answered the call with my usual cheerful and professional tone, identifying myself and the company and asking how I could be of help; the voice at the other end chilled my blood as soon as my name was spoken. "Mimi..." It was Michael. I immediately knew something was wrong by the way he sorrowfully spoke my name and my heart stopped. I took a sharp intake of breath and asked what was wrong, without even acknowledging I knew it was him on the other end of the telephone. As he began to speak, to share the news that caused my world to end, my body went numb. Sounds in the background of the room evaporated into nothing; I could only hear his voice.

I remember hearing the pounding of my heart in my ears; a frantic beat which matched the pace of the crumbling of my life. I remember the utter despair, anguish and pain in his voice as he broke the news to me. I remember my chest feeling tight, as though the weight of the news was crushing my lungs preventing me from breathing. I remember taking shallow and rapid breaths as I began to shake my head and utter disbelieving "Nos," down the telephone. I vaguely remember hearing my workmates try to gain my attention and ask what was wrong. I felt the colour drain from my face and my body turned as cold as ice. I remember hearing someone, I could not tell who, point out that I was shaking.

And then the tears started to fall, silently, down my face; burning my ice cold skin with their agony. Michael had told me more details than I had heard. His first sentence was whirling around in my head, rushing from one synapse to another in order to search for a place where his words made sense. The sentence found no fitting home inside my brain. I was too numb to act; the pain in my chest, the compression of my lungs, the stabbing pain I felt searing through my heart was indescribable, unbearable, and preventing me from achieving any movement.

I did not know what to do. How to react. What to say. How to feel. What to think. None of these options, questions, had an answer. I remember feeling like I was the only person in the world; that everyone else had faded into the ether, and the weight of the world was now upon my shoulders. This news, this devastating sentence which Michael had somehow summoned the strength to deliver to me, had crushed my life. Ended my world. And now the devastation set in.

Zara and Robert had been in a car crash on the motorway. Robert was on a life support machine in hospital. Critically ill.

Zara was dead.

Zara... was dead.

Chapter 15 – Realisation

Before I knew what I was doing, I was in my car. I had somehow explained to my boss at work what had happened, in a garbled sentence, and that I had to leave and I grabbed my handbag and was somehow suddenly in the car. Michael had told me to go to the hospital as soon as I could and that he would meet me there. I could not remember how I had got to the car, or indeed how I had got to the road I was driving on, and before I knew it I was in Zara's home town at the hospital putting coins into the parking meter before going inside to meet Michael. It was only then I remembered a long time ago Will saying he was amazed that a place with an Accident and Emergency Unit could possibly charge people for parking when we had arrived here to greet Tara after her birth.

Tara.

My world started to spin again for this child my little girl my Goddaughter the apple of my eye my niece the pain I felt doubled trebled quadrupled when the realisation hit me she had lost her mother I had lost my best friend she could lose her father I did not know what to do and the tears started flowing rapidly again from my eyes as the first gasps of pain escaped from my mouth and turned into howls and before I knew it there were a pair of familiar arms wrapped around me just after I had entered the ward where Michael had told me to meet him and I do not remember getting there but I remember my crying and howling in pain and I buried my head into a welcoming shoulder and grabbed onto his arms for strength and support although I do not know where I found the ability to be able to grab his arms but I did because he was the only thing that was holding me up not that I wanted to be standing up I would have quite happily fallen through the earth into oblivion at that moment I ached with the agony of this tragedy the worst thing to ever happen in my life the worst thing to ever happen in Tara's life the worst thing to ever happen in the world ever and I just did not know how to deal with the pain and I started sobbing the palpable hurt in my soul my chest my lungs my heart my brain being consumed how did this happen who was responsible how could I fix it how could I avenge this how could this happen why me why Zara why Michael why Robert I know they say life is not fair and at that moment I could not have agreed more with that statement the pain and anger rage really flowed through every nerve and every vein I possessed in my body and it was so immense I felt it in my fingernails I could not believe this had happened and I felt my body giving in to the pain and my weight sinking to the floor to match the position of my heart as I broke Michael's hold on me and leant against the wall with my knees bent almost in a seating position with my head down and thinking that if I did not stand up right there and then of my own accord I may never stand up again and as my mind started racing I remember frantic movements from my arms and my gestures were over the top and my mouth was allowing words to spill out of it in a random order and I made no sense because none of this made sense and right then and there for a brief moment I wanted nothing more than the void that had devoured my heart to swallow me up and let me join Zara because the void she left was too large to comprehend my best friend how was I going to live without her how was I going to cope without her in my life how could I understand that I would never see her again how would I be able to breathe without her how would I be able to tell Tara what had happened to her beloved Mummy how would I be able to tell Robert what had happened to his soul mate his wife his other half how would I be able to tell him without it killing him would he even make it Michael had said that he was critically ill and that pained me even more the friendship I had with Robert had blossomed and was as solid as a rock I loved him more than I had the words for how could I even think about him not living and then as I thought about him not living my legs gave way again and the familiar arms wrapped around my waist to try and keep me upright because it was worse than before and I was almost on the point of fainting and then I just wondered how on earth I was going to cope and my head was muddled and I could not think straight and my breathing was irregular and it hurt my chest to breathe in and the physical pain only just registered with me even though I knew it was the worst I had ever felt and would ever feel again and I just did not know what to do and somehow I remember being made to take steps further into the ward towards the side room and before I knew it I was in the room where Robert lay battered and bruised and broken with tubes and wires and drips and monitors coming from every inch of him dripping and beeping and the smell of hospitals hit my nose offensively and I felt sick to my stomach because this was so unfair so unfair that Robert was like this that his wife had died oh my God Zara was dead and Robert does not even know how would I tell him how would I tell Tara?

I looked up at the owner of the familiar arms which were still around me and chocolate brown eyes met mine filled with the same pain and hurt and agony and anguish in them as I had in my soul. Michael was the only person in the world who knew how this felt. And then I remembered.

We had made a promise, years before; a life altering promise.

And now we might have to keep it.

Chapter 16 - Remember

The memory had struck me as Michael's eyes had met mine. On the day that Zara met Will, she had asked me to be her child's legal guardian along with Michael should anything ever happen to both her and Robert. I had immediately agreed, never thinking that it would be necessary.

A few months after the christening, I remember we were reminiscing about our younger days as we were out for a day shopping, and Zara had told me that she could not believe how wrong we had been back then about our future as a foursome. I had replied that it was sad that things had not worked out in the fairy tale ending that we had imagined, but that I would not give up my situation for the world. I had told her that I was blissfully happy with Will. That we were complete. That we were each other's missing halves, just as she and Robert were. She told me she understood and knew that, and that she had been extremely dubious when I had told her about Will, and that she had been worried about me, but she could see the first time she met him that what we had was the real thing, just as she and Robert were. I told her I knew. I had wondered why she was bringing this matter up; I thought we were accepted as a unit without restraint by Zara, and I did not understand the relevance of the conversation.

Just as I was glowing with the thought of Will's love, Zara had shaken my world with a request that had frightened me to my core for more reasons than I could comprehend. She told me that she and Robert had been talking, since before Tara was born, and that the topic had been frequently discussed since the christening. I had frowned in bewilderment, puzzled at what Robert and she could have discussed repeatedly without her mentioning anything to me during our visits down there, or on Monday nights when she and I had had our catch up phone calls, or for me to even notice that she had something so significant on her mind. She told me that having a baby had forced her priorities to change and I could understand that since I had found I had experienced incredible amounts of love and feelings of protection towards my niece since the instant I met her. Zara had then gone on to explain that she and Robert had been led to question their own mortality, and the preparation for Tara's care should anything happen to them. I had tried to stop her from saying anything else; I did not even want to imagine anything happening to Zara or Robert, never mind the possibility of something happening to both of them, but she had interrupted me. Zara had leant across the table and took a very firm hold of my wrists and looked me straight in the eye. She took a deep breath and told me that she wanted me to do more than the promise I had made. She wanted to legally ensure that Michael and I would take care of Tara if anything happened to her and Robert. She laid considerable emphasis on our names, and it shook me to my core. She told me that she would not trust anyone else to bring up her daughter as well as she could but me, and she then elaborated and said that if anyone would bring her up to remember her mother and father as she would want Tara to remember her and Robert, it was Michael and I. I had been speechless. I had not been able to answer her. I wanted to say yes, of course, really I did. I knew I would never let anyone else take care of Tara if anything happened to Zara, I knew that from the moment I met her I would do anything for that girl, and that she had my heart completely the second her hand clasped my finger, and a significant part of me had understood that I agreed to this when I said yes to being Tara's God Mother, and that my promise to ensure I looked after her meant some sacrifice on my part, but at that moment I could not help but feel resent at Zara's request.

How could Zara expect Michael and I to bring Tara up if Will and I were married?

And then I had realised what Zara was asking of me.

She wanted me to give up my life for Tara's.

Chapter 17 – Numb

I was numb. I had not been able to believe Zara, my best friend of more than a decade, a friend so close she and I were practically like sisters, would ask me to sacrifice my life's happiness, my *everything*. I had wondered whether she had considered Michael and I might be able to look after Tara without me having to give up my life with Will. I had wondered if Robert was asking Michael the very question Zara was asking me now. I had wondered what Michael's reaction might have been. But most of all, I had hoped Zara and Robert would never ever have anything happen to them so that this situation would be a possibility. I had even sent up a silent prayer asking God to not let anything happen to two of the most fabulous people I had ever known. I could not live without my best friend, and I knew that Tara would suffer in immeasurable quantities if she were to be without her parents before she was a fully-grown adult. I had been enveloped by disbelief, but I had known I was the only person she could ask. I had known if the roles were reversed, I would want Robert and Zara to raise my child. I knew I would not trust anyone else to do a good enough job. And I had known that I had to say yes. Of course, I would say yes, make it official, officially accept the responsibility and carry the duty, and indeed I did. But it was not without a heavy heart. I had asked her what she would like me to say to Will, and she had said she did not know. She had asked me if I remembered the day she and Will met, and I had said yes. She asked me if I remembered her trepidation regarding whether or not to ask me to be a God parent for her baby after her meeting with Will. I said yes, because I did now, I had quite forgotten about it until that moment. Suddenly it all became clear. Zara was anxious about asking me to be a God parent for the baby, because I had ended my relationship with Michael.

The numbness I felt increased.

I had been near silent on the drive back to Zara's house, after the shopping trip. I had gone into the kitchen to fetch a drink for myself, and stood leaning up against the breakfast bar, eyes unfocused on the wall ahead of me, deep in thought. My restless, random, roaming thoughts had been interrupted by chocolate brown eyes looking at me with trepidation. I could tell by the look on his face that Robert had indeed asked Michael the same question Zara had asked me whilst we were out shopping. I had looked at him intently. I took a deep breath and sighed heavily, my lips closing together as my eyebrows lowered in a resigned frown. I had closed my eyes and leaned my head back and opened my eyes to look at the ceiling to look for answers, inspiration or a sign of *something*. I did not know what. I sighed again as I closed my eyes and found my head was slowly shaking from side to side. After a while, I returned my gaze to Michael's face, and tears pricked at the corner of my eyes, as I took in his countenance. I had known then he had agreed to Robert's request of him. How could he not? He was under Tara's spell as much as I was. He loved her just as I did. We both knew, since the day we met her in the hospital ward where she was born, that we would do anything for her. She was ours. Not a word had passed between us, and as I closed my eyes and slowly shook my head, lowering it, I felt his arms wrap around me and pull me into his chest. It was warm. Familiar. Comforting. His hand cupped the back of my head and he turned his face to kiss my temple. "I love you, Mimi" he said. I told his shoulder that I loved him too; and I meant it. I remember telling him I hoped we would never have to uphold our promise. He had agreed; he said that he could not imagine losing his best friend. It had terrified me to think about it. I had never really given much thought to our mortality. The joys and innocence of youth. Will and I had said when we got married and bought our house, we would of course write our wills to coincide with our life insurance, but that was about as much thought as we had ever given it. Somehow, this request had made mortality so much more real.

Again, the numbness returned.

Tears had started to fall from my eyes, and I did not want Michael to see. I had turned and faced away from him, looking through the window at the garden of Robert and Zara's house. Typically English, it was the site of many a barbeque to come, no doubt. Michael asked why I was crying, he was wondering if it was the thought of something happening to Zara which was making me so upset. I said yes, it was partly that. I had not expanded the sentence any more, but I had been sure he had understood that a significant part of my anguish was also at the prospect of having to give up my life with Will to take care of Tara should she lose her parents. I knew Michael could never really understand what it would be like to give up half of his heart. He and I had never been what Will and I were. We were two halves of a whole. Michael had loved me, as I had loved him, possibly even a bit more. But he was not my world. He was not my reason for being. He was my friend, but he was not my soul mate. He had not dated anyone, as far as I knew, since I had ended the relationship. Or at least not that he had told me about. I felt dreadful that he was not in a place where he could search for his, female, equivalent of Will. Although, the thought did strike me that he probably would not have to search, that when he was ready, when love was ready for him to be happy, his match would be put in front of him, just as Will and I were for each other.

It was that thought which had brought me back to reality. How was I going to tell Will what I had agreed to all those years before? Would I tell him before Michael and I signed the papers or afterwards when nothing could be done about it? Would we argue? Would he resent Tara for the promise I had made? Would he understand that Zara and Robert intended for me to sacrifice my world for their daughter should anything happen to them? I was not sure he would be able to tolerate the thought.

How was I going to sacrifice my *everything* for the additional centre which my universe orbited?

Chapter 18 – Misery

Michael and I stood in each other's arms at Robert's bedside for a long while. How long a time we stood statuesque there I do not know. The tears which burned my face were ceaseless; they pooled on my décolletage, pausing over my heart. It was as though my tears found a path to the source of my pain. Michael's arms were locked around me, holding me tightly to try to stem the emotion which tore through him. It didn't strike me until many years later that I seemed to be much more distraught than he was at that time. The reason for his detracted grief did not occur to me at that point. We stared at Robert, willing him to get better, willing him to wake up. Michael pulled from his pocket his Rosary beads and began to recite the words which offered reassurance in the face of the tragedy. He said these prayers under his breath, I could not quite make out the words – I did not know the Hail Mary - but I was sure I understood the intentions; but if Robert did awake, we were faced with having to tell him about his wife. Dead. I knew the reality, but my mind and my heart and soul did not want to accept it. My body and brain wanted to reject the notion that this was real. Somewhere, in the back of my racing mind, I hoped that this was all a nightmare and that I would wake up. I realised then; I had as much chance of waking up from this nightmare as Robert did from his coma. A spine-chilling shiver ran through my body. There was a nurse by his bedside constantly, monitoring everything. I caught his eye for just a second and a sad look flickered briefly over his face. It was then I *knew*. I knew Robert would not survive. I tried to stop myself from crying even more, to prevent Michael from knowing, as silly as that sounds; he would have to find out eventually. I do not know why I wanted to preserve his heart, prevent the reality from reaching him. I suppose it was because my heart, being so shattered with the news of Zara's untimely and tragic death, was not something I wished Michael to feel. Even though I knew he would. But it did not work. I could not hold back the tears; the grief had not even begun to set in. I was still running on autopilot and was not fully aware of my actions and thoughts. I was only aware of my raw feelings.

After a while, I do not recall how long it was, but it felt both an age and such a short space of time simultaneously, we were asked to leave the room so that the nursing staff could perform some tests on Robert. Michael pulled me from the room, gently I recall, but my body felt like lead; weighed down with the grief that had gripped, crushed and broken my heart. I glanced at Michael's face, his chocolate brown eyes red, and no doubt stinging, from the crying he had been doing that I had not been aware of. I was too consumed by my grief to have noticed anything happening to other people around me. I remember Michael mentioning something about calling Robert's parents and I remember muttering that I would call Zara's. I knew both sets of parents would be on their way to the hospital, the long journeys ahead of them from remote parts of the idyllic countryside would seem even more horrendous as they tried to combat rush hour traffic to get there. I called Zara's parents; they had already been told of the accident and knew their daughter, their beautiful daughter, was dead. I spoke to Zara's mother and just cried on the phone, words spilling from my mouth in no order or sense as my grief commanded my speech. I knew that she understood. She was the only person other than Robert, myself, and Tara who loved Zara the most. I remember she asked me where Tara was and I said I did not know, but I assumed Michael did. I glanced over at him as he was on his mobile telephone to Robert's parents and he nodded slightly to tell me he had somehow managed to find out the information. Even now, I do not know how he managed to gather the mental strength to be aware of Tara's location; where she was and who was looking after her. Zara's mother asked me how Robert was, and I turned my head away from Michael and lowered my voice to try and prevent him from hearing that the prognosis was not good. I told her that Michael was on the telephone to his parents right now, answering questions and giving details. Zara's mother sobbed down the phone and I was resigned to just listen. I could do nothing else.

Two hours later, Michael and I were at Robert and Zara's house, numbly tucking Tara into bed, trying to maintain a brave face and act naturally and normally. We had driven to her school to pick her up from her after-school club; Michael had called the school to tell them what had happened, and they said they would keep her safe until we could pick her up. Her teacher had gone above and beyond the call of duty that day on our behalf. Zara's parents had remained at the hospital to deal with the official necessities regarding her body, and were staying with their friends nearby for the night. Zara's father was not a man of good health, and her mother struggled to take care of him on her own. They had help from the NHS, but not as much as he required. It had been many years since I had seen them, the christening had been the last time in fact, and I had understood completely why Zara had asked Michael and I to look after Tara, and not her parents. I asked Michael in the car whether we should break the news to Tara that night or the following morning. He had taken a deep breath and suggested we leave it until the morning. I understood why. I had been wondering the same thing. Did we tell Tara about her mother only to have to give bad news to her again the next day, or did we wait to see if Robert made it through the night and had a better prognosis in the light of the morning? I agreed with Michael; it was better to let her have the last good night's sleep she could before presenting her with the tragic news.

I remember walking downstairs after pulling Tara's bedroom door closed, my feet feeling like lead hitting every soft carpeted step, being able only to move at a glacial pace, my breath exhaling from my body with the same weight as each step I took. I went into the lounge and sank down into the deep sofa, tilted my head back and let the tears run freely from my eyes once more. I felt Michael sit down beside me and he held my hand; his fingers interlocked with mine. I turned to face him, putting my arms around his waist and leaning my head into his chest. I wept. As did he. I could feel his sobs running through him underneath my body as his arms moved to my shoulders to hold me tightly against him. There was nothing but pain in our lives. Heartbreak.

It was to get even worse. We were disturbed from our restless slumber in that same position on the sofa by a telephone call at three o'clock in the early hours of the morning.

That which earlier I had internally foretold had come to pass.

Robert had died.

Chapter 19 – Despair

Michael had left to go to the hospital as soon as he had put the telephone promptly back into its charger. I felt alone. I stayed in the house with Tara, hoping against hope that I would know what to say to her if she awoke in the night or early morning before Michael had returned, whenever that might be. Half of me had wanted to go with him to the hospital, to say my goodbyes and to weep for Robert. The other half felt despair because I had known this was inevitable. My heart ached already with the worst pain I had ever felt and yet suddenly, somehow, the pain had intensified. I did not know I could feel that much pain. It consumed me. I had lost my friend; Michael had lost his best friend. Tara had lost her parents. My mind was whirling, filled with thoughts of grief, sadness, despair, emptiness, confusion, injustice, questions, unheard demands, wondering if the prospect of Robert dying rather than living without his other half was actually easier for him and then being filled with disgust that I could allow such a thought to cross my mind. I was not sure he would have wanted to wake up if he had known that the other half of him was dead. I knew I would not want to if it were me in his position.

Then the awful realisation hit me like a ton of bricks; as much as I thought my world had ended, my world – my *everything* – had not suffered the same desolation that Tara's had. My world had not ended, despite my grief and agony; the reason for my existence was back at home - and yet he had no idea what was happening. I had not even called him to tell him I was going to the hospital in the first place. I had been gone for almost twenty hours and Will had no idea where I was; he did not know what had happened, he could have been thinking anything had happened to me. A wash of frantic hysteria and guilt drove me into a frenzy of activity as I rushed around Robert and Zara's house in search of my handbag. Misplaced anger arose inside me when I discovered, to my dismay, that my mobile telephone's battery had run out; something else which I really needed that had died that day. Tears sprang once more from my eyes, racing towards my chin, burning an unnecessary path as they journeyed, I was not sure why. I quickly grabbed the house telephone and called my home. The telephone rang for a long time before Will's groggy but urgent voice answered. I could barely say more than his name as I struggled to hold back tears so that I could try to explain what was happening. Immediately he knew that something was wrong. I told him I was at Zara and Robert's house. I told him I was with the baby. I told him that there had been an accident. I told him nothing else because I could not force the words to come out of my mouth. It was as though my body was refusing the final acknowledgement of saying out loud the devastation it knew was true. But he knew. Will could tell by the way my voice caught in my throat that something terrible had happened. But he had a relief in his voice that it had not happened to me. He told me that I should stay where I was and that he was on his way. I pictured him rushing around the house putting his clothes on haphazardly whilst he was reassuring me that my other half, my *everything* would be at my side as soon as he could possibly be. But that worried me; eventually I would have to tell him about the promise Michael and I made and the implications that would have on my life with him, on our life together. On our love.

After hanging up the telephone, I sank to the floor, my knees unable to hold my shaking body up under the weight of renewed grief, and my already broken heart shattered once more into a million unrepairable pieces. Filled with despair I was not aware of the howling and emphatic sobbing that accompanied my tears as I wept, consumed by the sorrow. It was not until I heard a faint coughing from upstairs that I realised I was making any sound at all, and that it could disturb Tara. I am ashamed to say that my selfishness forced my silence, the selfishness which I had once vowed to end; I did not want to have to be the one to answer her questions about her adored Mummy and Daddy, I did not want to speak to her alone. I shuddered as I felt the cowardice run through me, like a dark, unrelenting virus, listening carefully for any indication she may have awoken. I heard no further sounds, no rustling of bed covers, no turning or moving of the mattress. For a brief moment, relief crept over the guilt. I felt torn; half of me wanted to go upstairs to check on her, to hold her tight and let her know someone was still here to love her, but the other half did not want to see the face which I was now responsible for. I hated myself for allowing the selfishness to take hold of my heart once more. I decided that it was best I go and check on Tara, and so I crept upstairs as quietly as I could. Peeking around the door of her bedroom, I saw her angelic face sleeping soundly. My heart dropped in my chest as I felt an overwhelming urge to run and embrace the child who was now the centre of my life. I had always known she was an additional centre for my universe to orbit, but now she was to become the sole focus of my existence.

I did not know how I was going to accomplish this great feat. How could I replace Will, my *everything,* with anyone else; even my beautiful, perfect, angelic, orphaned niece? How could I embrace her in my arms, in my heart and in my life? How could I embrace the fact that I was now her guardian along with Michael?

How was I ever going to keep my promise?

Chapter 20 – Heartbreak

I had often wondered why no-one ever mentioned the little things that occur when people are heartbroken: why nobody ever mentioned that they needed to visit the bathroom, or that they quenched their thirst. In Britain, tea consumption trebles during a crisis, but when people recount their tales of heartbreak, the making and drinking of it is never mentioned. It was only during this time that it dawned on me: these things become automatic when your world falls apart – you never realise you are doing it, these tasks become just a basic function, like breathing, over which you no longer have any control. Looking back now, I cannot tell you how many times I used the bathroom, or drank, or even if I ate anything or brushed my hair. I assume my body had taken care of the absolute basics, running on autopilot, but I cannot say with any certainty.

It was still dark when the quiet tapping at the door disturbed my crying. I was not sure what time it was. Time had no bearing on anything that night. I knew it was Will. The temperature of the house fell as I opened the door to him, letting in the coarse chill which accompanies an early autumn morning; the darkness extinguishing all heat the sun could have hoped to have provided for the earth earlier that day. I knew Will would be supportive, and I knew I would collapse into his arms and be selfish and lap up the comfort he would offer. I knew I would take undeserving pleasure from his strong arms being around me, and that my head finding its place on his shoulder would offer me a little ease. I knew that I would cry, weep, and that he would tell me that it was fine to cry and that I should let out all my grief. And I knew that I would. I would take advantage of all he would offer. I also knew that when Michael returned from the hospital Will would comfort him, and I knew Michael would be grateful. I knew that when Tara woke up, Michael and I would tell her what had happened, and Will would be in the background, offering emotional support to all three of us, in his own way. But I also knew that before all that, I had to tell him what had happened.

I remember sitting Will down on the sofa, in the living room which seemed full of duller colours than it used to be, sitting facing him with one leg folded on the seat between us. I remember he naturally turned to face me in the same position. It was so difficult for me to utter the words that I needed to say; we were so clearly meant for one another, a perfect mirror image and match, like magnets drawn to one another through an invisible, undeniable field of energy. I remember him taking hold of my hand, his other hand brushing a tear from my jaw line before it dropped from my face onto my collarbone. But what I remember most is the blackness which covered his face - his complete, absolute understanding of me, detecting the impending doom; the despair he could sense was approaching, that would consume him, and me, and lay waste to all we had created together was a violation of his perfect features.

My head was whirling with fragments of the beginnings of sentences I was considering using to tell Will everything he needed to hear. Whoever knew that thoughts could make you dizzy? Even now, I cannot quite remember exactly how I started, which sentence I settled on to deliver the devastating blow to our devotion, or how I managed to tell him about the promise I had made, how I managed to force the words out of my mouth, but I do remember how I finished. I finished with breathing as irregular as my broken heartbeat, forcing words past the lump in my throat, which I was sure would be permanent: "I love you, Will, more than anything in the world, and I always, always will."

The look on his face mirrored the feelings in my heart: absolute despair, destruction and devastation. I knew this was hurting him as much as it was hurting me. More so, even, because his was the innocent heart in all of this. I told him I was sorry, and that he would never know how sorry I was; still, to this day, I am not sure anyone can understand how much guilt I carry for breaking his heart.

I was being cruel, so very cruel; we both knew it. I do not know how he could still stand to kiss me, how he did not detest the very sight of me, between our lips pressing against one another I voiced these thoughts, but at the same time I knew he could do nothing else but kiss me. Perhaps this was the reason why my outwardly shared thoughts received no reply other than his mouth meeting mine in quiet desperation. In truth, he had not said a word, no denial escaped his lips, no pleas asking me not to do this. Nothing. Nothing which might have been expected from an external perspective. I knew he would not, could not, ask me to not do what I was doing. I knew he was too heartbroken but at the same time I knew he would not ask me not to fulfil the promise I had made. I knew he would not say out loud how much this hurt him, how devastated he was for reasons of his own, not only the death of his friends. He was too much of a good man for that. He was the perfect, perfect gentleman. But grief makes people behave in strange ways; it divides typical, logical thinking from the actions of the receivers of bad news. The desperation of the situation manifested itself in our final act of love. I was selfish. I wanted him more than anything, more than breath, more than bringing Zara and Robert back. If I had wanted them back more than I wanted Will, if they had never left, I would not have been faced with this situation and I could have lived my perfect life with my *everything* as I had planned to do. But I could not think logically, realistically, I could not think like that. I just wanted him; a deep, carnal need to be with the man who made me complete. Much like people never talking about using the bathroom, I had always wondered how people could still continue to be intimate with one another when grief consumed them so much. Stupidly, I had believed that if they were truly that upset, they would not be able to think of anything else but their grief and dealing with their loss. It was not until being in that situation myself that I realised that comfort came from being as physically and emotionally close to the person whose heart completed your own. There are some life lessons that you can only learn through experience, no matter how much you are told by others, or read from a book.

And so, roughly, with great need, desire and hunger, amongst tears of grief for both our friends and our lost love, Will and I took solace in each other for the final time, in the lounge of Zara and Robert's house, with the sleeping baby upstairs and the promise I had made to Zara to protect the child hanging over our heads like a noose as we rocked and writhed against one another, searching for release; release from the anger, from the pain, the grief, release from the selfish enjoyment of having one last moment together. Each thrust was the hammering of a nail into the coffin of our relationship. His crystal blue eyes, now obscured with redness, gave in to the mounting sea of salty water as the gasp of desperation escaped from this mouth as he reached the final peak of his need for me. His head pressed against my shoulder, his mouth against my chest; I remember the vibrations against my skin as he muttered, "Mimi, I love you, I love you," over and over again between firm kisses. I can still remember, even now, how that felt: glorious. Even through the sadness, to feel the impact those words have on your skin is an astounding sensation. They say that babies are the only ones who know what their mother's heartbeat sounds like from the inside; to feel the words "I love you" against your skin is akin to that intensity. My hands were in his hair, holding him to me, whether this was in an attempt to offer comfort, or a need for him to be close to me to gain comfort, I am still not sure. I remember wondering if he could feel my streaming tears, matching his own, fall onto the top of his head as they hurriedly left my face.

The devastation death brings disguises itself differently depending on whose life it desolates.

I do not know how long had passed before Michael returned, but the sun was beginning to start a new day, struggling to pierce the dark, autumn clouds to bring light to the earth. Michael's eyes were red; clearly a combination of lack of sleep and an emptiness of energy only complete grief can bring. His shoulders slumped as he leant up against the front door, closing it quietly to prevent waking Tara. Finding the last scrap of strength he had, he wordlessly fell into my arms; arms of friendship, of comfort and of shared pain. A veil of sadness descended over us from which I would never completely be removed. Will was in the kitchen, putting the kettle on to make a cup of tea for us all: a last shot of courage before we awakened Tara to tell her the devastating news.

To be perfectly frank, I do not know how we got through it. It is one of those moments in life which I remember with both cruel crystal clarity and an overwhelming cloud of fog. The memory causes a sharp and painful sensation in my heart, and a dull ache seeps through my mind causing confusion. Michael did most of the talking, I just remember holding the fragile child in my arms. She was too warm from sleeping, sticky skin a product of the safety of her bed. Hair slightly damp due to dehydration. Silly things ran through my mind before Michael started to talk; did she need a drink so that she would be awake enough to understand what we were saying to her; was it a good idea to tell her this in her bedroom or would it make the bedroom a bad place for her, and would we have trouble getting her to go to sleep in her own room from now on; should we have let her eat her breakfast first? I realised I was half trying to care for my beautiful girl, and half trying to put off the devastation for her, and us again. She was too young. She was too young to be dealing with this, she was too young to be experiencing this. She was just too young. Michael had a very calm tone to his voice; I remember thinking that he was the best one to give the bad news, but he did seem to be bearing the brunt of more of this tragedy than anyone. I remember him telling Tara about Heaven, and how Mummy and Daddy were going to Heaven. I remember her starting to fidget, clearly affected by what she was being told. It was almost as though I could feel the emotions traversing her little body. Confusion. A glimpse of denial. Sadness at never seeing Mummy and Daddy again.

And then her tears came.

There is a piercing cry children have. It sends chills to the bone. It sends panic through a parent's body. It causes fear. It makes hearts stop, for a split second, between the cause being ascertained and action being taken. It is either when they have done something that has caused a bump or a bruise, or a scratch or a scrape, or a serious injury; but Tara's piercing cry was because her heart was breaking. The sound stabbed my already shattered heart, and I have no doubt that it did the same to Michael's, too. I held her, tightly, in my arms; sobbing with her. Rocking her gently. Her head was pressed into my left shoulder, my lips firm against her forehead in a vague attempt to offer a reassuring kiss. I remember Michael placing his hand on her back; her body looked so tiny beneath the span of it, whilst I sat stroking her head, trying to make her feel better, offering words to try and tell her everything was all right. I do not know why I thought that was a good idea; I still do not understand why we rush people to get past the emotions they are feeling. Why do we not just let them experience the sadness that they're going through and let time take its course? Why has it been handed down through generations that it is what you're supposed to do when presented with a crying child; to tell them not to cry and to dry their tears? Why do we not see that grief is a process that must be endured to come out of the other side in some semblance of the identity we had before it overwhelmed our lives? I did not understand why I was trying to offer reassurances to this little girl then, why pointless words were coming out of my mouth, when I certainly had no idea how everything was indeed going to be all right as I did not think it was possible; and I still do not understand why I did it, now. The impact our parents have upon us is lifelong, whether we realise it or not.

But would Tara's parents have had enough impact on her to last her lifetime? Or was it up to Michael and me to shape her as a person from then on? Would this grief define who she was for the rest of her life?

The thought truly terrified me.

Chapter 21 - Goodbye

Mimi, you have brought such colour,
laughter and sweet life to me. You have
given my life its purpose; my heart is so
full of you.

I love you.
Forever, and only, yours,
Will.

I still have the crumpled piece of paper in the back of my material memories box, hidden away in the lower drawer of my dressing table. The splattered discolourations on the paper, where the ink of the lines has seeped into the blank spaces between them, a sign of how many times I have cried oxymoronic tears of pain and joy over the beautiful, wonderful words Will wrote to me. For me. For us.

Tara had eventually cried herself back to sleep, Michael and I holding her whilst she did so. His embrace was reassuring, but the tightness of his grip told me how much he needed Tara and I. We were all he had left of his best friend, too. Just as he and Tara were all I had left of Zara. I remember a blur of pink out of my tear-filled eyes; it was the fake fur trim at the bottom of Tara's lamp. I had turned my face towards it to hide my tears from her; my eyes betraying my sadness by being able to see the joyful colours in her room. At some point, Will had left us and had gone downstairs, gathered his coat and was waiting at the door as Michael and I descended; drained. Will's head hung, his face pointed towards the floor; he was drained, too. Michael reached the bottom of the staircase before I did. He extended his hand to Will, in solidarity, in friendship, and to offer comfort. Will had become friends with Robert and Zara, too. They hugged, briefly; an awkward one-armed motion which had become popular in recent years between men. Neither of them seemed to be so accustomed to it that they could naturally embrace with ease. "Look after her." These were the words I remember Will saying to Michael. Michael assured Will that he would. Looking back now, I have no doubt Michael assumed Will was talking about Tara. But I knew differently: Michael was being told to look after me.

Michael went into the kitchen, to make yet another cup of tea no doubt. Will and I were left standing in the hallway, a tense, heavy, emotion-filled silence filling the gap between us. We indulged in one last embrace, one last kiss, one last tear each. One last, "I love you," before he left. The pain hit me like the first destructive wave of a tsunami. Even now, I can still feel the touch of his lips on mine, on the end of my nose, on my forehead, and on the top of my head. The heat of his breath sending one last shiver down my spine. The bitter chill of the outside air attacking as the door ushered in the autumnal temperature.

And then he was gone.

Sacrifice takes many shapes.

My legs crumpled under me. I do not remember hitting the floor, I cannot be certain I did. But I do remember Michael's strong, comforting, familiar arms helping me up. He sat me on the second stair. I remember how I leaned into him, devastation demolishing what was left of my already depleted strength. I remember briefly thinking that it was not fair for Michael to have to be everybody's rock in this situation. But then, selfishly, the thought crossed my mind that he was getting much more out of this than I was. That was an awful thing to think. He could not have been happy with the situation and the way things were turning out. He would have wanted any other scenario than the one we were presented with. I do not know how long I wept for, eventually the sobbing was silent, reduced to convulsions coursing through my aching body. *My everything* was no longer part of my life. All my dreams and hopes and plans for our future had died along with Zara and Robert. My life now had to be centred around providing Tara with a stable, family, life.

Saying goodbye to Will, to Zara and Robert, to everything I had ever known in my life was the hardest thing I have ever done. They say time is a healer; I do not find that to be true. The pain is still as raw today as it was then. The pain does not lessen, you simply find a way to cope and incorporate it into your life.

In some ways, leaving a note for me in my handbag was cruel. Not that I am at all, in any way, suggesting Will to be a cruel man or that he meant his incredible gesture to be callous. He was the epitome of kindness to me. I know he meant well and, in the darkest hours of my life, the note has helped reassure me that I am loved. I did not find it immediately. I did not go into my handbag for a couple of days after Will left my life. Left me with a hole that only Will's love could ever have filled, could ever have mended. When I did discover the note, the tears ran like a river once more, renewing the pain. It had been one of the nicest things Will had ever said to me. He had never had problems expressing the depth of his love for me, not since the first day our eyes met. The cruelty was not intentional, but nonetheless to give me something as a constant reminder of the intensity of Will's love for me was a bitter-sweet gesture.

I was entrenched in a perpetual sadness.

The funeral was difficult. Funerals are never easy, but this was the most difficult I have ever been to in my life. Seeing the coffins side by side, each covered with flowers - a visual representation of how much these two, young people were loved by those in their lives – was dreadful. Trying to explain to Tara what was going on was a battle, the words stuck in my throat, choking me; Michael could convey to her much more easily than I, what was going on. The priest had sat with Tara and Michael before the funeral to speak to her, to tell her what would happen during the Mass. The same priest who had married her mummy and daddy, who had baptised her just a few years before, was now helping her say a final goodbye to her precious parents. The funeral was well attended: all Robert's friends from work came to say goodbye, Zara's too. Extended family: parents, cousins, aunts and uncles. Neighbours, people from the gym and all the different groups that they had both belonged to. Book clubs, music groups, parenting groups, the rugby club, and of course most of their parish attended as they all knew Zara and Robert and had been friends with them. It was a polaroid of their life in the church, a sea of black in a snapshot of their existence. Of how much importance they had had on the earth, how many people they had influenced and affected and brought happiness and joy to in one form or another. How many people's lives had been made better for them being alive. It was an overwhelming day, lots of people saying how sorry they were, how they could not believe what had happened, how short life was. Lots of people asking how Tara was coping, how Michael and I were coping with looking after her; never failing to mention that if we needed anything to just ask them. We both knew they meant well; but neither of us had adequate replies prepared, nor could we think of any at the time.

Once more I observed the comfort Michael gained from the Mass prayers; the words seemed to solidify his resolve to get through the day, and through the difficult time we found ourselves in. I remember being envious of the comfort that his faith brought to him. I remember thinking that Michael did not seem quite as lost as I was; I remember thinking that people think that faith is tested during difficult times, and whilst that can certainly be true, what I saw in Michael, and Zara and Robert's family, was faith bringing comfort to them. Taking the edge off the difficulty, making the pain a little less raw; almost easier to handle. I think this may have been due to believing, knowing, that their loved ones were in a better place. I even noticed some of this reassurance beginning to bud in Tara. Her little mind far too young to truly comprehend all that was being told to her; but still, there was a glimpse of a little less burden on her fragile shoulders as she realised that Mummy and Daddy were in heaven. It was then that I realised that Michael and I must ensure that we raised her to include the church as a fundamental part of her life. It was what her parents wanted for her. We needed to continue it.

I promised myself I would do whatever it took to ensure that my precious goddaughter would be raised exactly how her parents wished.

Chapter 22 - Childhood

It took Michael and I a while to get into a routine for Tara. After a discussion about normality versus space to absorb the impact of the events of the car accident we concluded that she should be at home, with us. We kept her home from school for a couple of weeks, in the end, rather than just a few days as we had originally thought and talked about; we wanted to give her time to grieve before she had to go back and face the questions of the young children who did not know any better to not ask what had happened to her mummy and daddy. Through those two weeks, the nights were the hardest. Lying on the bed, silently crying in each other's arms, taking it in turns to comfort Tara when she awoke with cries and tears, in the middle of her own nightmare. Her head teacher and class teacher had both been very understanding when I had spoken to each them on the telephone. Michael had suggested it might be better for me to speak to them than for him to; I had agreed. Stereotypical roles notwithstanding, I did not want him to have to bear the burden of dealing with everything in our situation. The toll it was taking on him was already beginning to show in the dark circles under his eyes, the dryness of his skin, the chewed nails and the slight hanging of his head which had never been a part of his posture previously. I explained what had happened and what the plan was for Tara in the near future, and briefly mentioned what I hoped would happen long-term for her. I informed them that Michael and I had not yet begun to put things into motion, but that we would be hoping to soon. I stressed the importance of providing a solid, stable home, and as smooth a transition to it as possible. I also said that when she did return to school the teachers should not wrap her up in cotton wool; that she would need to deal with life and learn its lessons. I remember thinking that I knew she might hate it at the time, the discomfort it would cause, but one day she might thank me for it; that it might help give her inner strength and allow her to cope with anything that came her way later in life. They offered the standard reassurances, saying that they would help Tara catch up with any work she had missed, but also offered some advice on how to help her keep on track at home. We wanted to give her time to get used to having two different adults in her house full time, each of us able to negotiate compassionate leave from our respective jobs. We wanted to make sure she could cry when she wanted to, without being looked at by anyone but us. I almost wanted her to get the worst of her grief out of her system before she returned to school. Michael had briefly mentioned the prospect of taking Tara away for a week, a short break away from everything that reminded her of Zara and Robert. Although, before I could even utter any syllable, to offer any portion of my opinion, he quickly corrected himself, revoking the idea from the realm of possibility; he realised that it would only delay the inevitable, and that Tara needed to adjust as soon as possible to her new situation. We all did.

It certainly was a shock for us all, although I can only truly convey my own perspective in an entirety; I had only ever had to look after a house with two adults in it, and Will – being a modern man - had done half the housework. Not that Michael did not help, he did; but I did not realise just how much work looking after a child full time was. Tara had stayed at our house for weekends before, but she had come with a selection of clothes pre-packed, favourite toys and a small selection of books, crayons and colouring books to keep her occupied if I had ever run out of things for her to do. And so, all I had ever had to do was make the occasional sandwich if we had not gone out to eat. I cannot count the amount of times I had heard mothers complaining about how much extra work children were, and how many times I had silently turned my eyes upward and inwardly thought that they should have realised before they made the decision to have children. That it was their own fault; if they did not want the workload they should not have had the children. That they should have understood the burden and the responsibility they

116

were willing to shoulder; and that it really was not as difficult as they purported. And that it was just their tough luck; they had made their proverbial bed and now had to lie in it, co-sleeping with their child or otherwise. But it was true: the washing; cooking; cleaning; ironing; bathing; doing hair every morning; entertaining; listening to stories; inventing stories at bedtime, or in the car; the teaching of new words and quizzing recently learned ones; keeping on top of any missing toys or favourite clothes; describing and explaining each and every aspect of each and every task undertaken within any given day; helping with painting and colouring; transporting to and from music lessons and horse riding lessons, gymnastics and dance sessions; ensuring swimming costumes were packed in a bag and not losing the cap so that Tara did not have to go out with wet hair running the risk of a cold which might make the whole household ill; making sure either Michael or I could collect her from school and drop her off each morning; making sure that if we went out to a pub it was child friendly with a playground to keep her happy for half an hour whilst we enjoyed some peace. It took a long time to become familiar with a routine and to admit the mothers were right, that looking after children was the hardest job on earth.

The logistics took a long time to work out, also, adding to the heightened stress which was brand new to both Michael and I; neither one of us had ever had to deal with the rigors of adulthood in quite that manner before. Will employed the services of a solicitor to buy me out of my half of our house. I knew why he was communicating through a solicitor; it was too painful to talk to each other knowing that we had already said the last goodbye. I worried how he was going to afford the mortgage all alone. It was a lot of pressure on, and a lot of money for, one single person. I would have been happy to just let him have the house to do with it as he wished, sell it or rent it out; but he wanted to ensure that I had enough money to support Tara and for emergencies in the coming years. Another bitter-sweet gesture from him.

Christmas had weighed heavily on my mind, also. As the days grew colder, crisper, damper, darker, the season to be jolly was descending with dread upon me. Tara just seemed muted. Her spark had been quelled with the death of her parents. Of this, there was no doubt in my mind. She had been so animated in previous years, excited by the twinkling lights, the music from shops and the interesting adverts on television. That year, she was subdued. I had expected nothing less. The question of whether we should or should not celebrate at all was one I raised quite quietly in the kitchen with Michael. I had been pondering what to say, practising how to broach the subject with him repeatedly in my mind. Eventually, one particularly overcast afternoon, after several deep breaths to steel my resolve, I descended the stairs and went into the kitchen where we had had so many poignant exchanges before. I noticed that I could already see the street lights on in the distance. It was the first time I had noticed how early they had illuminated the dark streets. It had been a long time since I had noticed anything external to the house, to Tara, and to the grief we were all dealing with. I told Michael I appreciated that it was a significant event for him, as a Catholic, the season of Advent and Christmas. For me at that time, it was less so. It was about presents, giving and receiving, and doing something nice for those in your life. The limit of my understanding revolved around the notion that Christmas was supposed to be a magical time for children, lots of Christmas films, over-eating and too much cooking, a refrigerator full of left overs, a sink full of dishes, and a time of celebration and gathering of friends and family for much of the nation.

Family.

What family did Tara have? She had her Aunt Mimi and her Uncle Michael. She had grandparents, granted, but they were poorly in their own right, and the grief was making their health worse; they were still dealing with the death of their beloved children. Each set saw their own child in Tara's face. In her mannerisms. In her soul. It was all just a little too raw. Too raw to slap a smile on their faces, to pretend to be all right. During their conversations with us on the telephone, when they had been passed back to me after speaking to Tara, the cracks in their voices betrayed their determination to be strong for the only reminder of their respective children. Their British stiff upper lips succumbing to the overwhelming grief of the situation. I asked Michael whether he thought it was fair to even recognise Christmas that year, whether Tara should be expected to go through the rigmarole or whether we should just leave her to have some time in peace over the Christmas holidays from school. He told me he could see my perspective, but that Tara needed to understand the true message of Christmas. That at church she had a second family. That she was loved by God. That God would be the comfort to help her through this tragedy in her life. That this would bring her closer to God, that she would understand the idea of a bigger picture sooner than most people. That this would eventually help her develop into a well-rounded, mature young lady. That she would be the good person we both, we all – her parents included - had hoped she would be when she was born and when we became her god parents. He was very patient when he discussed his point of view with me, his priorities for her spiritual life. He understood that I had not grown up with the same understanding of the world as he, Zara and Robert had had; and the one Tara was beginning to have before her parents' death. He truly did honour the vows he made when he became her Godfather. It was a long, enlightening, conversation. But then I thought of when she would return to school. The conversations she would inevitably have with the others in her class. The questions: what did she have for Christmas? Who did she see for Christmas? Did she see the new film on the television? I realise that this, combined with the benefits of knowing she had a second family at the church who loved and cared about her very much, was a reason to celebrate Christmas rather than ignore it.

For the first time, I truly began to think like a parent.

And so, we did. We gave her a few small gifts, went to the celebration of Mass, I prepared a small Christmas lunch and just spent the day doing whatever she wanted to do. I had wondered whether Michael and I should have given Tara a gift from her parents. I wondered if it was something which would confuse her too much, and eventually I decided against it. I do not know if Michael thought the same thing, I did not mention it to him, preferring to avoid a taxing debate around Christmastime. At one point, she went to the sideboard in the dining room and slid open the bottom cupboard door, letting out the musty air which had been trapped within. She spent a long time looking through the photo album at photos of herself from when she was a baby, and pointing to her mummy and daddy, saying their names. "Mummy heaven... Daddy heaven." These are the words that, in her angelic voice, still stick in my ears today. It was then I knew she understood where they were, what had happened and that they were never coming back.

I knew then she understood that the childhood she was supposed to have would never happen.

That it was lost forever.

Chapter 23 – Beginning Adoption

In due course, in the New Year, the wills of my dearest friends were read. That was an experience of overwhelming, intense, numbness, and confusion and was accompanied by a considerable dose of denial. The musty smell of the solicitor's office smelt liked a hundred years of tears as I realised the men and women working there must have seen so many distraught people in the years of their working lives. Michael, once more being the rock of the situation administered to the legalities of Tara inheriting her parents' house and who would act as guardians for her; and began the process of us legally adopting her.

At the start, we were both completely in the dark; neither of us had knew anything about the details of the process. We knew it was long and arduous, sometimes; but, like most things, you can never truly understand what is involved in something until you go through it yourself. Michael made lots of telephone calls, I remember thinking that it was a good thing the new mobile telephone contracts had come out which included some minutes and texts otherwise he would have faced a huge telephone bill. He used the Internet, also, to try and find some information, too. Back then it was not nearly as useful as it is today, of course. I called Tara's school to ask them for any information or ideas they had; they guided me towards calling either an adoption agency or a social worker through the council. We were lucky the school had members of staff who could recount tales of other people who had been through the process. I remember scribbling over two pages of notes from the different phone calls I had made.

In time, we learned about the questionnaires we would need to complete; the financial backgrounds we would need to disclose. We found out about the medical histories we would need to submit. We had lots of paperwork sent to us, meetings with different people; at times, it was hard to keep up with all the appointments, information and telephone calls. It was all so confusing. Appointments were put onto the kitchen calendar, but it was still a whirlwind of commotion. Michael told me that he thought it was for the best, to be done as quickly as possible, to protect Tara. I asked him about the chances of us being approved, or whether the authorities would want Tara to be with a family member. I remember the thought made my breath catch in my lungs. A lump form in my throat. Tears fill my eyes and blur my vision. I was so confused. I felt almost swept away in the mayhem and the aftermath and wanting to do the best I could, we could, for Tara. Michael told me that because Robert and Zara had each stated their wishes in their wills, that the Godparents should look after Tara, there should be minimal disruption to her routine, and minimal disagreement.

I was less optimistic about the proceedings than Michael; I am still not sure if the events were just taking their toll on me, or if the tiredness I was tortured by was becoming ingrained into my body in the form of worry lines and a persistent need to thumb my right temple and run my fore and middle fingers over my left eye with a slow, shaky hand. The redness of my eyes was a permanent fixture in my face, something no amount of mascara could cover; a cemented reminder of the sadness which had swallowed my life. And the sadness which had stopped Tara's from the path it should have taken. The most constant, reoccurring thought running through my mind was whether she would be too adversely affected to have a good life. Since the second we had met her, that was all Michael and I had wanted for her; a good life filled with happiness.

Would we be able to give it to her?

I remember it had been a very cold, rainy Saturday. It was that sort of rain that attacks you as you try and walk through it; the ice-cold droplets hurt your skin if they make contact. The type of rain that is not only present, but loud; loud on your umbrella, loud on the car windshield, loud on the windows of the house, loud going through the drainpipes on its way to the drains. I sat in the lounge; Tara was in bed. I was drained of almost all my energy. It had been a very long week at work, and I had not been sleeping very well since the accident. I was past the point of being ready to sleep, but I was dreading yet another night of sleeping alone. I missed Will's body next to mine, the crook of his elbow being beneath my neck, or his shoulder being my pillow. It was a big shock to be alone at night. The bed was just too cold to sleep. The sleeping arrangements were strained in the house. Neither Michael or I wanted to sleep in the room Zara and Robert had shared. In fact, we had not touched the room other than to sort out the most important things. I had washed the clothes in the laundry hamper, hung them up etc. It was something neither one of us could bring ourselves to face. That night, Michael was pottering around in the kitchen, preparing vegetables for the next day's Sunday lunch. I was surrounded by papers, re-reading and reading things I had either overlooked, or not seen, before. My mind was swarming with little titbits of information. My head hurt in a way that painkillers could not contend with.

I had long hair, back then, and grabbing a fist full of it and supporting my head on my clenched fingers was a common pose. Sitting on the sofa, legs crossed, hearing only the sound of the rain as I read my eyes spotted two separate pieces of information.

The first one hit me like a thunderbolt in my heart. In the 'Home Study' pack, on the fifth page was a section headlined: "PREVIOUS RELATIONSHIPS. Brief description of any previous significant relationship/significant events." Brief. How could I have briefly described my relationship with Will? Brief? How can anyone briefly describe the other half of themselves, of their heart? I was so astonished I could not even be upset; I do remember I did not cry. I did feel like the world was playing a cruel joke on me. Was it not enough that I had already had to

123

sacrifice my everything for a greater purpose? There was not a day I did not think of him, and even now, each day, he consumes a large part of my thoughts; I was certain I was at the forefront of his mind, also. Now I had to drag it all up again to tell strangers who, at that point I was convinced, could not understand the love we had had, and had had to walk away from. My head hurt even more. I felt like my brain was in a vice, slowly being squeezed for someone's perverted amusement.

But that was nothing in comparison with the second piece of information in the pack. I had tucked the 'Home Study' pack away, trying to tuck away what it required of me to the back of my mind. Briefly, just for a split second, I wondered if Michael had read that particular page. Of course he had. But I could not feel any resentment towards him for not warning me of it. He probably did not know either how to broach the subject with me, or how I would react to it. At the time, I think I was too tired to act. But that changed when I read the second piece of information. In the 'Preparing for Permanence: Understanding the Assessment Process' under the section 'Legal Information, police checks and local authority enquiries', on the bright white, smooth A4 paper, crisp between my fingers, was a sentence which did not hit my heart like a thunderbolt. It pierced it with a nail.

If you wish to adopt jointly with your partner you must be married. If you are living in a stable relationship but are not married, only one partner can adopt.

You must be married. Must be. Married. Must. Married. Only one partner can adopt. Only one.

I read the words over, and over again, until they almost lost all meaning, in the way that words can when they are spoken repeatedly until they are just sound without purpose. The words

124

on the page simply became simple shapes, images, without any true denotation. And then they became a blur. Blurry because they had lost all meaning, blurry because I was looking at them through tears tormenting my eyes.

Without warning, adrenaline caused by anger surged through me, forced my feet to take me through the hallway to the kitchen. The tiredness I had been overwhelmed by had now dissipated into pure, undiluted fury. In an uncharacteristic gesture, I slammed the paper down on the kitchen surface and glared, wordlessly, at Michael, ignoring the pain searing through my hand and wrist. I had never had a temper before. I frightened myself by how cross I truly was. With Michael, with the situation, with life. My head was full of rage and questions. My eyes glared, piercing through him trying to stab their way to the truth. The same question I had asked myself earlier, whether Michael had read this, flashed at the front of my mind: did he know? Had he read this? Why had he not told me? Had he not seen it? Was he waiting for me to find it myself? Was he too worried to raise the issue with me? Was he wondering what would happen if he had told me? Did he think it was better for me to find it myself? Each question was trying to force its way out of my mouth to be asked, demanding an answer for itself. My tongue was tied. I could not speak; such was my seething.

Anger is a process, I suppose. I have heard people talk about it being one of the many stages of grief, but I think anger is a process in itself. I do not know why my first reaction was to be angry towards Michael. Was it his fault that the adoption process required people to be married if they both wanted to adopt a child? No. Was it his fault either of us were in this situation in the first place? Of course not. I suppose it was just because he was there, and he was the only person who might understand an iota of what I was going through. Of course, he had not had to sacrifice in the same way that I had, or the same amount; nevertheless, he had had to sacrifice his potential future. But the process I went through was to just be angry at everything to begin with. The whole situation. And then my mind narrowed to the trigger of my current rage. I remember raising my voice as I almost spat the word "married" at him. Then the words came tumbling out of my mouth. I complained and ranted about how I was already going to get married, how I had my life set up and I had *my everything*. How I had had to give up Will already and asked: wasn't that enough? My blood was boiling, my broken heart pieces beating a heavy metal drum beat in my ears, I could feel each piece trying to break my ribs, escape my body. I paced up and down the kitchen, my feet stamping like a petulant teenager.

My selfishness had returned with a vengeance.

I remember him trying to calm me down with a firm, stern, almost determined, tone of voice, which I had never heard him use before, saying that if I was not quiet, I would wake the baby. Neither of us had called Tara that for a while. It was then it dawned on me; I realised that he was angry, too. I was not the only one whose marriage and future had been torn apart. I had hurt him, and he had never truly got over it. Perhaps this was something he was happy about? Perhaps now he thought we would have to marry. For the sake of the baby, for Tara; to adopt her. I tried to shake my head and dismiss those thoughts. I suppose they had niggled at the back of my mind since Will and I had had to end our lifetime together because of the accident. Confusion consumed me. I did not know what to think, what to say, or what to do. My mind was dizzy with thoughts.

In almost a whisper I asked Michael if he had seen it. I did not specify what. I almost wanted to catch him out. I do not know why, what it would have achieved. Some justification for my anger, perhaps? I was not sure. He mumbled that he had seen some things that he thought might upset me. The accusatory voice in my head reared again at that point. I know he had not made the rules, but a large part of me felt as though Michael had done something on purpose. What that something was, I did not know then, nor do I now. I asked him which things he thought would upset me. I asked him why he had not told me about them, what the point was of leaving me to discover them myself. I asked him what he would have done if I had not spotted them as I was reading through all the information, what would he have done if I had not read those sentences? I was truly bewildered. He told me that he was trying to figure out how best to tell me, how best to bring up the subject of having to explain to me that I would need to tell the adoption panel about Will. How best to tell me that only one of us could adopt Tara if we were not married to each other. He told me that we had made a promise to Zara and Robert and that within that promise was the requirement to raise Tara together. He told me he could not go back on his word. That it was his duty to keep his promise. That it was his duty to look after his Goddaughter. That she needed to be raised with the same standard of parenting as Robert and Zara had begun to provide for her. He said that legalities were legalities and a necessary step to do our duty and keep our promise, and meet the standards expected of us for her. For him, it was a foregone conclusion, it seemed.

He was beginning to lose patience with me. He told, almost ordered, me to go upstairs and look at the baby, sleeping in her bed. He was angry with me. Angry that I could not immediately see what, in his head, needed to be done, and automatically agree with it. He was angry that I had not come to the same conclusion as him sooner. He was angry that my mind had been consumed with, and confused by, other issues, that I had not seen the bigger picture of what was best for Tara. He was, simply, angry.

As I ascended the stairs in darkness, not wanting to turn on the light for fear of waking Tara, I felt as though I was climbing up a mountain of uncertainty. Of sacrifice. Of duty. The carpet seemed particularly rough beneath my feet that night. The fibres scratching the insides of my toes as they sank with each step. My shoulders slumped with every step I took. My head fell just a little more with each inch I moved forward; the tiredness was beginning to reclaim its grasp on me. And, as I peered through the door, slightly ajar as always, acceptance washed over me. The smell of talcum powder and freshly folded laundry hit my nose. The smell of innocence, of childhood. Of normality.

I wanted to adopt Tara, to be her legal guardian. To be a solid, steady influence and role model in her life. To keep my promise to my best friend, her mother, Zara.

I could not go back on my word any more than Michael could.

Chapter 24 - Conversion

I slept deeply that night for the first time in a long time. I woke up as the alarm rang, in Michael's arms. For a brief second, something inside my head entertained the idea that the nightmare of the accident, leaving my life with Will and having to accept that Michael and I would now be married after all, was a dream. My mind then mused at whether meeting Will at all was a dream, and that I had been with Michael all this time. At some point in the night he had got into bed next to me. I did not know why. It had not happened before. The weight of his arms was much heavier than Will's used to be; the smell of him stronger than Will's gentle, soapy scent. Michael's body was warmer than Will's used to be in the mornings. It was an odd feeling, but one I supposed I was going to have to get used to. Seven o'clock, Sunday morning. It was time to get Tara up and ready for church.

Usually I did not attend Mass with Michael and Tara. I usually dropped them off and then collected them an hour later and we went to brunch. But that day, I went with them.

There is a distinct smell to a Catholic church. I had been in other churches during my life, for friends' weddings, and funerals and other people's christenings, but none of those churches smelt quite the same as a Catholic church. It is a comforting smell, almost like a homey musk. I have always thought it was very welcoming. Despite this, I was lost; it was all so confusing. I could see Michael's glances towards me throughout the Mass, no doubt he was wondering what I was thinking, and if I was following what was going on. I did not know when to stand, sit, kneel, what to say and when. We were sat towards the back of the church, next to the nave. I had the Order of Service card in front of me, and the piece of paper with that Mass' readings on them, and the hymn book, but I was still lost. There were certain things that everyone seemed to know how to say, but I did not.

It was all so overwhelming, so foreign to me. I felt very alone when Michael took Tara to receive Holy Communion and for Tara to receive a blessing from the priest, sat on my own watching all the proceedings around me. Every other member of the congregation had moved towards the front. I was left alone. At the end of Mass, we did not leave the church, but sat waiting for the Priest to pass by where we were sitting. Michael told me that this was usual for he and Tara to do; the Father liked to check in with Tara and see how she was, and how Michael was coping.

I looked at the priest tentatively as he approached us, a polite half-smile on my lips. I had seen him, of course, at the funeral, and at Tara's baptism and the wedding of Zara and Robert. But this was the first time I had said more than the conventional pleasantries. After speaking to Michael, Father Philip spent a lot of time talking to Tara. He was so kind to her; it was an endearing thing to witness. As their conversation drew to a close, Michael took Tara to the front of the church to go and light candles in memory of Zara and Robert. This seemed a familiar practice for them; they stood in front of the statue of Mary with their heads bowed in prayer. I asked Father Philip if I could have a word with him. Michael had clearly told him who I was, and a bit about our situation as he was very willing to sit down with me and talk.

Father Philip had warm, friendly brown eyes and greying hair around the temples. He must have been around fifty years old. He had clearly been a priest for a very long time; his homily was given with humour and confidence, he knew the grown-up children of his parishioners very well suggesting that he may have baptised some, if not most, of them and certainly played a part in many of their confirmations. I told him about the situation I found myself in. I told him how much of a shock everything had been to me. I told him that yesterday Michael and I had had an argument about the legalities of adopting Tara. Before I knew it, the whole story and almost all of my feelings had

130

spilled uncontrollably out of my mouth and I was, once more, in tears.

The church had emptied; out of the corner of my eye I had spotted Michael taking Tara out of the church before I had become upset. I suppose he surmised what I would say to the priest, and presumed that the events of yesterday were still too raw for me not to be upset by them. He wanted to shield Tara from hearing anything which might upset her; I assumed they went to wait in the car.

Father Philip kindly offered me his handkerchief. I was not aware that they were even made any more, never mind that people continued to use them. Dabbing my eyes, I completed my tirade of talking by telling the priest that I was going to have to marry Michael and that because he was Catholic and would still want to come to church that it would have to be in the church. I knew some of the rules; without permission, Michael could not have any marriage to someone outside the Catholic faith recognised by the church, and therefore would not be able to receive Holy Communion. I remember rambling that of course, the priest would be able to apply for permission, but for me it did not seem the best course of action because I thought Michael would resent me for it. I went on to openly ask the rhetorical question regarding Tara: how could I help nurture her faith and life in the Catholic church if I was not Catholic myself? I was very aware that it was not a good enough reason to convert, but that I thought I was left with very little option other than to do so. I am sure that they give lessons in patience in the seminary; Father Philip had done nothing more than say that he understood and murmured a few agreements throughout my speech. As I ended my outburst he told me that he thought being thrust into the role of motherhood was an unimaginable challenge, fraught with difficulties, that Mary had at least had some months warning to prepare for the coming of Jesus and to be His mother, rather than the overnight responsibility I had had to assume. He surmised the burden on my shoulders must be more than I ever thought was possible. He was so understanding. So calm. So nice. I immediately felt better and remembered that a problem shared really is a problem halved.

After a pause of a minute or so, in silence – although it felt much longer, he told me of a course called RCIA that I would be welcome to attend if I felt like converting to Catholicism might be the option for me. He said there was no pressure, and that the course was designed for people in my situation – those considering converting – to find out more about the teachings of Christ, the Catholic Church and to make an informed decision about whether this was right for the individual or not. The course, told me, would run once per week to allow time for what he called catechumens to reflect on that week's teachings, to do any reading from the Catechism, and to formulate any questions they had so they could be answered the following week. All the new words and terms I was encountering seemed bewildering to me, overwhelming even. It was a feeling I was becoming all too familiar with, much to my chagrin.

Of course, as with anything in life, there was a down side. Father Philip said these courses began in July, so that catechumens could have almost a year of teachings before Confirmation took place during Easter; the course he was currently running was almost at an end. I felt like my face fell a mile. I remember closing my eyes, trying to hide my frustration. Having clearly seen my reaction, and understanding my predicament, Father Philip said that for me he would make an exception. That he would re-start the course on a different day for me to attend. I think that was the first time I thanked God for anything and meant it.

I agreed, readily, to Father Philip's idea. I was grateful he would go to such lengths to try and help me, Tara and Michael. I shook his hand and arranged to see him once a week on a Tuesday night, after Mass, to go through the teachings and lessons of the Catholic Church. He suggested I attend alone so that I could make up my own mind, form my own opinions and not be coloured by my primary motives for attending church and considering converting. At the time, I was nervous. I had struggled to follow the procedure of Mass that Sunday. I voiced my fears to Father Philip and, with a kind chuckle in his voice, he told me not to worry, that he would find someone nice to sit next to on a Tuesday Mass and that they would help me understand when to sit, stand or kneel, and why those actions were done at that time. He also suggested that I continue to attend Sunday Mass with Michael and Tara, to help her see that church was a place for family, and a place where she was loved and cared for by more than just her god parents. I agreed.

It was not a process without its difficulties, attending the RCIA course. I had so many questions that at one point I had to write them down, so I would remember them all. So much of what I had grown up with, was different than the teachings of the Church. It was a challenge to understand the perspective of the Catechism fully. Father Philip was endlessly patient, clarifying things for me and in some cases pre-empting some of the questions I had. I understood the reason for the long process of RCIA, it takes time to understand a mindset and then to decide whether, or not, your fundamental values and perspectives align. Father Philip told me that many Catholics struggle with at least a few aspects during different points in their lives, and that it was all right to question and to look for answers. Free Will includes free thinking.

The more I attended Mass on my own, sitting next to a lady called Sarah, the more I felt comfortable enough to integrate aspects of Catholicism into my daily life, at times without even thinking. Before long I had joined Michael in saying grace before meals at home with Tara. I had joined them both in saying the Rosary before her bedtime. It took me a long time to learn all the different prayers, and even longer to analyse their meaning. I spent many nights sitting opposite Michael, either in the lounge, dining room or at the breakfast bar in the kitchen, trying to learn all I could as he went through the forms of the adoption process, trying to get as much completed as possible in preparation for when we could finally go ahead with the proceedings. The house was a sea of paper. Michael was patient with me when I asked him questions, even Tara was able to answer a few, her face lit up when she found she could teach Aunt Mimi something.

Eventually, as Easter approached, Father Philip asked me if I wanted to convert and be confirmed at Easter alongside the other catechumens. After a deep breath, and a mental check, I said yes. I told him I felt in my heart this was the right thing to do. For me, for Tara, for Michael. I understood that the teachings were the ideal way to live one's life. That, granted, not everyone was able to do this for all of their lives, all of the time, but that working towards it was what made you a better person. That small steps were the way towards becoming a good, or better, person.

And I truly believed every word I said.

I was starting to see the bigger picture, to rebuff the selfishness which had consumed me for most of my life. I was beginning to live for someone else instead of myself for the first time.

I had to choose a Confirmation name. This was a challenge for me. As much as I had learned, I did not feel I knew enough about all the saints to make an informed decision. Again, I turned to Father Philip for help. In his friendly voice, tinted with wisdom, he told me that learning about Catholicism, about Christ, was a life-long task and to not put too much pressure on myself to know everything all at once. He told me that I should look at what I wanted to do with my life and who I thought I would need the most guidance and intercession from. My priorities were to be a good wife and adoptive mother. Father Philip told me that St.

Rita was the patron saint of marriages, and that St. Anne was the patron saint of parenthood and that if I was going to be asking for help and guidance as I embarked upon, and tried to maintain, these roles in my life, that choosing either or both saints would be beneficial to me. Despite all my learning I did not know that one person could have two Confirmation names, but I decided to hyphenate them: Rita-Anne.

My Confirmation day was lovely; a glimmer of positivity in the dark sea of heartbreak I had, until then, been drowning in. We went to church, I asked Tara if she wanted to oversee the taking of photographs after the Mass on Michael's new digital camera. Eager for some responsibility, she readily agreed. Both she and I had had new out-fits for the day, a treat from Michael. Mine, a white high collared blouse and long, flowing white skirt, Tara's a mass of pink with white flowers stitched on and a matching headband. She was every inch my little princess that day. Mass began, and I was to make my first Holy Communion immediately after being confirmed. Kneeling in front of the Bishop, and having the sign of the cross made on my forehead as my chosen names were said, I felt a wash of warmth go through me. I cannot really explain it, but it was not a feeling of discomfort in any way. More of comfort. Safety. Reassurance. Welcoming. After I was confirmed, I was asked to take the bread from the back of the church to Father Philip at the altar. After the prayers were said I was asked to receive my first Holy Communion along with the other catechumens. It is such a warm feeling when you receive Holy Communion; I was surprised by it. Nobody had told me to expect it. I tried to look on this as a new start in my life, as the beginning of my role as a future wife and adoptive mother. At the end of Mass, most of the congregation came to shake my hand and welcome me to the Catholic family and the church. It was so nice; everybody was so welcoming.

Father Philip stood for photographs and Tara was more than happy to take as many as he would allow. She was particularly impressed that the images were in front of her immediately and that she could zoom in on the faces. These, new, photographs were much different than those she had of her parents, entombed in an album.

Tara, Michael and I went for brunch after Mass. Tara was enjoying her fruit plate with a small croissant, a Belgian waffle and an American style pancake. From the corner of my eye, I caught Michael rolling his towards the ceiling; I could almost hear him saying that they were not proper pancakes, that they were too thick, and they should come with sugar and lemon. Michael was more than somewhat of a traditionalist. I was more concerned about the refined sugar she was consuming in abundant quantities, and the effect it would have on her mood later in the day. I was quite certain that she would not sleep well, that night; every mother knows, despite whatever the scientists try and tell us, that sugar and children do not mix, and that they should avoid it as much as possible in their diets – not only for the benefit of their teeth – if they wanted to be healthy, happy and live without a cloud of distraction in their brains.

Tara had been given some pictures to colour in, and some wax crayons by one of the staff. She was happily colouring in the hills and trees of the landscape scene, chattering away to Michael about what colours she wanted to use. I was only half listening to their conversation, my mind replaying the events of the day and the lessons and teachings I had learned to get there. As I was running through the events of the last six months, and the plans for the rest of the day, I stirred my freshly squeezed, with pulp, orange juice in an absent-minded fashion. My mind began to wander towards what I should make for lunch when my head snapped across to Michael. I had heard the word "bridesmaid" being said, and an excited affirmative from the lips of Tara.

Suddenly, marrying Michael was at the forefront of my tumbling thoughts. Flashbacks of my telling Will I thought we should wait until Tara was old enough to be our Flower girl at our wedding surged through my memory causing tears to unexpectedly attack my eyes. Tears at the loss of the marriage and life I should have had, that I had foreseen when his eyes had met mine on the day we fell in love. Everything I had dreamed of had vanished into the tears which filled my eyes. It was all I could do to paste a smile on my face as I gazed at the girl whose eyes had become as large as saucers, as only children's can when they are excited about something special. It was the first time since her parents' death I had seen her look like she had her spark back. It was the first time she had seemed happy or energised about anything.

And with that excited look on her face, I knew that the wedding would be a good thing for Tara; it would cement in her mind that she still had a family, still had grown ups who loved her. Still had a pair of parental figures to guide her life until she could run it for herself. And that was more important to me than anything else. It was my duty to provide that standard of care for her to the best of my ability.

And with that excited look on her face, I knew I was going to need the ring back that had once felt so heavy on my left hand.

Michael and I were getting married.

Chapter 25 – Court

I had been quite preoccupied with the process of RCIA, juggling work and Tara's home life, alongside trying to wade through the sea of documents associated with Tara's adoption in preparation for the day we could put the wheels into motion to become her legal parents. Not that we could ever hope to replace Robert and Zara, but we knew we needed to go through the legalities, for everyone's benefit. Too preoccupied, in fact, for me to realise that the date of the trial was upon us.

The police had conducted a thorough investigation into the accident which had murdered my best friends. I had heard they had sent the forensics team, that they took thousands of photographs documenting the site of the crash, and that they had interviewed all the witnesses they could and had arrested the suspect. I had heard fragments of information from others, in passing, about the progress of the investigation; however, I was, probably wilfully, ignorant of most of the goings on, of the intricate details of the process of prosecution despite being updated each time both sets of parents had received updates from the designated Family Officer of the Police's progress. When they had begun their case, I had barely been able to pay attention, too entrenched in grief to want to hear the details of my best friends' last moments: of what they had had to endure, of what they had experienced as their last, conscious, moments on this earth. I wondered, presumed, that their thoughts would have been of each other, and of Tara. To let the thoughts of it into my mind was to allow my already shattered heart to be ground into powder. If I refused to hear it, I could refuse to admit the dreadful events which my best friends had had to experience. I am certain you understand; it was almost a type of self-preservation, and I am sure that you could imagine yourself doing something similar. Nevertheless, the time had arrived in which I would have no choice but to listen, to hear, to be confronted with the facts, to almost relive what had happened that fateful, autumn afternoon.

I had never been inside a criminal court room before, but it appeared to be the same as I had seen on British television drama series which took their representations of realism quite seriously. It had a musty scent, no doubt caused by the old carpet, the leather seats and old furniture polish. It smelled official; the heavy scent of justice and guilt hung in the air like an axe looming above the proverbial guilty person's head. And daunting. Even for someone who was simply visiting, a witness to the process of justice; there only to see those who were guilty get what they deserved.

We sat in the gallery, to the right of the room, the judge above us on our right-hand side, casting a shadow over the witness stand, opposite the box in which the defendant stood. There was another area for the public, above the ground floor, by which people must ascend a staircase outside of the court room to access. The green leather appeared to be extremely old, yet not as worn as much as I might have expected, had I been able to consider more carefully my surroundings.
The judge entered from a wooden door behind the bench, everyone was commanded to rise, and the proceedings were called to order.
It had been proven through blood testing that the driver had been under the influence of both drink and drugs, two things which I abhorred before the accident, and afterwards more than I had the words for. We heard during the trial that the driver had been four times over the legal limit for alcohol, and the blood contained a cocktail of illegal drugs. I still cannot abide the idea of anything being in one's system other than that which has been prescribed by a medical professional; even then, I believe, it is wholly inadvisable to be behind the wheel. Life is too precious.

The driver was a woman, a girl really. Eighteen years of age. Not that much older than Tara, in the grand scheme of things. Her name was Felicity. To me, it did not sound like a name which screamed drink and drugs; it sounded like her parents were good people, respectable, educated, and had wanted a good life for their daughter when she was born, and named her in accordance to their feelings when she came into their lives. As I sat in the courtroom, I remembered when I first discovered it was a woman, girl, behind the wheel, how shocked and confused I was. Horrified, even. Stereotypically, I suppose, I had expected the culprit, murderer, to have been a reckless man. Perhaps one of those boy racers one hears so much about in the news, or one of those youths with an ASBO. *The Daily Mail* was full of derogatory news about the youth of the day, tarring them all with the same, criminal brush. So, I had expected the murderer to be called Nathan, or Zach, or Callum, or Leighton or Lewis, or Ethan, or Ryan, or Brad, or Josh, or Joseph. Or perhaps a middle-aged man going too fast, and being drunk behind the wheel of his mid-life-crisis sports car; perhaps a Nigel, Colin, Brian, David or a Kevin.

Instead: Felicity.

The first time I saw her was when she stood in the dock, escorted by two police officers: a man who looked to be on the border of retirement, and a woman who looked to be my age. They both had neutral, expressionless faces looking towards the judge, as though they had seen these kinds of cases hundreds of times before and knew that there was a chance that justice would not be served; as though they knew better than to react and to cast judgement or hope for the appropriate outcome. She was a slight girl, with a look about her of not enough to eat; dirty blonde hair which looked both from an at-home bottle and extremely greasy, as though it had not seen a shower for a week or two; clothes which looked as though they had seen better days, and were bought from a market rather than any good clothes shop. They did not look as though they cost more than twenty pounds for the whole ensemble, if, indeed, she paid for them at all. As judgemental as that may have been, I had no reason to believe she was anything other than a criminal; I did not, in fact, want to accept that she, in any way, shape, form or fashion, was a law-abiding citizen. She spent a long while rolling her eyes and looking disinterested in what was going on around her; she paid little attention to the legal team below her, who were working to defend her actions, or those in the gallery watching. She did not look our way once.

The first time I saw her, I knew in my soul she was guilty.

The first time I saw her I detested her.

The first time I saw her my mind was filled with murderous thoughts.

She stood when the judge entered the court room, because she was made to by the male police officer who stood to her side. He had to prod her, then grab her arm and lift her up as he rose to meet the judge's presence. It was then that I had decided she was nothing but a disrespectful cretin and should be sentenced to life imprisonment. It was then that I wished the country had never abolished hanging. I had to steady myself, grabbing hold of the cold leather of the bench beneath me, when I saw her wipe her nose on the back of her sleeve, making an extremely disgusting accompanying noise; she had not even the decency to bring a disposable tissue with her, or a handkerchief.

My stomach lurched and churned at the sight of her.

My hatred intensified.

As the trial began, I had to grab Michael's hand to help focus my attention on not screaming at her across the court room. His was as hot with rage as mine. I needed something to ground me, to stop me from launching from my seat towards her, to exact some sort of revenge by taking her life as she had taken Zara's. Robert's. I had never before been violent, but a primordial rage raced through me merely for being in the same room as their killer. My body stiffened, tense with anxiety and horror. Her demeanour remained that of total disinterest. She was either a sociopath or could not, or would not, grasp the magnitude of the situation and the trouble she was in, nor the potential consequences.

On the opposite side of the courtroom, where the additional seating was, seemed to be a group of people there to support her. Perhaps five or six, a mixture of young men and women. Nothing more than children, really. They were mostly of the same appearance as her, young and immature looking, in awful clothes with dirty looking hair and skin. One boy seemed particularly gaunt, much more so than the others. His skin was a dirty brown colour, the type one might assume has not seen soap for several years.

There was, however, in the corner of the room, and old couple who seemed to be extremely upset. They looked a little too old to be her parents, and a little too involved to be unrelated. They looked distraught, clutching each other's hands, heads close together as if trying to console or question what was occurring. I tried my best to ignore them, wanting to know nothing about her life at all, other than what was to happen to it through the punishment I so desperately wanted her to receive.

The prosecution laid out a damning case, the barrister used a serious, emotionally charged, tone in her opening argument, a few of the jury, I noticed, looking swayed by it. I hoped they felt towards alcohol abuse and drug taking the same way I did. The defence barrister offered a feeble excuse that Miss Felicity Brimley-Smythe had been coerced into a life of crime, drink and drugs through falling into the wrong crowd, and that, due to a lack of mental capacity at the time, she should not be charged on two counts of murder, rather the lesser charges of vehicular manslaughter and driving whilst under the influence of drugs and alcohol.

This, I found to be incredible in the worst kind of way. Blood pounded in my ears, almost drowning out the rest of the defence. It was an insult. A slap in the face. It was as though her legal representation had stomped all over the graves of my best friends and spat on their memory for the simple fun of it. Although Michael and I both knew that he was doing his job, and that he probably did not believe Felicity should face these lesser charges, we both bristled at the end of the barrister's plea to the jury. Logic does not apply when lives have been lost. Michael was as incredulous as I was that this may come to fruition. I willed the jury to be harsh, to find her guilty and put her in prison for the rest of her miserable and pathetic life.

I even sent up a silent prayer for God to work His will through the jury to exact a suitable punishment.

There were experts called on both sides, over the two and a half weeks that the court case ran for. Those who said that her judgement was not impaired, those that said it most certainly was. Those that said she must have had an inordinate amount of alcohol in her system to cause such a crash, those who said that she was simply not paying enough attention. One even tried to blame the autumnal weather and the time of day; I am certain I do not have to explain to you how I felt when that so-called expert gave her opinion! Eyewitnesses were called, and most found in the favour of Zara and Robert; there was nothing my friends could have done to avoid the crash, each stated they had tried to help them, but that it was a lost cause. One, older lady, said that she was quite sure they did not suffer any pain. I understood that this was to try and reassure their families, and us, but in reality,

143

all it did was damage the case; if the jury thought their suffering to be any less, then Robert and Zara's murderer may not receive the punishment she so clearly deserved.

It was at this point that I wanted to scream at the girl standing in the dock that the damage was irreparable, that the ripple effect of this child's actions had ruined the lives of more people than she could count: that a little girl was without her parents because of her; that two sets of parents had each lost their only child; that two, precious, lives were over far sooner than they needed to be, should have been, because of her choices; and, that Michael and I had had to sacrifice everything we had each been working to build for our own futures because she had not had the self-restraint and common sense to say no to drugs and to not get behind the wheel of a car after having an alcoholic drink.

She was not called to the stand to defend herself; I believed this was because she could not offer any sort of defence. I wondered if this was because of her barrister's advice, or if she merely cared not one iota for the damage she had done and could not realise the potential consequences as a real possibility. Interestingly, there was no mention of her home life, no attempt to blame poor parenting; of course, this would only have held water if she had been younger than eighteen. At her age she should have known better; she was, after all, an adult.

The jury deliberated their verdict for an hour. After two weeks of sitting through day after day of overwhelming, compelling evidence, debate, and discussion, it was a swift decision that left me completely disillusioned with the justice system. I wanted to scream at them that they should go back, reconsider, that they had not debated long enough if they had come back with this ridiculous verdict. I wanted to take the stand myself and explain the extent of the trauma this specimen of vermin had created. It seemed that they had taken her age into consideration, youth and inexperience in life, and found her not guilty of a double murder, but guilty of the lesser charge of vehicular manslaughter.

Silent tears streamed down my face, burning with hatred at these twelve people who could not see what damage had been done, and chose to be too forgiving to a woman, child, who should have known better. These twelve people, who seemed to ignore what was as plain as the noses on their faces, ignored the details and facts of the case; she, Felicity, had been idiotic enough to take drugs and because she did that, Robert's and Zara's lives had been ended. She should have known better than to take drugs. Why do people do that? Why do people not treat their bodies with more sanctity than they do? Why do people abuse the only set of skin and bone they have been allotted? Surely, they should know better? Surely, everyone should know better? Surely, the jury should have known better than to let her get away with it? Everybody should always know better!

Michael, too, was crying – something he rarely did. Silent sobs escaped his lips, sniffles occupied his nose. I am certain he reached into his top pocket for his handkerchief to dab at his face and blow his nose without realising what he was doing. Michael and I were stunned, Zara's mother and father wept into each other, Robert's parents were muttering protests of unreasonableness, that it was not fair, that the sentence was not harsh enough. We were all shocked into statues in our place in the gallery; we had to be prompted by those around us to stand when the judge left the court room. I had not even heard the sentence, too consumed by my rage to truly listen and hear; it was not until afterwards that I realised that Felicity Brimley-Smythe had received a custodial sentence of just ten years, with parole no sooner than six years.

Six short years.

That's all their lives were worth.

I was disgusted. I felt the bile shift inside me, threatening to escape.

Felicity Brimley-Smythe had been led away before I could look at her face. I do not know if the gravity of what she had done dawned on her before she was taken to prison. I wanted to kill her, I wanted to rip her head from her body, to peel off her skin piece by piece with my bare hands and make her scream in the same agony Robert and Zara must have felt, to replicate for her the pain and suffering Tara felt at losing her parents, to tear out her heart the way Tara's had been, the way mine had been; to do all those things you see in the films when people exact revenge in the worst way with no conscience because they have been hurt so very much, because of the immense crimes which had been committed against them.

I wanted to choke the life out of her. I wanted to exact the revenge that the justice system had not delivered. I wanted to take my thumbs and press them each side of her windpipe in her throat and cut off the blood supply to her brain, what little of one she seemed to have. I did not want her to exist in the same world as Tara. She did not deserve it. Tara deserved to live in a better world; one without criminals. Desperate thoughts raced through my mind; how on earth do people move past this and continue with their lives? How were we to do that for Tara?

I knew it was going to take a long time to process the events of those weeks.

And we only had each other to rely on.

And only wedding planning to try to distract us.

Chapter 26 – Till death us do part

"By the power vested in me, I now pronounce you husband and wife."

With these words from the mouth of the priest at the altar at the head of the church, an echoing coming from the high, hollow ceiling, a rush of emotion ran through me. I cannot say that much of it was positive emotion; a feeling of sadness, despair and anguish flowed through me. My emotions were threatening to spill out of me in the form of tears, conspiring to ruin the moment, the day, and reveal my anguish. That was the last thing I wanted, to let my true, mixed feelings jeopardise the beginning of renewed stability for Tara. Better to let my British stiff upper lip do its work and keep the traitorous emotions hidden.

With those words, the exchanging of rings, and the signing of the marriage licence, Michael and I were married. Bound to one another. Joined, in front of God, for all the world to know. Mr and Mrs. One, married unit. Till death us do part.

It was a quiet Saturday, mid-morning wedding; we invited only our respective parents, obviously, and Tara's grandparents. Partly because they would be reassured that their granddaughter would be looked after as their children had wished, partly to help with the babysitting during the day, and partly because Michael and I wanted to make sure they understood that they were part of Tara's family unit and had just as much importance now as they would have had if the car accident had not happened. Everybody in attendance understood the significance of the day, of the wedding, of the marriage which would follow. Everybody in attendance conveyed subdued emotions.

I wore a simple ivory coloured skirt, camisole top and an embroidered, tailored jacket. I had matching, ivory court shoes which pinched my little toes ever so slightly. I did not think a white dress was appropriate. Call me old fashioned but there are some traditions I like to uphold, you understand. Michael looked handsome in his charcoal grey suit, with matching ivory cravat. Tara, on the other hand, had a calf length white dress, complete with flower sash, flower headdress and a bouquet of flowers to carry up the nave. She looked even more my little princess than she did a few months earlier on my Confirmation day. It was more important to me for her to be the centre of attention, than either Michael or I.

I smiled a lot that day, not because I was happy about marrying Michael - it was hardly my dream - and not solely as a default expression as a means to hide my inner turmoil, which I swore to myself I would never reveal to anyone, but because it was the first time I had really seen Tara come out of her shell and it made me feel a little better. It eased my anxiety just a little; perhaps if she was this happy with the idea of a marriage, Michael and I might be on the right track towards ensuring she was happy in the rest of her life. She had been increasingly excited during all the fittings for her dress, she had chosen what she had wanted, colour and length and so forth, ribbons and sleeves. She had asked lots of questions of the seamstress who made her dress, and had begun to take a real interest in things again. She was curious about the way dresses were made, and how they were made to be poufy, the way she wanted hers. We had gone shoe shopping and she had picked out a pair of shoes she said she liked. She told everyone she met that she was going to be a bridesmaid. She even started skipping up and down the shoe shop, almost giddy with delight.

Our small congregation of guests, including Father Philip, joined us for a quiet sort of wedding breakfast in the same pub in which Robert had proposed to Zara. A wave of nostalgia hit me as I entered the smoky, mahogany furnished, deep red lounge, interrupted before it could fully form by a frown encompassing my forehead as Tara's cough reached my ears as the smoke invaded her lungs. I remember glancing over at Michael, as he made his way across the thick, spongy carpet to the oak tabled booth in the corner of the room, to find a similar expression on his face, as he turned to move the chairs, and knowing he was thinking about the upcoming smoking ban, impatient for it to come into law. It was rather an unpopular thing at the time with some, but, for Michael, it was too little too late; his father, my new father-in-law, had suffered terribly from a lung condition for years. A non-smoker, his life had been affected by those around him; the culture he grew up in, his friends and family having little knowledge of the dangers of smoking, had caused men of his generation to suffer greatly. Every aspect of his life had been affected: exercise was challenging; walking up and down the stairs was a struggle; if he had a cold, Michael's mother was fraught with worry in case he did not get through it. In Michael's eyes, it was all unnecessary, and the concern on his face was immediately present as Tara coughed. His furrowed brow a sign of his increasing parental perspective.

The staff at the pub noticed Tara's dress, with all its big skirts and multitude of ribbons and flowers, my outfit and Michael's suit, and that our guests were also dressed for the occasion and very kindly brought over a bottle of champagne and some flutes as a gesture of good luck and best wishes. They even brought over a small, sturdy, glass of sparkling apple juice for Tara so she could feel included. I know that they meant well, but I was torn between wanting to celebrate the beginning of a renewed stability for Tara and mourning the passing of my lost life. We toasted to absent friends, to family, and to the future. Our parents toasted our future as new parents ourselves, wishing us wisdom and strength. It occurred to me then that they were becoming grandparents, and that through the despair of the accident, some joy might be felt somewhere, by someone. My eyes, which were beginning to fill with tears – overwhelmed with the throng of emotions I was experiencing - met Michael's before they moved to Tara. He had an odd look on his face which looked vaguely familiar, although I could not place it at the time.

Eventually, after we had all indulged in quite a delicious carvery-style lunch and a slice each of surprise, decorated sponge cake for dessert, which all sets of parents insisted Michael and I cut together, everybody said their goodbyes, pressed cards and gifts into our hands and exited the car park in differing directions. Father Philip offered one last blessing on our family, and our marriage. Michael and I were stood, watching them all depart, with Tara in front of us; each of us with one hand on one of her shoulders, our other appendage being used to wave. Although it was a rhetorical question, Michael asked if we should go home. Before I knew what I was saying, I had said yes. I was so tired. I was too tired to realise that I had finally, wholly accepted Robert and Zara's house as my new home. All the emotion of the last few months had drained me, and my wedding day had been the final straw. I wanted to go to bed and sleep for a year. For a lifetime.

Michael drove us home, the short journey taking all too long for my tired, weary brain. I vaguely remember helping Tara to brush her teeth, to put on her pyjamas and that Michael and I tucked her into bed; a goodnight kiss on her forehead from each of us as we said our prayers before she snuggled down into her pink duvet cover, turning on to her left-hand side to go to sleep. Our wedding night was not the typical event that most newly married couples experience. I took a quick shower to erase the makeup from my face; the black mascara leaving watery trails down my cheeks and over my wrists as I wiped my face, gradually giving in to gravity, resulting in droplets escaping downwards from my elbows. Robert and Zara had not succumbed to society's trends and installed a power shower, believing they cost far too much money and used too much water and that ordinary showers did the job just as well. It was one of the many things I missed about my home with Will. We had not been nearly as conscientious as Robert and Zara. I went into the bedroom to find Michael pulling a vest over his head and down towards his blue pyjama trousers. As tired as I was, a half smile crept over one side of my face; usually his pyjamas were like his socks, a tad on the obscure, whacky and luminous side. I tried to hide as much of myself under my towel as I could, used my hairdryer to dry my long locks quickly before I woke Tara. I do not know why I was so shy around Michael, we had been each other's firsts, but I was. In what I am sure was a bid to protect my privacy, Michael left the bedroom to fetch a glass of water from the kitchen leaving me to hurriedly get ready for bed. This was the first night that Michael had changed in the bedroom, usually choosing the bathroom instead. But we were married, and so there was no real reason any more to avoid sharing things.

I crawled into bed with the last of my energy, what little I had had that morning being depleted by the events of the day, turning off the bedside lamp on my side of the bed. My side. Michael and I had sides of the bed. We were a true married couple after all. I think I must have fallen asleep before Michael returned because the next thing I remember was the alarm clock going off, my eyes snapping open with a start, seeing Michael's face inches from mine. I shook him gently on the shoulder, his warm skin beneath my icy fingers, whispering his name. After stirring with some odd, almost middle aged, stretching sounds, Michael's chocolate brown eyes met mine with a small smile. We exchanged good mornings, again with a coy whisper.

There was a moment between us filled with awkwardness and acceptance; this is how we would start every morning for the rest of our lives.

Till death us do part.

Chapter 27 – Family Formalities

Michael took all of three days off after the wedding before he recommenced the adoption process. I was in the process of informing all the necessary companies about my name change, and ordering different bank cards and so forth during the immediate aftermath of the wedding; a task which was so overwhelming in itself it gave me a newfound respect for Michael's bearing the brunt of the adoption work. It was odd getting used to calling myself a different name, especially since there had been a time I knew with every fibre of my being that I would never use Michael's surname and would only use Will's. But what did I know about the twists and turns of life, back then, when I had met Will and ended my relationship with Michael? Nothing. It turns out I knew nothing at all.

The following few months blurred into an even more intense whirlwind of interviews, telephone calls, emails, faxes, letters and meetings. There were signatures, which felt strange with Michael's surname after my initials, lots of reading, and I am almost certain we kept Royal Mail's profit margins intact for a while with all the post we sent and received. Each overwhelming moment we interacted with the process tightened the inside of my body; apprehension squeezing my heart, causing a permanent panda-look to settle beneath my eyes. My energy was completely spent. Each time I looked at Michael, my husband – I was still getting used to that word - I saw that beneath his organised, calm and cool exterior he was just as anxious as I was that everything would go well, that we would be approved to be Tara's adoptive parents. He was just as tired as I was; each night we collapsed into the same bed, our bed, now, falling immediately asleep.

All the way through the process, I will admit, I had a dreadful, thought hiding beneath my consciousness: if we were not approved, then the marriage would have been for nothing. I suppose there was a lot of regret in my heart at that time. I was still hurting over the loss of Zara and Robert, and my life with Will, still furious over the ridiculous verdict of the trial, and I still hurt for Tara. After Mass each Sunday, following brunch, we took Tara to her parents' graves. We spent time with her there, and we also gave her time alone. She told them about what was happening, her friends, her school, her favourite toys, what was going on in her cartoons and favourite television programmes, and how much baking she had been learning to do with Uncle Michael. Each week I lamented having to go at all; not because I begrudged Tara the chance to process her grief, but that any of us had to go through the experience at all. I always felt a fresh punch in the stomach, a weekly reminder of my lost happiness. The selfishness which I had sworn to eradicate from my personality had not been entirely eliminated.

The pessimistic thoughts which had consumed my everyday life, eventually - thankfully, proved redundant. Although, I was not proved wrong for what seemed like an eternity. After many legalities, and gripping tightly of each other's hands, Michael and I finally went to the panel and were approved to officially adopt Tara. We had become parents. We were the guardians of Tara's childhood.

The relief of the process being over with a positive result was fleeting; when the realisation dawned on me that I was now a parent I felt the weight on my shoulders increased tenfold. I never understood that being legally and morally responsible for someone, a child, could be a tangible burden.

We sat Tara down and told her the news, over a homemade milkshake in the kitchen. She was quiet for what seemed like a long moment before tentatively looking up at us under the weight of her long eyelashes with her big, innocent eyes, and asked us if she had to call us mummy and daddy now. From the fragile tone she spoke in, I could tell this question had been one she had been wondering about for a while. Michael looked at me, his eyes dark, eyelids quivering. He did not know what to say to her, this little girl whose life was now in our hands; the apple of his eye, the life in his heart. Swallowing, I reached across the table and took her fidgeting fingers in my hands and told her that at no point would she ever have to call us anything other than Aunt Mimi and Uncle Michael. That her mummy and daddy would always be hers, and nobody could replace them, but that all that this meant was that she would be able to stay in her home forever, and that she would have people who loved her taking care of her until she was old enough to take care of herself, and that we would probably still want to take care of her even then. I also told her that at no point would we stop going to visit her mummy and daddy and she would always hold them in her heart, that she could always talk to them in her prayers, and that she could always, always look at the photographs she had of them whenever she wanted to.

Tara sat, for a moment, taking in my answer. Her head oscillating upwards and downwards with a slow, steady pace. She seemed to understand that nothing would change any further in her life. She then asked if she could go and play upstairs in her room, hopped down from the chair and climbed the stairs quickly.

I turned my head to look at my husband who, with his cheeks blowing sideways, was slowly exhaling the breath which had weighed heavy in his lungs.

Childhood is always more stressful for the parents.

Chapter 28 – Passing Time

As the years passed, and Tara seemed to grow before our very eyes, we settled into a solidified family life. Uncle Michael reluctantly agreed to decorate Tara's room with princess pink and white colours, with glittery stars adorning the walls, and later, as she turned twelve into a subtler purple colour; with plenty of bare spaces on her wall for the posters of her favourite film and television stars. She even had a couple of her favourite musicians up there. We went on family holidays: Greece, Italy, France, Canada, Germany; we tried to make sure that Tara knew as much about the world and saw as much of it as time would allow. It had been one of Robert's wishes for her, that she be exposed to unfamiliar cultures, people and ways of life. He had had much the same when he was young and considered it to be one of the most humbling experiences of his life; he always told us in the pub that he felt it had contributed to his character, enhanced his personality. Of course, after the third time of being told this in a night Michael had been audibly rolling his eyes. How we still missed his voice telling us about his worldly experiences!

In a way, we were lucky; tragedy meant we could afford to take Tara on the holidays because there was no mortgage on the house to pay. The life insurance policy Zara and Robert had had, paid off the remainder and Tara inherited the property as their next of kin. With the money Michael and I had from each of our house sales, and our salaries from our respective jobs, we were able to live a comfortable life. Especially since we did not have the expense of setting up a home, or making any significant purchases; our lives had amalgamated quite easily. Of course, life would have been easier if I had climbed the career ladder as I had always planned; however, I chose to change my priorities and focus on raising Tara well. There were three promotions for which I did not apply at work, much to the confusion of my coworkers; however, those who knew of my situation were quick to offer support, and did not pass judgemental comments. I tried to ignore the frowns in the coffee corner, the whispers and questions I overheard in the cloakroom. I understood their confusion; I had been adamant I was going to be successful in my professional life. However, circumstance had forced my hand. Despite my lack of upward progression, we were able to send Tara to one of the three private Catholic schools in the county, spending time visiting each one with Tara to understand the ethos of each school, the academic performance and the pastoral support on offer, should Tara require any. They were all extremely welcoming, but eventually, the decision belonged to Tara; she chose the second of the three schools we had visited saying she liked their science laboratories and the extra-curricular options they provided. Michael and I were proud of the balanced decision she made, despite her youth, and supported it without reservation.

When Zara's father passed away shortly after Tara turned nine there was a muted fog surrounding her; I had no doubt that her mind was filled with the memories of what she went through when Zara and Robert died. She spent a lot of time at her friend Anne's house, whose maternal grandparents had both passed away within the previous twelve months. Spending time with someone of her own age who had been through the same thing helped her realise that grandparents do not last forever. It was Anne who came with Tara and I to the department store to select a suitable dress for the funeral; plain black, knee length with long sleeves perfect for tucking a handkerchief underneath. A rounded neckline with a black, lacy collar lying flat for about half an inch over the material of the dress; its edges scalloped in half-moons, giving it a more delicate appearance. Kindly, Anne complimented Tara on her appearance, she told her how smart she looked, and how proud her Grandpa would have been of her. I was relieved she was such a comforting presence in Tara's life, that she offered the innocent optimism only a child can. Tara coped well at the funeral, chin held high, accepting hugs from all the friends of her grandfather; she helped her grandmother all day, I suppose she thought being useful was a better option than merely sitting and dwelling on the sadness of the event.

However, when Tara wore the dress once more, on the fifth anniversary of her parents' death, her demeanour was much more subdued. All the family went to church, where a Mass was said to remember Robert and Zara; then, we went to their graves, recited prayers and the Rosary, and laid flowers. It was a day of mixed emotions; comfort from the fond memories Tara had of her parents, and raw, piercing pain as she remembered how much she missed them, and realised how much of her life on which they were missing out. Her remaining grandparents spent a lot of the time, unintentionally, reminding her of this by telling Tara how much she had grown up, how proud her parents would have been of her. They meant well, but sometimes older people do not realise the damage words cause, especially at such a young age, when the brain remains in a sponge-like state, absorbing all around it. Those still of the mind that sticks and stones may break bones but words will never hurt, sometimes, cannot be more wrong. And so, Michael and I spent the day trying to remain strong for Tara, to quell the tears that threatened to spill from our eyes so she would not see our grief; neither of us wanted to appear as though our grief surpassed hers. She was, of course, the most entitled to grieve. Granted, there is no word for a parent who has lost a child – no word could encompass the pain – but Tara had lost out on ever truly knowing her mummy and daddy. She had missed out on being raised by them, on spending time with them, on being guided by them. To be reminded of this, almost cruelly, was almost as horrific as them being stolen from her in the first place. Michael and I wanted her to realise it was absolutely acceptable to be upset, with whatever the cause was that day. Tears at a time of sadness can mask a multitude of causes. We had a brief time together as a family at the grave side, and then we all left Tara on her own so she could speak to her parents in private.

The cold, damp bench which stood at the side of the main path through the cemetery, uncomfortable beneath my legs, was our designated waiting place. Small talk has always been something at which I was not skilled. The weather, typically autumnal, had unleashed a downpouring rain upon the area; puddles, full of the grey skies above, collected in the uneven dips of the cemetery path. The hedgerows were becoming brown, losing their crispy orange and golden leaves to the muddy earth below. Death hung in the air. The cold, musty smell of rot, inescapable. The weight of an approaching winter felt heavy upon my shoulders. Desperately, I wanted to speak to Tara's grandparents, to tell them off, almost, for upsetting her. For not knowing her well enough to avoid making harmful comments, however unintentional they were. I was trapped in the elder section of the millennial generation. Too respectful to tell them, too angry to allow the issue to go unspoken. Glancing at Michael, I could see from the lines furrowed in his brow he was of the same opinion. However, the last thing either of us wanted, and indeed the family needed, was to argue. Cohesiveness was necessary for a stable life for Tara. Delicately, I asked them how they thought Tara was coping with the day. I received a mix of responses, from all places on the scale from terribly to exceedingly well. They then spent some time discussing their differing opinions with each other, which served only to cause frustration within me. My mind was a mixture of dizziness at all the backwards and forwards heated debate I was witnessing, and anger at it happening at all. How could they argue about what each other thought rather than trying to find a way to help her cope? I was aghast, both at their conduct of the day and how little respect they seemed to have for the anniversary – although, I suppose, their grief could have been influencing their behaviour, for Tara and for the job that Michael and I were doing in trying to raise her. Were they not old enough to know better? Michael, though, asked them why they thought she might not be coping very well. It was only a short sentence, but a powerful one. They fell silent, for a while. He then asked if they thought anything we had said had made the day even worse than it needed to be for her; mentioning that adults' words impact small ears much more so than ones of the same size, that children are like sponges and take extra consideration over everything they hear because they are learning to understand the implications of what is being said. Nothing came in reply to his questions, but the message within was received and understood. I reached for his hand, wrapped my fingers around his knuckles and gave a little squeeze of solidarity. He made an excellent parent.

In comparison, a few years later, Tara's Confirmation day was a celebration for the entire family: two grandmothers attended, and her last remaining grandfather. Most of the other members of her class were being Confirmed, also, that day, and so she spent a lot of it away from Michael and I. We were glad to sit away and let her enjoy the day, the moment with her friends, and create her own memories. We knew the family meal after the ceremony would suffice for us. Michael took lots of photographs on his newest smartphone, emailing them to Tara's secret email address to which he was planning on giving her the password when she turned eighteen. He had read about the idea on the Internet and suggested it to me not soon after we became her legal parents; I had hesitated at first, wondering if some of the things we might send her were too morbid, too damaging. Michael had been quite direct in his argument, suggesting we would regret not doing so later in life; telling me that Tara was a well-rounded child, emotionally and intellectually mature enough to deal with what she would read. Eventually, after much discussion, I relented and agreed that he was probably right, and that it would be a memento of which she could be proud; especially after we had both passed on, she needed, he claimed, at least one lasting memory of one of her sets of parents; also – she might even start the same tradition for her own children.

159

Tara's grandparents gave her traditional gifts; a Bible, a Rosary, a necklace with a pendant of her patron saint.

At the end of her Confirmation day, after Tara had said her goodnights and gone to bed, I sat in the lounge and kicked my heels off, wiggling my toes, still imprisoned in my stockings, in a bid to find them some comfort, contemplating how very much different my understanding of the day would have been if my life had not changed in the manner it had. Of course, I would have attended the day, with Will at my side, we would have smiled, hugged, taken photographs, congratulated and chatted. I would have understood it was important. However, I was not certain I could have fully understood what she had accepted in her life if I had not gone through it myself. I understood why Michael had been saying prayers at Robert's bedside when we went to the hospital, why he seemed to have been able to deal with Zara and Robert's deaths better than I had. The rock that he had been to me was because he had the rock of the Church to depend on and was able to draw strength from everything he had learned in his life as a Catholic. I was pleased Tara would have the same sense of reassurance throughout her life as Michael had had in times of crisis and heartbreak. My mind had meandered through these thoughts and I did not realise I must have been frowning as I was thinking, because Michael, dropping down onto the sofa next to me and rubbing his legs, asked me what was the matter. Taking his arm in my hands and snuggling into his shoulder, I reassured him that nothing was the matter, that I had been reflecting on the day and the changes that had taken place since Tara had been born. With a slow sigh, in a demonstration of solidarity and friendship, he pressed his nose against the top of my head, moved his lips forward and kissed me.

My hand moved to his chest; his heart was beating hard with rapidity, I could feel it through the thin, crisp cotton shirt he was still wearing. His head did not move. My hand moved atop his chest, which expanded with deliberate, deep breaths. I wondered

160

briefly if he could still smell the apple scented shampoo in my hair. My fingers, almost absent-mindedly, began caressing Michael's torso. He gently moved his other arm, his hand covering mine with a gentle squeeze before he entwined our fingers. I moved my head back and was greeted by his warm chocolate eyes, filled with questioning and confusion. His eyebrows moving so slightly together, I knew he was wondering what was going on. We had never consummated our marriage; our days, weeks, months and years had been busy, draining, and we just collapsed into bed each night, desperate for sleep.

There were so many reasons for this, on my part at least, most of them confusingly contradictory to one another, the most prominent of which were knocking at the door of my conscious mind: I did not want to erase Will, nor my last time being intimate with him from my mind, or replace the last time I had experienced intimacy with anyone else; to me, it would be as though my life with Will had never happened, and would damage the feelings he had written in the note which was now hidden away in the material memories box in the lower drawer of my dressing table. It would be as though I was cheating on him, on the memory of us. A significant part of me also did not want to be intimate with Michael because I had thought it would mean I wasn't grieving any more for my best friends, for Tara's loss. More pressingly, all our focus had been on providing a stable life for Tara, adopting her and establishing a family life in which she could thrive. It was not until that night I realised, and accepted, that Michael and I were also entitled to our adult lives. We were married, and had been for several years; a woman's prerogative, they say, is to change her mind, and I knew Michael's love for me still existed. He would not refuse my choice. Why could, or should, we not experience every part of our marriage? I knew that if we were to indulge it would be the polar opposite of the first time we were together, or at any point in our short relationship. I also knew there would be none of the emotional merging as there had been each time Will and I were together;

161

that could not be possible. It simply could not happen. Michael and I had loved each other in a different way when we were teenagers in comparison with the way we loved each other as husband and wife; Will and I were two halves of the same heart, meant to be together but brutally ripped apart by cruel circumstance. But surely Michael and I were entitled to this aspect of our adult, and married, lives?

And so, with a hand encased in his, I raised my fingers towards his face, and trailed my index finger from his ear, along his jaw, to the underside of his chin. His hand left mine, and searched for the back of my neck as he leant into me, with one last, intense, gaze before his eyelids succumbed to the imminent meeting of our mouths. I cannot say the feeling was passion fuelled. Nor can I compare it to anything I had experienced before; neither with Will nor Michael before him. As I wrapped my arms around Michael's neck, my hands eventually exploring his hair, his strong hands pressed against my back, keeping me upright against him. The pressure of his hands conveyed how long he had wanted to hold his wife like this, how long he had waited to be man and wife in every possible way. Taking hold of the sofa behind Michael, I moved my leg to straddle him, my need for this indulgence surpassing any shy or coy actions I may have wanted to take; I raised my skirt up over my thighs to part my legs and lower myself to rest on his lap, Michael's desire for intimacy already present beneath me. My hands went back to the crisp shirt covering his racing heart in his chest, and I began to free his skin from beneath the buttons. As the cool skin of my fingers found the hot skin of his chest, a small sound of satisfaction emitted from his throat, through closed lips. For a split second, I wondered if I should change my mind, whether this would mean far much more to Michael than to me, whether this was a step too far. I shook the thought from my head; in that moment, there was no reason not to make him happy in every way possible. There was no reason important enough to not experience every area of our marriage.

Michael's hands moved to my knees, his fingers swiftly skimming their way up to the top of my stockings, under the hem of my skirt, worn for the special occasion. Kneeling up, I moved my mouth once more to his, my hands either side of his face, directing his affection towards me. The small part of me which felt I was taking advantage of his affection for me was silenced by the larger part of me which was in desperate need of it. Michael's hands slid around the backs of my legs, making the most of the slit in my skirt to explore higher. His fingers crept slowly, but with a purpose, towards the inside of my thighs, meeting my skin above the top of the sheer stockings that were being held in place by a black garter belt I rarely wore. Slowly, agonisingly slowly, Michael began to move his fingers upwards, teasing me. I had not wanted to feel this much desire, but there was no denying the effect physical contact was having on me; it was becoming evident in my moistened underwear. I could feel the pooling at the apex of my thighs. My lips increased their pressure on Michael's as he slipped his index finger under the elastic, moving aside the only thing covering me. Another small sound of satisfaction emitted from his mouth as his finger found the source of the damp condition of my clothing. As he did, an unexpected gasp of air rushed into my lungs; I had not expected to be as eager for this as my body clearly told me I was.

Slowly, I sank down onto his finger, enjoying the fire it ignited as I took more of it inside me. My breath began to labour in my lungs, it was difficult to keep it even and smooth, and to be as quiet as possible so we did not disturb Tara. I did not know how parents managed to indulge in intimacy on a regular basis without disturbing children. Not until then. It is one of the more challenging aspects of parenthood. I found myself moving my mouth away from Michael's; leaning back until his digit disappeared within me. After what seemed like an eternity of ecstasy, Michael pulled his arm upwards, guiding me, moving his finger inside me as he did, making me moan; he wanted me to be kneeling up again. With trembling thighs, I happily obliged, leaning backwards for a more fulfilling sensation. Slowly, tantalisingly slowly, he began to swirl his finger as his other hand pulled clumsily at the buttons of my blouse, his mouth hungrily searching for the skin of my décolletage. I had been clasping his shoulders as the shock of his swirling had surprised me, but I realised I needed to assist his pursuit of my skin.

In that moment, I yearned to undo the buttons of my blouse slowly in an attempt to make this moment last for Michael, but my fingers hurriedly pulled and fiddled with the plastic circles betraying my intentions. This was not, apparently, a time to wait. This was a time to enjoy. Indulge. Hurry. The blouse finally opened, leaving my skin awaiting the onslaught of Michael's mouth. My skin, fiery hot, was met with an even warmer sensation; his tongue swirled in the same rhythm as his finger, causing more uncontrollable gasping. I ran my fingers underneath the lacy top of my bra, freeing my breasts, the underwires presenting them for his devouring. Michael moved his swirling tongue to one, and then the other, never halting the moving finger within me, causing my lungs to pant with each rotation of his tongue. My fingers grabbed fistfuls of his hair, my wedding and engagement ring glinting as they caught the light, directing his attention where I desired it the most. The sensation was soothing, as intense as it was; like taking a long, cold drink on a hot summer's day and feeling it pool as it reaches the stomach, the cold spreading like wildfire. Relief. I had not realised how much I missed this part of my life, how muted everything had been after the accident, in comparison.

A throbbing between my legs became too powerful to ignore and I began to writhe my hips. Michael understood my need and extended his thumb to press against the spot I needed it the most. He paused, momentarily, as he felt the pulsing against the pad of his thumb, gazing at me, mouth ajar. I do not think he could believe the racing pace he was causing. He seemed in awe of it.

164

Of me. Firmly he moved his thumb side to side, making me writhe further. At that moment, I could not wait any longer. Reaching back, I took hold of his wrist and held his arm still. Taking my cue, he slowly withdrew his finger from me, despite my groans of remonstration, allowing me the freedom I needed to move back and undo the buckle of his belt and trousers, to slide his zip down. My mouth captured his as my hands worked busily to free him.

As my fingers lifted the waistband of his boxer shorts, moving them down, he sprang free. I shuffled forward, too impatient to wait, and writhed against him; desperate to feel the same relief his thumb had been providing just moments before. We gently moaned together, as the most sensitive parts of each of us met. Hot fingers moved my skirt up to my waist, firmly holding my hips and guiding them, not that I needed any direction, to the place Michael needed them the most. As I took him, gradually, inside me, thoughts of how familiar it was flooded through me. As I gently started to rock my hips, Michael's mouth returned its attention to my chest, causing me to repeatedly gasp as an electric feeling flowed through me. His thumb also retook its place, increasing the pace of my rocking. I knew it would not take Michael long to reach the peak of his pleasure, I knew he was ensuring I would not go without. Ever caring, considerate, loving Michael. My husband.

The gasping my lungs had been doing turned once more to panting, the moaning his throat continued to make vibrated against my skin through his mouth, increasing the electrifying sensation I was experiencing. It became a circle of intensity, one action increasing the others, which in turn increased the initial one. It felt like hours that we were in the cycle of pleasure; I am not sure whose release came first but we each reached the peak of our enjoyment within what felt like seconds of each other. My lips clamped together to try and muffle the moans, Michael's did the same, as I collapsed into him, slouching so that my face was buried in his neck and his in mine. In the hollow of my ear I thought heard him whisper, "I love you, Mimi," but I could not have been sure; the sound was too faint, and I did not want to question him. Pushing it aside, and shaking my head to try and lighten the mood, a smile crossed my face and a giggle escaped my lips as a funny thought ran through my mind: I was out of shape and should probably join a gym. There is nothing quite like the workout of being intimate to remind oneself of low fitness levels. Michael pulled his head back to look at me, puzzled by my jovial display. I explained what I had been thinking, he chuckled, agreed he should probably do the same; if we were to continue to exercise every aspect of our marriage, we should probably exercise our bodies to keep up with the demands of physical intimacy.

Despite the passing time, we were, after all, not all that old.

Yet.

Chapter 29 – Teenage Trials

Tara was growing up well, adjusting to Secondary School, making more friends, keeping up her good reports and good marks in her classes and balancing her extra-curricular activities with schoolwork, chores and spending time with her family. She and Anne became closer; it seemed they alternated weekends at each other's houses. Each time Tara had stayed at Anne's house, Anne's parents commented on how well-mannered and well behaved she was. These are the comments which make parents proud. They also serve to reassure that they are not doing such a terrible job of raising their youngster. In time, we became friends with them, also, and so life was blossoming for us all, for a while. Michael and I were proud of, and impressed with, the young lady Tara was becoming. When it came time to select her options at school, she wanted to choose scientifically based subjects; she wanted to become a doctor. Michael and I discussed at length the reasons why she wanted to pursue a career in medicine; both of us agreeing it was more than likely due to her experience of losing her parents and the doctors not being able to do anything to help. Michael suggested her motivations would be to prevent somebody else experiencing what she did. It was honourable, he said, noble. I concurred. We did not, however, discuss this with Tara. Neither of us wanted to revive all the memories for her, or for us. We still visited the graves of our friends each week after Mass. We still said prayers for them each night before bed as a family. But we didn't feel there was any need to put Tara through the re-living of the events just to discuss her chosen career path.

When she had turned fourteen, Tara went on a school trip to Austria. Skiing. She was to room with Anne, both of whom were delighted at the prospect; I was concerned that neither would get a wink of sleep throughout the entire trip and I would be subjected to an extremely tired teenager upon her return home. I was also terrified, panicking that she would end up breaking her leg, or worse. Every time the telephone rang whilst Tara was away my heart froze before I jumped with fright and ran quicker than Linford Christie to answer it. Michael, shaking his head and chuckling with amusement each time he witnessed my maternal apprehension, was equally, internally, worried. His mirth hid it well; I did not bother to hide my fear, unconcerned with outward appearances of being overly protective. My little girl had been through too much in her short life to have something happen to her.

We collected her at almost midnight, halfway through the half term holiday, from school upon her return, her suitcase heavy with dirty laundry, and souvenirs for her Aunt and Uncle, and a few for friends not from school. Anne and she shared a hug as they parted; clearly having enjoyed their time together on the trip. Tara also returned with a surprise for us separate to the souvenirs: she had a boyfriend.

The journey home was silent; Tara, being – as I predicted - tired, dozed in the back seat of the car, Michael and I stared straight ahead out of the windscreen, the lights flashing their orange glow above us as we drove beneath them. Without looking at him, I knew exactly what he was thinking as the same thoughts, questions and fears coursed through my mind, too. As I turned my head and stared out of the passenger door's window my hand reached towards him and gripped his as it rested upon the gearstick. His warm skin beneath my cold fingers a reflection of his quickly beating heart, unnerved as he was with the news. As we pulled into the driveway, Michael whispered to me from the corner of his mouth a warning that we were not going to discuss this with Tara tonight. With my head falling forward, my vision directed towards my shoes, I knew he was right. I would have to bite my tongue. Pursing my lips, I nodded in agreement. Gently, Michael shook Tara's shoulder before retrieving her suitcase from the boot. I took her coat and hung it up as she ascended the stairs as slowly as she might climb Everest; the travelling tiring her out. Michael took the suitcase into the kitchen; I wearily unzipped it and took out an armful of clothing to put into the washing machine, shoulders slumped, trying to get on top of the housework before the next day. I was not accustomed to staying up so late, and the impact of the news had extinguished any excited energy I had had. Michael disappeared to lock up the car and came back with a glass of red wine for us, each. I took only a small sip, not wanting to have the after-effects the next morning. Michael drank half of his glass, telling me he needed some help expelling the memories of a teenage boy's thoughts from his mind. I replied that I, too, was remembering what we were doing at Tara's age. The thought now terrified me, that in the modern era with more and more peer pressure, she might repeat our mistakes, or do something even worse. Mistakes: they hadn't been for us at the time. Neither of us regretted our decisions when we made them, but we would not for even half a heartbeat want the same experiences for our little girl in her teenage years. It was only years later that I had come to regret what I had succumbed to as a teenager.

That night, I climbed into bed and lay entwined with my husband, craving his comforting arm around me, for a short while at least. Our intimate lives had continued after our first consummation, perhaps not with as much fervour, or with any significant frequency, however we were both sated in our physical needs. Throughout the night, despite our fatigue, we both struggled to sleep tossing and turning, flipping pillows, huffing and puffing, getting up for glasses of water, trips to the bathroom and so forth.

In the morning, we both felt the banging of our heads as each foot hit the stairs as we plodded and shuffled into the kitchen. I had not been capable of more than a quick shower and throwing on an old skirt and beige three-quarter sleeve length t-shirt; I looked as big of a mess as I felt. Almost on autopilot, I began arranging the cereals, placing the bread into the toaster, fetching the milk from the refrigerator. Michael went about finding a new filter and putting it into the coffee maker, along with the coffee from a new, metallic red package; the smell enough to begin to wake him up to a level of functioning he seemed happier with. Clearly, he could not face the discussion with Tara without caffeine. To his benefit, she did not wake up before he had no choice but to depart for work, and so, any primary discussion about the bombshell she had dropped the night before would fall at my feet. It was at that point I regretted booking the day off work so that I could be with her the day after she arrived home. I envied Michael's day at work, even as busy as it was going to be.

There had never been any indication Tara would have a boyfriend before the trip; to our knowledge she had never had any close male friends, choosing to spend her time with girls her age from either school or one of her other commitments. She had mentioned in passing the boys in her class but had never dwelt on, or divulged, many details of them. I will admit to panicking and wondering if she had been keeping secrets from us as I did from my parents when I was her age. I will also admit to wondering if I should make an inordinate amount of noise whilst doing the housework to rouse her from her teenage sleep in a bid to begin the retrieval of information. At that point, I did not even know his name.

Eventually, mid-way through daytime television, the repeated heavy thud of slipper encased feet met my ears as they descended the staircase. There was a slight pause next to the hall cabinet followed by an increasingly loud shuffling sound as the grips scuffed against the carpet. I was sat on the sofa in the lounge, the television filling the silence with some panel of women having a heated discussion about childcare costs. I was only half listening as I prepared myself for a conversation with Tara. Shuffling into the room, she pushed one hand over her face and through her un-brushed hair as the other weakly pushed the door of the lounge almost closed. She lazily crossed the room to sit next to me on the sofa, curling her legs underneath her as she did, which lead her to naturally lean towards me for, what had become her routine, morning hugs.

Happiness is being a parent of a teenager who is not too old for shared displays of affection.

We exchanged good mornings and I asked if she had slept well. She replied, in her unique teenage way, that she was still tired. She enquired about breakfast; I suggested brunch might be a better idea. Nodding, she sat up and plodded through to the kitchen and sat at the island. I busied myself making an omelette for her, cutting up the mushrooms and finding some red and green peppers from the vegetable store. I had always enjoyed cutting up mushrooms, the soft but firm texture between my fingers making me feel like a much better cook than I was. Occasionally, in my self-boasting mindset, I felt I was approaching chef-dom. I am certain I do not have to tell you just how far away from the truth that whimsical idea was! Slowly, Tara retrieved the fresh orange and mango juice from the refrigerator that Michael and I had made in the juicer the previous day, pouring herself a measure in her favourite glass, the one with the purple flowery design. In the reflection of the cabinets, from the corner of my eye, I could see her looking over the top of her glass at me, my back to her as I prepared her meal. I remember wondering what she was thinking, whether she remembered what she had told her Uncle and I the previous night, and whether she regretted telling us. I wondered if she was apprehensive about what we might say, or think, or feel. I supposed she had every right to be; this was a momentous change in her life from our perspective. And, indeed, from her own.

171

I had, of course, had 'the talk' with her several years before, the basics of the birds and the bees, the biological changes that would happen to her, and the optimum way to live one's life in accordance with Catholic beliefs. But as I passed the blue plate and cutlery to her, topped with her omelette, I remembered how little I had paid attention when I was young when my mother had had the same discussion with me, without the Catholic references of course, and how I was shocked and confused when my monthly cycle first began. I also remembered the difference between Michael's willpower and that of Zara and Robert's when we were in our respective relationships, and I prayed that self-control was genetic rather than learned behaviour.

Tara ate slowly, despite her obvious hunger, the sounds from her stomach positively ferocious in their grumblings. I watched her, as I sipped on a cup of Earl Grey tea which I was hoping would steady my nerves. The choice of which approach to take bounded back and forth in my brain like a Wimbledon final; should I take the friendly, cool Aunt approach, or should I be serious? Again, I wondered how on earth other people managed to be a parent at all, knowing every single decision made would impact and have a ripple effect upon the rest of the child's life, no matter how minimal. Every little decision, action, word, counted towards the whole, end, product of the adult into which they would become.

I began by asking about the holiday; we had been given an itinerary at the meeting at school, but I wanted to hear from her what was good, bad, indifferent, what she had enjoyed and what she had not. If there had been any funny incidents which she wished to recount. Tara told me about the lodge, about her friends with whom she was sharing a room, about the ski instructors, about how her friends fell over a lot, how she only fell over twice, and she spoke a lot about the weather. She seemed amazed by how bright and sunny it had been, and how much the snow had hurt whenever she had not worn her goggles outside. I remember thinking that we were both putting off the discussion, trying to avoid the subject. I remember thinking that she seemed to be avoiding any mention of anything other than her friends I already knew. I also remember acknowledging I was being a coward in not confronting her more directly. At the rate the discussion was going, I felt I would never find out the information I needed to know. Need to know is an interesting concept; how much did Michael and I, actually, need to know? Did we tell our parents everything about our relationship when we were Tara's age? Absolutely not. Does any teenager share everything with their parents? I imagined at the time, and still do, that that is highly unlikely.

When the effects of her breakfast were evident, the meal having performed its task of restoring her teenage energy, Tara bounded towards her suitcase, next to the washing machine, to retrieve the numerous gifts she had bought from its non-clothing compartment. Delicate crimson tissue paper nestled inside a large brightly multi-coloured paper bag enclosed the different gifts she had purchased. She gently retrieved the top two; one for me, one for Michael. Her mouth twisted in disappointment when she told me what she had bought for Michael; she was beginning to discover that men can be difficult to buy for and she told me she had struggled to find something nice enough for him. I told her that no matter what it was he would love it, because it was from her, but I understood her point. She had settled on a paperweight snow globe of the mountains she had visited. For me, something different. She passed me the small, heavy, tightly wrapped, parcel – I was surprised by the weight - with a smile and a bottom lip trapped beneath her teeth. I unravelled the gift, feeling the spirits of all my female ancestors running through me as the thought of saving the paper for later skipped through my mind.

It was then that I realised I had become old.

Beneath the layers lay a silver coloured bracelet, with charms associated with mountains and the Austrian countryside attached to the individual links. There was a tree charm, a ski boot charm, a log cabin charm, a tiny snow globe with actual water and artificial snow inside, and a charm of an animal I did not recognise. It was a delicate piece of jewellery and must have cost a sizable portion of Tara's spending money. It was pleasant enough, however I quickly realised that Tara was hoping for a substantial reaction from me. From the corner of my eye I spied the apprehensive look on her face, the right-hand corner of her bottom lip held tightly by her upper teeth and her posture angled towards me; I was able to see the fluttering of her eyelashes as her gaze rapidly alternated between my face and the gift. I had thought the time for mandatory overly enthusiastic reactions had ceased when Tara stopped bringing home paintings from school for the refrigerator; however, clearly, I still needed to play the role. You see, the role of mother, adoptive or not, is to support and encourage a child in all they dream to be, all they work to obtain, and all the kind, positive attributes they display in their behaviour. If this role is performed well, the child will turn into a productive, conscientious, member of society, fulfilling their potential. And so, like thousands of other mothers before me, I offered the, somewhat overly dramatic, necessary 'thank yous' and 'it's wonderfuls' with an accompanying hug to ensure Tara understood that the gesture she had made, and the item she had chosen, was appreciated. I asked her to help fasten it around my right wrist, and she gladly did so with a beaming smile, clearly pleased she had bought something which would be worn.

It was then, as the light from the window made it sparkle so the light hit my eyes, making them blink with pain, in an apparent slip of the tongue, I discovered the name of Tara's boyfriend. Amid telling me she was pleased I liked the gift, Tara mentioned that Henry had helped her choose some of her gifts whilst they were both shopping.

174

Like a television detective, I had unearthed the first detail in the investigation. I cannot tell you how much I wanted to play the role of cool aunt and not overreact to the detail of a name. I desperately wanted to coax information out of Tara, rather than enter into a confrontation; however, the best laid schemes o' mice and men gang aft a-gley. I believe the common turn of phrase, 'like a bull in a china shop', would aptly describe the bluntness with which I asked the questions in the following few minutes. I could not stop myself in the pursuit of information. I hunted it like I hunted chocolate during certain weeks of the month. I plunged into interfering mode: I asked who Henry was; how long they had been in a relationship; why Michael and I had not heard about this before; when we were going to meet him; what his parents were like; what he did for hobbies and for fun; whether they had kissed or not; whether they had done anything else, anything more than that; I asked about what grades he was getting in his classes; whether they were in the same set; what they had in common; and, whether she thought she loved him. My mouth ran away from me, my brain unable to stop it.

Teenagers hold grudges. It is quite amazing for how long they can sustain a bad mood. It almost warrants scientific study. Needless to say, the barrage of questions which escaped my mouth without my brain being fully engaged enough to prevent it sent Tara into a teenage tantrum with which even Kevin and Perry would have been impressed. Gone was the temperament of earlier, the relaxed brunch and post-trip pleasure. Rage raced through her; her accusatory rhetoric demanding to know why I wanted to know the details she clearly wished to keep private. Before I even knew I was replying, I had raised my voice and, punctuating each word with a matching forward thrust of my hands, shouted in such a short temper that I did not want her to repeat the same mistakes that I had made when I was her age. Her fingers gripped the kitchen surface as she seethed. It astonished me just how quickly her mood had altered; she had been angelic and innocent as she had watched

175

my reaction to her gift. And then, with one careless thought, one murmur from my mouth I had ruined it. I had caused the change in her temperament. I had flipped the switch. Tara told me I had no right to know these things, that it was none of my business; she practically spat the words at me from across the room. In the half-second it took for me to formulate the appropriate, responsible adult, response, but before I could force the words from my mouth, she summoned the stab to my heart I suppose I had always known would come one day.

As she stomped away from me, I followed her swiftly to the base of the stairs, standing with the front door behind me. I watched her stamping her feet, encased in pink fluffy slippers, up each stair escaping towards the sanctity of her bedroom. Crossing the upstairs hallway, she screamed the words back down at me with what seemed like all the strength she possessed; they crushed me as though they were a boulder the size of a house landing on top of me.

She told me I had no right to know what was going on her in life because I was not even her real mother.

And she was correct. I was not. With this, I could not argue.

But there was no consolation in the truth; in fact, it is true what they say: the truth really does hurt.

I was left aghast, speechless. The tears tumbled before my rational thinking took control of my mind. The sinking of my stomach told me that I knew that it was my own fault, I never should have pressured her into telling me anything. I had not even tried to think about her perspective; I had not reminisced to my time as a teenager and how protective over my privacy I had been. I had not listened properly to Michael the night before when he had told me not to talk to her about the matter, then. I should have waited for him; I should not have confronted her without him there. My head hurt as it began to spin with the torment of the truth, and I sank backwards to the front door.

The number of things that front door has seen is astounding. Weddings, funerals, grief, love. Parting. It was there that I began my own, almost-middle-aged, teenage tantrum.

My eyes, seeing over the top of the stinging tears which dwelled within them, settled on my keys which were sat in the bowl on top of the cabinet in the hallway. My car key, sitting on top of my house keys – not my house, Tara's, really - called to me and before I knew what I was doing, the unique sound of plastic and metal clanking into each other filled the hall. I threw my feet into the closest pair of heeled boots of mine I could find. In a second, I had opened the door, closed it firmly behind me and walked to my car, parked on the driveway. The car sprang to life as I turned the key, pulled slowly out of the driveway and onto the road. I am quite sure I did not know where I was going, I drove on autopilot; a combination of being tired and heartbroken once more.

The tears had not stopped, I had just stopped noticing. I no longer noticed the tightening of my cheeks as the tears turned my face a splotchy red. I no longer felt the impact in the hollow of my chest of the hot, salty water, rushing past my heart. Instead, I ranted in my car to myself, to God, to nobody in particular: I was sick of being hurt; sick of things going wrong; sick of having to be in a life I did not choose, did not want to have to choose; sick of being responsible; sick of being used; sick of being taken advantage of; sick of not progressing in my career and just having a 'job' because of putting my priorities aside; sick of not being happy, especially having known true happiness and having to give it up. Through side streets, down main roads, over dual carriage ways and empty country lanes lined with barely blossoming trees I drove and drove, and cried and cried, until I was drained. Again. That feeling was becoming far, far too familiar for my tolerance levels. It seemed that all I had felt for the last decade was drained. I did not realise at the time that I had been so unhappy, or that the unhappiness had, seemingly, accumulated by a magnitude. And in truth I probably was not; yet at that point in time, having been hurt by such a small person, all the animosity I did not know I felt towards my life burst through the façade I had cleverly constructed, crumbling into mere rubble.

It was only then I realised to where I had driven; without consciously choosing to.

I was outside Will's workplace.

Chapter 30 – Bliss

I did not stop to think. I exited the car quickly, walked through the main doors of the building, I did not glance at the receptionist; instead, walked swiftly, purposefully, in the direction of the corridors towards Will's office. The mixture of furniture polish, anti-septic cleaning solution and a musty scent of the aftermath of a vacuum cleaner made the air heavy as I strode over the deep green carpet of the corridor. Then, what darkness there had been - because of the tall doors with small windows, long brick walls covered in notices and posters, and little, singular strip lights - was replaced by a brightness which made me blink because of its intensity as I ascended a ramp encased in windows. It is strange how quickly our eyes get used to darkness. My footsteps' sounds altered as I walked where there was little support below, the dull thudding sound had changed to a hollow one as my heeled boots hit the bare floor, not protected by carpet. I pushed open the set of doors at the end of the long corridor and dashed up half the flight of steps before they could slam shut. At the top of the steps was another, double door; I pulled it open and slipped through, taking the right-hand side corridor. This corridor was brighter, with windows at the top of the wall; the floor was tiled and so my heels click-clacked all the way down to the third-to-last office on the left. Will's office. I did not hesitate before grabbing the handle and turning it. I did not even knock. I did not think about anything, not even why I was there. I just entered the room.

But it was empty.

There was a desk, a dusty telephone, a grey filing cabinet in the corner of the room, with the second drawer ajar but containing nothing, and a standard, black and green wheeled office chair up against the radiator underneath the window. But there was no Will. There were no papers on the desk, there were no notices stuck to the cork board attached to the wall at the side of the desk; no books or files on the shelves, and no signs the office had been used for a considerable time.

All there was, was silence.

I could not hear my own breath, and it was then that I realised I was holding it. In a quick, but heavy sigh, I let it out through puffed cheeks. Perhaps this was for the best. I turned on my heel and left the office, glancing at the empty name place holder on the door. I had not noticed Will's name had not been there as I had entered. I walked back down the corridor almost as quickly as I had moved through it earlier; I suppose I was trying to leave without being seen. To erase what I had done, where I had gone, and the consequences.

I watched my feet move in and out of my line of vision as I sprinted down the first half of the steps, I was only looking at where the next one needed to go so I could move as quickly as possible without slipping when a pair of brown loafers came into view a moment before my body bumped into their owner. I muttered an apology, not wanting to look up, but I could not move aside. Two hands held my arms, keeping me stationary. The owner of the hands said my name in question. I looked up and was met with hazel eyes and sandy brown hair; it was one of Will's colleagues. We'd met at a Christmas office party one year, long ago. I was struggling to remember his name. Sam? Steve? Simeon? I remember knowing his name began with an S but in my unhinged mindset I could not bring it to my mind.

He said my name as a question and then prompted me with his own, pointing at his chest. Sebastian. Yes, of course, I should have known that was his name. I must have looked a bit shaken because he did not remove his arms from mine for what felt like five minutes. He asked me if I was there to see Will, which I obviously was. I do not remember if I spoke aloud, but I remember nodding and betraying my desire to undo what had already occurred. Before I knew what was happening, I had been ushered through the double doors at the bottom of the next half of the flight of steps, and to the right. I only half heard Sebastian rambling on about room changes about twelve months ago and trouble with the telephone extension systems.

Six doors from the start of the corridor, on the left, was a door with Will's name on it. I could hear his perfect voice through the mahogany, see the top of his blonde hair through the tiny window, head tilted to the right as he spoke on the telephone, the front of his hair lit blue from the glare of a computer screen. Sebastian said his goodbyes, saying it was nice to see me, and left me alone in the middle of the corridor. I, still, cannot articulate the mix of emotions which consumed me during the next couple of minutes. I was frozen to the spot, deliberating whether to run away or whether to walk into the room. Questions relayed through my mind. What would it do to Will to see me? Would it break his heart again? Had he moved on? Was he married? Engaged? Did he have a family? Would he be glad to see me? Would he think I had come back to him? Had I come back to him? What was I doing there? Should I go? If I left then, would I be able to leave unnoticed? What did I want from him? Would it hurt me if I saw him again? Did I care? Could I just see him once and then leave? Was I capable of leaving? Did I even know what I was doing there, why I had driven there of all places? How had I driven there? Had I gone through any red lights? Had I taken any one-way streets the wrong way? I shook my head trying to rid it of the questions. I took a step forward, tapped my knuckles quietly on the door, pressed the handle downwards and walked through it without waiting for a reply.

And there he was.

My *everything*.

181

His eyes met mine as he put down the telephone and turned his office chair towards me. And all the love I ever felt for him returned to the surface of my soul. He was beautiful. Perfect. Time had been good to him; he had hardly aged. His blue, sparkling eyes as entrancing as always. His face, his beautiful face; his shoulders, his hair, and his arms. I had not realised until then just how much I had missed just being able to look at him. My heart hurt so much for so many, different, reasons; all I wanted to do was to be in his arms and to be kissing him. All I wanted was to be his and for everything to have been a nightmare and to have woken up from it, wrapped up in him, back in my old life. Back where I knew I belonged.

Looking at him, I was home, again.

I took a step forward and he rose up from his chair, moving towards me swiftly. My already extended arms wrapped around his waist, my head, turned towards his face, found his familiar, comfortable, perfect shoulder as his arms wrapped around me tightly and gently. The perfectly balanced scent of soap and aftershave filled my nose and I felt wrapped up in him. I do not know for how long he held me, but it seemed both forever and only a second simultaneously. However, it was long enough for a damp patch to have been created on his shirt from the tears I had not been aware were falling. His warm lips kissed the top of my head and I was undone. A wave of relief rushed through me; purely because I was, once more, where I belonged in this world. His voice was in my hair as he asked me what on earth I was doing there. The words of reply tumbled out of my mouth. I must have sounded quite the petulant child, complaining about my life, about what Tara had said to me, about how I felt, about everything I had given up, about how sick and tired I was of everything; I was ranting in the same way I had done in the car on the way to Will's workplace. My ranting then turned to apologies. I apologised for interrupting his work day, for showing up unannounced, for disrupting his life, for breaking his heart, for not telephoning to say thank you for the note he left me when we had to end our most perfect relationship, when I had to do my duty and sacrifice all that we had built together.

He pulled away from me, half way through my apologising, and held me at arms' length as he guided me to sit on the edge of his pine desk, facing the window over the radiator. I knew at that moment I had made a mistake, that I should not be there, that I should leave. But I was rooted to the spot, content in the feeling of his fingers around my arms and feeling the warmth of his skin through my clothes. Bending over, slightly, he moved his right hand to brush the tears from my left cheek first, and then used the back of his fingers to attend to the right-hand side of my face. He asked me to stop talking and start from the beginning; he wanted to know what I was doing there, why I had come to him and what had happened to make me so upset. I tried to explain without sounding petty and childish, I tried to explain without sounding immature; I was not successful. I could hear the petulant tones in my words as they left my mouth, and yet I could not stop complaining. I had, once again, broken the vow I made to stop being so selfish. I wondered if, perhaps, I just was not capable of being selfless, if I could only keep up the pretence for so long, if I had built my house on a camel's back and Tara's comment had been the final straw which had demolished it. I ended by recounting how I had gone to his old office and had tried to leave when I bumped into Sebastian and was shepherded to his office and acted before I could think about leaving.

In a short, sharp, but gentle sentence, he asked me if I thought it was a mistake to be in his office. Whether I should be there or not. My head was so unclear, I could not determine the intimation in his tone, whether he was pleased or disappointed to see me, nor generate any sort of reply. A large part of me was just so relieved and happy to hear his voice, his soothing voice, that I did not try to decipher his tone and its meaning. I knew, realistically speaking, that I should not have been there, that I

183

should not have left the house, that I should not have overreacted to Tara's comments, that I should not have, once more, disrupted Will's life. But I could not help but love being with him, seeing him again; just to bask in his presence. My love for him had not gone, diminished, or been replaced. I reached my hand up behind his neck and pulled him towards me, his forehead pressed against mine as I whispered to him that I just did not know what to do.

Our eyes were inches apart, staring deeply into each other; I had missed that shade of blue, but behind the sparkle, I could see the pain; my heart ached, and his eyes told me his did, also. I could see his love for me had not lessened. I could see that his heart had been just as shattered as mine when we had to part all those years before. I tilted my head up and stretched my neck up, so my lips met his. It was the most perfect kiss: gentle and familiar and spine-tingling in just the right way. I belonged once more.

I shuffled slightly backwards on his desk to anchor myself a tad more securely, and without thinking moved each of my legs to the side and pulled Will towards me so he was standing between them. Despite my best efforts, questions and doubt ran through my mind. Could I cheat on Michael? Was it cheating if I was, and had always been, head-over-heels in love with Will? If my heart and soul belonged to him? Was it Will I had been cheating on all this time with Michael? Probably. That was the conclusion I came to as I moved my hands over Will's chest, pausing my right hand over his heart, trying to feel it beating beneath his skin, before trailing my fingers down to his waist.

The feeling of familiarity washed through us as we entwined in each other. We had not missed a beat and fit together as naturally as we ever had. Arms and hands were everywhere, disrobing the necessary garments from each other hurriedly and with an urgency of need we had not enjoyed with each other for years. His fingertips met with the bare skin of my thighs as he pushed my skirt up towards my waist. My fingertips met with the bare skin of his lower stomach as I loosened his belt and undid his trousers. My mind flashed back to when we had first moved into our home and christened every room in our youth and the smiles and laughter which accompanied it; although that was missing now, the physical need we had for one another persisted in its intensity.

As I sat on the edge of the desk, Will's mouth journeyed across what little bare skin it could find and sent shivers through me. He started at my neck and worked his way down to the décolletage that was accessible to his firm, moistened lips. As they travelled from one breast to another, teasing what they found beneath the thin material of my underwear, I remember letting out a moan of many emotions: urgency, relief, passion, love, lust. Guilt.

My head moved away from Will, letting my back arch so he could have more access to what his mouth most clearly desired. I had to let one hand move from his waist to steady myself, as only one of his was supporting me, the other was holding my breast to steady it for his mouth to devour. I remember catching the mouse attached to his computer and trying to move it out of the way, so my hand could be flat upon the desk, and giggled when the thought of sweeping everything off the desk like they did in old, cheesy films, crossed my mind. I remember reaching out for his belt, which hung from his waist, and trying to pull him closer to me. All I did, in effect, was elongate the belt's overhang, but Will understood what I was trying to do and positioned himself where I wanted him to be.

Bliss. Bliss is the only word to describe what the feeling was like when Will was back where he belonged: around me, next to me, inside me. He slid inside me with such ease, it barely required any effort on his part. We fit perfectly together. I wish I could say that what we did took a long time, that we had the chance to

185

savour one another as we used to, that we were able to prolong our enjoyment for hours, that it was the most romantic thing we had ever done; but it was not. It was frantic: hurried, urgent and necessary. A mess of flesh, arms and mouths and hands everywhere. My legs trembled as he moved in and out of me, gasps escaped my lungs on their own, groans emulated from his throat with each forward motion he made. I was drowning in the waves of pleasure he was forcing me into and I loved every millisecond of it. I tried to commit to memory every motion, every touch, every sound. I did not close my eyes during any of it, desperate for the sight of him, to commit everything to memory, to bask in him and to savour the sight of his beautiful face and see into his soul. He had not closed his eyes, either. It was the most intense type of intimacy. I needed him more than anything and I struggled to get enough of him; my hands roughly grabbed his face, kissing him hard and urgently; my legs wrapped around him to bring him closer to me and deeper inside me. I wanted to do so much more with him in that moment, I wanted to use my hands and my mouth to make him feel as incredible as he was making me feel, but time was limited by necessity. He had not forgotten what I needed, and used his thumb exactly where I required it to maximise my enjoyment. He truly was the best man on earth. Unfortunately, it did not take us long to reach the climax of our mid-afternoon tryst.

And through gasping, groaning, panting, moaning, the heat inside me, and tears from each of us, we slumped down onto the floor; revelling in the feeling of our arms around each other, basking in the bliss which was created by our mutual adoration. I wept for a long time because I had missed Will with every ounce of my soul. I wept because I knew I would never feel that way again in my life. I wept because I would have to leave where I belonged. I wept because I could not hold him every day. I wept because I missed his heart, his soul, how he made me laugh, how we fit together perfectly. I wept because I missed his life.

I did not know how much time had passed as we made small talk; I asked Will to give me details of his life that I had no longer been privy to. I missed hearing about his hobbies, his friends, his family all of whom I missed greatly, his passion for things he loved. I missed his perspective on life. I missed his ideas and theories. I missed his opinions. I missed his approach to problem solving. I missed his ability to make me laugh, smile and be happy. I missed the sound of his voice.

But, after a while, the inevitable silence fell over us like a smothering blanket, covering us in an inability to make small talk any longer. Then, painfully, we each whispered the three-word phrase that connected our hearts forever.

"I love you."

Chapter 31 - Confession

Being an adult is awful.

As I reluctantly got to my feet, I leant my head against Will's chest with my hands pressed against his stomach, I knew that I would have to go home.

Home.

It was not my home; it was Tara's. I was at home with Will. That was where I belonged, where my heart lived. But my body lived in the house with Tara, with my husband, Michael, and had done for years. What other option did I have? I had to face up to my responsibilities. To the commitment I had made. To the promise I had made. I could not abandon Tara, no matter what she had said to me. I could not behave like the injured child any longer; I had to be the adult. I had to be the mature one. I could not be selfish anymore. I had to go back and look after her. To guide her to adulthood. I had to face up to the changes which were going on in her life, and try and steer her away from the physical mistakes I had made in my own youth.

Will whispered an imploration to stay as I stood up straight and his mouth became level with my ear as I wrapped my arms around him, embracing him as tightly as what little strength I had left allowed me to. I could hear the tears in his voice, the strain and struggle to get the words out before his voice cracked and rendered him unable to utter a single thing. I am quite sure he felt he was compensating for not requesting I stay with him when I had to end our relationship years earlier, after the tragedy which tore apart our lives. I understood back then, as I did on that afternoon, that he had not been capable of asking me to remain with him before; words failed him as his heart and mine had shattered in unison. But, that afternoon as the sun hid behind the clouds in the sky, making his office dimmer than it had been seconds before, I replied to him that I had to leave. I tried my best to explain the situation. Tried to convey that I had no choice. I asked him if he wanted Tara to be on her own with Michael. I felt at that point, of course, I was using emotional blackmail against him – which was quite unfair of me, I admit. I instructed him to imagine being in her position. I asked him whether he thought she had meant what she had said. He quietly replied "no" to the last question. I could tell then that he missed her, that he missed me as much as I missed him, and that he had been as heartbroken as I had been when we had to part after the accident. I was half infuriated with myself that the questions I was asking Will to answer had not crossed my own mind before I had left the house, and that I had not thought of the answers to them before I had allowed myself to become so emotional only to find myself in a situation where I now felt guilty. How could I have been so reactionary? So unaware? So closed minded and immature?

With a last lingering kiss, full of love and sorrow, my hand held his face, and gazed into his beautiful, blue eyes one final time. He walked me to the door, ever the gentleman, and held me for one final, tight embrace. His arms around my shoulders, mine around his mid-back. I inhaled all the scent of him I could trying to remember it as I did. I felt him match my actions at the top of my head. Manoeuvring my arm, I depressed the handle behind my back and opened the door, stepping out and walking away with tears streaming down my face. I could not bring myself to look back, and when I heard the door click faintly as I walked away, followed by a hollow thud against it, my already shattered heart disintegrated into nothingness.

Pain was becoming far too a familiar feeling in my life.

And so was guilt.

So was feeling despondent with myself.

I finally got to my car, and sat behind the steering wheel. The journey back had seemed twice as long as the journey to Will's office, despite the original detour I then realised I had made, earlier. I made some final adjustments to my clothes, trying to ignore that my underwear was becoming uncomfortable in the aftermath of my act that afternoon. The walk had seemed to take forever, and I was weary. I remember sighing heavily as the thought of what was going to happen next dawned on me. I switched on the engine, wiped the tears off my face with the back of my hand, and began to drive back home.

A section of my mind replayed the events in Will's office, part of the rest of it was focused on driving and the remainder was wondering what on earth I was going to tell Michael, and what I was going to say to Tara. Firstly, about where I had been, and secondly about what she had said to me and how I was going to talk to her about it.

I was almost back to the house when I saw the church up ahead, and the lights on through the stained-glass windows. I quickly indicated and turned right, into the car park. The car door shut with the conventional thud as I got out, and clicked as I locked the door. Before I knew it, I was at the door of the church, pushing the heavy oak aside by use of the twisted, iron handle.

Peaceful was the atmosphere inside as I dipped my fingers into the Holy Water and crossed myself, genuflecting towards the Body of Christ behind the altar. Glancing around, I saw the dim red glow of the confessional in the corner of the church, indicating an occupant within. Moving forward to the pew, I genuflected again, crossing myself once more, and knelt on the padded kneeler and prayed. I could not see anyone else in the queue and so knew I was next.

An old man, in a short, beige raincoat stepped out of the confessional after about five minutes and slowly, unsteadily, moved to the front of the church, and knelt in front of Mary to say his penance. He looked familiar, although I could not remember seeing him at church before and wondered if he was confessing to a different priest as I had heard some people often do. Shaking the thought from my head, and trying to focus on why I was at church, I stood up from my place slowly moved into the confessional, closing the thick, heavy mahogany door behind me. Kneeling down, I crossed myself and began the request for forgiveness.

I explained to the priest what I had done, and why I thought I had done it. I explained how the day had started, what had changed and what I thought caused me to do what I did. I explained to him how my marriage had come to be in the first place, and what I felt I had had to give up, and gave as much information as I could. I told him I was sorry for what I had done - and I was - that I was sorry for the hurt I had caused, both to Will and to Michael, for the reaction I had had to Tara's words and for the vows I had broken. When I was finished, the familiar voice of Father Philip spoke to me.

He reminded me that I was a role model, that I was the mother in Tara's life, and that I should look to Mary to be a better version of this. He asked me to meditate on what I thought Zara would have done in my position, had Tara said something hurtful to her. He asked me to consider what I wanted for Tara's future. These were such valid questions, and he was wholly correct. As my penance, I was told to meditate upon the Rosary, asking for guidance, help and the strength to be a better mother and wife. I was also instructed to tell Michael what I had done and to ask his forgiveness. I knew that was going to be the most challenging part of my atonement. I said my act of contrition, vowing that never again would I be adulterous, and received my absolution.

As I left the confessional, I, too, moved to the head of the church and knelt in front of Mary. The old man was still there, deep in silent prayer. Crossing myself, I began to recite The Apostles' Creed, in a hushed tone: the beginning prayer of the Rosary. I had often seen Michael use The Rosary in his prayers. I had often joined him, but never before had I said an entire Rosary as part of my penance. Not having one with me, I had to use my fingers to count the prayers, as I had often seen Father Philip do before Mass.

About half an hour later, as I completed the Hail Holy Queen, I felt more stable in my resolve to be a better mother and role model. I sat on the pew after finishing my prayers, surprised to discover the old man was still there. I had been so engrossed in my penance I had not paid him much attention. He had clearly finished his prayers, and was sat quietly, in the pew in front of mine. He turned to look at me, smiled awkwardly and said a brief hello. I returned the courtesy with a small smile. He asked me if this was my local church and if I knew what the priest was like. I gave him my opinion of Father Philip, which was nothing but positive; I explained how he had married my husband and I after overseeing my conversion to Catholicism. I told him he had baptised our adopted daughter, and confirmed her, also. The old man told me he had just moved to the area and was trying to find which of the local churches he liked the most. I asked him if he had a family with him, but he replied with such a sad "no" I surmised that he may have lost any he had had. I glanced at my watch and said I must be getting back home, as time was getting away from me, but that if he were to attend Mass on Sunday, I was sure he would be welcome and that if he wanted to, he could sit with Michael, myself and Tara.

Smiling, he said he might see us there and, together, we left the pews, genuflected whilst crossing ourselves and walked out of the church. Before I left him to go to my car, I offered him my name;

he did the same in return. His name was James Brimley. Brimley. Such an uncommon name. When I repeated it in my head, and let it settle, it was then that I realised where I knew him from, and why he had no family with him, and that he may have lost them to death, but in an entirely different way than I had originally thought.

Immediately, I wanted to rescind the invitation for him to sit with my family during Mass.

Immediately, I wanted to run away, away from any reminder of that creature.

Immediately, I wanted to be with Michael, to warn him. To find support. To find comfort. To find restraint and to prevent me from doing anything which I may later regret.

I drove home quite quickly, traffic was minimal, and the distance was short. Apprehensively, after parking the car, I walked into the house, closing the door quietly behind me. Ungracefully tossing my keys into the bowl, I wandered through the hallway to the kitchen. I reached across the sink to the draining board where I found the glass Tara had drunk her orange and mango juice from, earlier. I was pleased to see she had washed it, at least. I took it over to the refrigerator and took out the water filter, pouring myself a cold drink. Then, I slowly opened the freezer, and cracked some ice cubes free from their silicone mould. I leant against the countertop, steadying myself.

The muffled sound of modern music was above me; Tara was in her room, it appeared. I wondered if she had wondered where I had been, where I had gone to, or if she had even noticed I was not in the house; perhaps she had only ventured to the kitchen for what she needed before retreating to her room, not stopping to see if I was in the lounge as she did. Sitting atop the breakfast bar was the same crimson wrapping which had held my bracelet;

193

Michael's snow globe was yet to be given to him. I glanced at the clock, realising it would not be too long before he returned home from work.

When he swung open the front door, calling hello as he closed it behind him, Tara's music was turned off. If she had heard him come home, surely she had heard me close the front door behind me when I entered the house? I heard a quick rhythm of trotting feet from her bed, and down the stairs; he was greeted with a hug and a plea to come into the kitchen because she had something to give him. In that moment, she was four again. But the look she shot in my direction as she entered was unreadable. She swept the gift from the breakfast bar and, with stiff, outstretched arms, presented it to him. His briefcase was quickly placed down on the floor as he took it, first in one hand and then both, and began to tear at the paper clumsily. The thought which raised one of my eyebrows was that he was a typical man and, that, that paper could have been saved for later. He studied the snow globe carefully, asking Tara if this looked like the place she had stayed on her trip. She gave him details, a summary of what she had shared with me that morning. Michael told her he liked it very much, pulled her in for a hug and kissed the top of her head whilst he said thank you.

Turning to me, he asked what was for dinner. Since I had only just returned home, I had not begun to cook. I walked past them both, fetching my purse from my handbag in the hall. I took out a crisp, new looking, twenty-pound note, and told Tara that she needed to go to the local chip shop and buy our evening meal. In honesty, it was not that local; a good ten minutes' walk each way at teenage speed – the food would probably be on the cooler side of warm by the time she returned - but I knew I needed the time to speak to Michael without Tara around. Awkwardly, she looked in my general direction as she took the money from my hands, but refused to meet my eye. I told her if she did not think she could remember what each of us wanted, to write down on a sheet of paper from the notepad on the refrigerator what we wanted, and to take that with her. This she did: fish in breadcrumbs for Michael, with a small portion of chips – no vinegar. Fish and chips for herself, and for me, a sausage and small chips. No vinegar. I did not like the taste of acid in my mouth.

As Tara left, I turned to Michael and braced myself for the conversation which now had to take place. He was still somewhat engrossed in the paperweight which had created a smile on his face that bordered on adorable. I told him that I had not started the evening meal because I had not long been in the house; I told him I had gone to confession that evening. He looked at me, quizzically. It was not often that I went to confession, never mind tell him about it, so I understood why he was confused. I told him that I had had a really, rough day, and what had happened. He was angry when I recounted what Tara had said to me, and asked me, interrupted me really, why I was being so nice and letting her have a chip shop fish supper if she had said such awful things to me. I told him it was because I did not want her in the house when I informed him of my reaction to what had happened.

And then I recounted the afternoon's events; not in the detail I have told you, of course, but in enough detail so that he understood what had happened. As I endeavoured, in vain, to keep an even voice, I told him I was sorry, I told him I wished I had never left the house, I told him I wished I had not been selfish. I told him I should have known better, should have known not to overreact. I told him I had not realised how things had been affecting me. And I told him it would never happen again.

When I looked at him, his face was as white as a sheet. The colour quite literally drained from his face before me. I could see his demeanour go through several emotions: disbelief, denial, questioning, fright. He was speechless. He did not utter a

195

word. And then I saw anger in his face. Teeth clenched, frowning eyes and flaring nostrils glared at me.

Shattered glass lay across the floor of the kitchen, water and fake snow seeping and spilling over the cold tiles beneath us. The cracking and splashing sound echoed in my ears.

He had thrown the snow globe down in temper onto the hard, kitchen floor.

Immediately, we both bent down to clear up the mess in a panic; we both understood what it meant to Tara to give things to us, and how much it would upset her to find the gift had been broken. In a fuss of fetching kitchen towel, and a mop, our hands were clumsily bumping into each other. He grabbed mine, holding it firmly in his own. And then, increasing his grip, until he was holding my hand too tightly, uncomfortable to the point of pain, with damp eyes almost betraying him, he asked me two questions. He asked me how on earth I could do this to him. He asked me if I was really that unhappy.

I could not answer either of them immediately.

Half of me wanted to scream and shout at him, to tell him how I was miserable, and how it was not fair and to repeat the ranting I had done both in the car and to Will earlier. But I bit my tongue; Michael did not need to hear that. This was my chance to protect and look after my friend as he had me all this time, all these years. And, I did not want him to have the same access to my true feelings as Will did; that was something for my everything to have of me, alone.

The other half of me wanted to shout and scream at him for being so presumptuous; how could I do this to *him*? Was he out of his mind? Did he truly believe that this was anything other than a marriage of convenience that we'd found ourselves in? That it

196

was the means to an end to adopting Tara and being there for her to keep our promise to her parents, our best friends?

I was seething. Shaking with rage as tears of anger spilled out of my eyes, I snatched my hand away from him. I remember glaring at him, for just a second, with a look that must have been more intense with warning than any anger he was feeling because he flinched when my eyes bore into his. But I bit my tongue; Michael did not need to hear that.

Closing my eyes and taking a deep breath, I exhaled and told him that I was really, truly upset by what Tara had said to me earlier and, whilst it was true, it had begun a chain reaction that had exaggerated the negatives of the situation. I told him that I would not be seeing Will again, and that part of my penance was to tell him the truth; Father Philip had said that our lives, and our marriage, was difficult enough already, without my misguided actions further complicating matters and making it even more challenging. Hiding the truth would have increased the challenge, tenfold. And, of course, he was correct. Michael and I needed to work as a team, to bring Tara up to be a good person, to do our best jointly, through honesty and open communication. I had let the team down.

I did not answer his questions; I told him I was sorry, which I was, and that I felt guilty, which I did. I asked him, too calmly, to try and forgive me.

I do not know how I expected him to do this, his feelings for me had always been of a different nature than mine for him; I had clearly hurt them and to forgive my actions would take a greater amount of effort on his part. With a deep sigh, he told me not to worry about that, right then, but that we both needed to deal with what Tara had said to me before anything else took place. His ability to prioritise and focus had always impressed me; I had always wanted to emulate it, but – until that day – had not been able to, successfully.

In what I thought was an encouraging move, but with a nagging doubt of him putting on a brave face to maintain the façade of our situation, he asked me how I thought we should deal with the matter. The thought that perhaps he was testing my resolve and commitment to our family crossed my mind. I suggested leaving Tara to it; she had clearly been apprehensive when she took the money from my hand, just a short time before, so perhaps she was feeling guilty and would come to the conclusion that she needed to apologise for the way she spoke to me through her own reasoning. Michael asked me, shocked me really, if I thought I should tell her what I had done that afternoon as direct a consequence of her words, for her to begin to understand the notion of the ripple effect and how much of a part she played in everybody's life in which she featured. For a second, I really did think he was losing his mind. It was not Tara's fault any of us were in that situation; I suppose I could see the argument for her being more aware of her actions, but the place she found herself in was not of her doing. Then, I thought he was suggesting it as part of my penance, punishment, really. I asked him when he had learnt about the ripple effect, and how; was it under stressed circumstances, and did he think it would help her considering how much trauma she had been through in her short life? I certainly did not. Although, I will admit, it was not solely as a means of protecting Tara that I did not want her to know what had happened. I did not want to confess to her what I had done that afternoon: I did not want her to see me as a cheat, those were the types of people we joked about and made fun of whenever we indulged in morning television during the week; I did not want any negative female role model in her life, and I certainly did not want to be one; and, I did not want her to be confused and to think about Will unless absolutely necessary.

Whilst I appreciated we could discuss things to do with parenting Tara, I often wondered, occasionally despaired, whether Michael's approach was all it could be; at that moment the question in my mind was whether he should have taken a more proactive, stern role – or was that just my preconceived notion of a father's role? Where that idea had come from, still eludes me. Was it because my own father had been the stern one, and my mother the angelic-like, nurturing figure in my life? Was I trying to replicate that for Tara? Was it because that's how I saw Zara, also? Robert had certainly not been overly stern with the baby. Or was it a result of the time in which I had grown up? If that was the case, surely Michael, being older than me, would have been more willing to take on the disciplinarian role more naturally? Easily? There are so many layers that comprise each person; who could ever say for certain what makes anyone act in the way they do?

The consensus was to let Tara dwell on her actions and think about her behaviour. If I am completely honest, I was pleased because it allowed me more time to process everything which had terrified me that afternoon. I told Michael he should clear away the shattered snow globe into the recycling bin, near the bottom where Tara would not see it, and to put some cardboard over the top; he was then to tell her he had already put it in the boot of his car, so he could take it to work the next morning and did not forget it, so it would have pride of place on his desk. Since Tara never visited his office, she would never know it was not there.

The next task I had to broach was the other event of that afternoon: meeting James Brimley. I told Michael that when I had been to church, that there had been an old man there, and that I had recognised him from somewhere. I told him I was not sure where, and that I had struck up a conversation with him after I had prayed the Rosary. I told Michael that the man had told me he had no family with him, but that it was not because of any typical reason. He looked at me with a quizzical expression, and then I repeated the man's name to Michael. His features faded to white, shock I suppose, as he put two and two together and did, indeed, come out with four. He was mortified, horrified and felt sick all at once: a relation of the monster which had murdered our friends was a member of our church. We assumed James Brimley was Felicity's grandfather; he was too old to have been her parent. I had to confess to Michael that before I recognised, realised, who the man was, I had invited him to sit with us at Mass, should he choose our church, because he seemed so sad and lonely.

Once more, Michael became furious with me. I was furious with myself; I could not blame him for his emotions.

Before we could discuss anything any further, Tara returned with the evening meal.

Dinner that night was strained; barely a word spoken between the three of us. Tidying away the wrappers from the fish and chip shop, after we had all eaten, into the recycling, I saw the remnants of the snow globe; I hoped my actions had not shattered my family, much as Michael's reaction to them had destroyed the souvenir. I excused myself immediately after tidying up, went upstairs and stood under a hot shower, trying to wash away the remainder of the day. After half an hour or so, I eventually left the sanctuary of the hot water, put on my dressing gown and went to my, our, bedroom. Rubbing my hair dry with a towel, I spotted the laptop on the ottoman at the end of the bed. I did not know what it was doing there, I had not left it there myself.

I reached out and lifted it onto the bed with me, tucked my legs underneath the covers and switched it on as I continued to try and wring out the water from my hair; it has always been far too porous for my liking. After it had loaded up, I clicked the

Internet button and logged into my email account. I clicked the compose button and began to type.

Tara,

When I first saw you, you became a centre of my universe. You were so perfect, sweet and cute; the image of your mother, and I knew I would do anything to protect you. But, I was young, and grandiose. The thought that I would ever have to do anything which actually involved responsibility never crossed my mind. Your mother was my best friend, and I loved her more than any other friend I have ever had. When I promised her that if anything ever happened to her and your father your Uncle Michael and I would look after you, I never wanted to believe that the possibility may come to pass. I did not think, for a second, that anything would ever happen.

True love, true soulmate love is rare; your mummy and daddy had it, and your Uncle Will and I had it. To be two halves of a whole, and to find the other half to your heart is something most people never get to experience. But I did. And I had never been happier. I loved my life, I loved my everything and I loved the people who were my friends. And you, my goddaughter, my baby girl.

But when the accident happened, my world fell apart. I had to give up the most valued thing in my life: your Uncle Will. Please do not think that you were any less precious to me, you were not. But soulmate love is different than

201

Auntie love; it is the reason one exists. I hope you will find this for your life, one day.

To be hurt by someone you love is unbearable. I do not say this lightly: it is the truth. I hurt your Uncle Will when I had to end my life with him to look after you after the accident, and you hurt me today when you shouted at me the most hurtful thing I have ever heard. You told me I had no right to know what was going on in your life because I was not even your real mother. Do you remember that? Have we been able to move on and reconcile? Or do you still think that the years I have spent being the best mother I could be to you were not enough? I email this to you now so that you know, now that you are an adult, that even adults have feelings; that you hurt mine today. And that had consequences.

Today I cheated on your Uncle Michael, broke the marriage vows I made to forsake all others and keep myself only unto him. Before today I had had no intention of doing so, and I did not leave the house with the intention of doing so; I just fled because of the pain you had caused me. I was not the adult I was supposed to be, right then. I fled, and before I knew where I was, I was at your Uncle Will's workplace. And he and I were together, once more. I will not give you the details, they belong to both he and I. Besides which, I still think you are too young to hear such things, even though you will be an adult when you read this. You shall forever be too young, in my eyes, to hear things like this.

Do you even remember him? Your Uncle Will?

I really do hope you and I have not let this one sentence ruin our relationship; I hope you apologised to me, and I hope you meant it. And I hope I forgave you, whole heartedly. I hope when you're reading this you struggle to recall the day, the words.

I hope you do not think badly of me for doing what I did. I appreciate you might think me to be rambling, here, but I have not yet dealt with all the day's events.

Tara, your Uncle Michael and I have always loved you, and always will. More than you could ever know. I loved you enough to sacrifice everything I had ever wanted. Uncle Michael loved you enough to marry me despite knowing I did not want to marry him. I know I do not write these emails often, usually after lovely events, as you have probably already seen, so you have something to look back on with fond memories, but you needed to know today that what you choose to say can have everlasting effects. If you have not learned by the time you read this, please make a concerted effort to do so now.

All my love,
Aunt Mimi.

And with that, I pressed the send button, closed the laptop, switched off the bedroom light, scrunched down in the bed covers, and went to sleep.

Chapter 32 – First loves

The next morning, I awoke with a heavy head, fuzzy eyesight and a pain which shot and stabbed its way from the back of my skull to my forehead. For a second, the day before seemed like a bad dream. Alas, it was not. I turned my head to see two chocolate brown eyes looking at me. Groggily, with a dry and sore throat, I asked Michael how long he had been awake, and why he had not woken me up. He replied that he had only just awoken, and that he was sure we were awake before the alarm by a considerable amount.

He asked me if I felt any better. I did not know how to answer that question; better than what, exactly? Better because of what? I told him that my head hurt; he suggested I might be dehydrated. He was not curt in his tone, but clearly needed his morning coffee. I rubbed my face and held my head in my hands for a moment, dreading the day before me. I decided I was going to go into work early, to catch up on what I had missed the day before. I washed and dressed quickly, leaving Michael in the shower; I brushed my teeth and went downstairs. I put two slices of multi-grain bread into the toaster, plunged the handle down and began to pour some fresh juice into a glass.

Tara must have been roused by the noise of us both as I heard her feet thud through the ceiling above me; it would not be long before she would be downstairs. Grabbing the toast from the toaster, I hurriedly smothered the best butter from the silver butter dish next to the refrigerator over the toast, put it in some aluminium foil and transferred my juice to the travel flask I sometimes used for my morning commute. I hurriedly grabbed my handbag from the hall, threw my coat over my arm, picked up my car keys from the bowl and made my way to the door. Just as I was there, Michael reached the bottom of the stairs, reached out his arm and pulled me to him. He kissed my right temple, and told me to have a good day at work. I said I would see him later, and that I would let him know if I was going to be late, if I had a lot to catch up on from the day before. I thought I heard him make a comment under his breath as I left, but did not stop to ask what he had said; I feared hearing the answer.

Work was busy, I did indeed have lots to catch up on from the day before; I worked straight through my lunch break to catch up and spent most of the time on the telephone and trying to multi-task. I was pleased, if I am honest with you, because it prevented people from asking me how my day off was, and how Tara's holiday was and so forth. I would not have known what to say to the question; I was not a good liar. How could I have avoided telling people that I had cheated on my husband and run into the grandfather of the killer of my best friend, and, more worryingly, invited him to sit with us at Mass? When the time came to leave to go home, I was reluctant to depart. So reluctant, in fact, I almost wished for heavy traffic. But not quite.

When my journey home came to its end, I found the house was eerily silent. No music from upstairs, no voice from the television. No lights on, but with the lighter evenings since the clocks had gone forward, it was not necessarily unusual. I would have usually called hello, to see who would answer, however, I refrained and opted to wander around to see if anyone was in. Nobody was in the lounge, and, when I made my way into the kitchen, I found it, too, to be empty. I grabbed a snack from the snack basket, a small bar of my favourite salted caramel chocolate, and walked back into the living room to sit on the sofa. After a short while I began to frown, repeatedly glancing through the window to see if I could see Michael's car approaching or pulling into the driveway. I checked the telephone answering machine in the hall; no message left. I searched for my mobile telephone deep inside my handbag, those things were so small back then, they were easily lost; Victoria, with whom I worked, accidentally sent hers around in a washing machine cycle, because it had been in a pocket in her chinos and she had not checked thoroughly enough before laundering her clothes from the day, before bed; not even the eco-friendly 30-degrees prevented it from being irrevocably ruined. When I finally found it, I realised it had been set on the lowest volume whilst I was at work, and so I had not heard when Michael's text message had come through. Back then, of course, people were not constantly attached to their devices, as they are today. They were not quite so integrated into every aspect of one's life. Michael had sent a message saying that he was taking Tara out for dinner, and to not prepare anything for them at home if I had returned from work earlier than I had said I would.

Wearily, having decided another early night was probably for the best, I climbed the stairs. One long, hot shower later, I dried my hair and climbed into bed.

I prayed the next day would be better than the previous two.

The intrusive buzz of the alarm clock awoke me the next morning from a dreamless sleep. I scrunched up my face, unwilling – and unable – to open my eyes. I realised that my left arm was weighed down and too hot for normality. Eventually, I summoned the strength to lift my eyelids; in front of me, a mass of blonde hair filled my field of vision. Tara.

All the residual anger I had had, left me. In that moment, she was my little girl again; I wrapped my arm around her shoulders, kissed her head to wake her and whispered good morning. Tara was even less of a morning person than her Uncle Michael, and, so, it took her a while to rouse from her sleep and remember where she was. Clumsily, she turned over and looked at me. I do not know why I was expecting a grumpy good morning, but I was. Instead, I was offered an apology. With a croaky voice, not entirely caused by the morning's dehydration, she told me she

206

never should have said what she said to me, that she was grateful for all her Uncle Michael and I have done, and continue to do for her, and that she would never say anything like that again; she said she had learned that she needed to think before she spoke or acted – a lesson I was keenly aware of that morning.

I am a big believer in not saying "that is all right" after somebody apologises to you. I was then, and I still am now. It is not all right. Forgiveness does not excuse the act. Forgiveness does not, necessarily, include forgetting. An apology and forgiveness create a mutual pact to try and move forward from whatever occurred. But forgiveness is not always a release, it is not always deserved. Forgiveness does not mean that the injuring party should stop trying to make amends. Forgiveness does not mean all is healed. An apology does not automatically mean relationships return to a previous, happier, more stable state.

I thanked Tara for her apology. I told her I appreciated how hard it must be to admit being in the wrong, especially at her age. I told her that her words had hurt me, and that actions have consequences she might not be aware of at her age. Consequences she might not be able to understand until she was much older. I told her that she needed to take this as a learning opportunity; that, yes, I was not her real mother, but to ask herself if this would make either me, or her mother, proud. I told her to ask herself if she could be proud of her words. I told her that if she thought she could not be proud of them she should not say them. Hypocritical? Yes. I could not be proud of my actions, and yet, I still undertook them. But the purpose of parenthood is to ensure that you try to instil better behaviours and morals into the next generation than you, yourself, have. That was what I was trying to do at that moment. A brief thought flashed through my mind; I was trying a lot harder to be a good, and effective, parent than James Brimley clearly had. My child, and her children, would not grow up to be reckless and a murderer.

After nodding, sincerely, she stretched and sat up. We both got out of bed and got ready for the day. Michael, looking the worse for wear, exited Tara's bedroom, scratching his head and rubbing his face. Tara used the bathroom as I stood opposite my husband, and pressed the palm of my left hand to his face. He moved his arm, his hand encompassing mine, his fingers touching my wedding and engagement rings. I thanked him; clearly the dinner with Tara was to discuss her behaviour and what should happen next. He was a good father to her. He recited part of our vows to me: for better, for worse. I hugged him, my arms wrapped around his broad shoulders, pulling him to me with my head on his shoulder. His warm lips kissed my forehead, and a little, light, relief eased the weight off my shoulders slightly.

Perhaps he would be able to forgive me.

Life returned, somewhat, to normality during the following few weeks. Tara went back to school, work and home lives passed without any real interest. About a month after the holiday, Tara broached the topic of Henry with us. She asked if she could bring him home for dinner one night. Learning my lesson, I kept my mouth firmly closed and let Michael do the talking. He agreed, suggesting Henry come for lunch on a Saturday, instead, and perhaps we could all go bowling in the afternoon. Michael then told Tara he would be happy to drop Henry off at his home, afterwards. It was clearly not up for debate or alteration; it was what would happen, if Tara wanted Henry to meet her family. We were unanimous in our resolve that Tara would not live her teenage lives in the same way we had; we had had so much more freedom, and with it, made so many more mistakes than we wanted Tara to make. The topic had been the focus of many a conversation in her formative years as we grappled with the role of being her adoptive parents. However, it was a different time, back then, when we were young. Generational attitudes shift, alter; our parents had been raised in the 1960s and 70s, and had different ideas about relationships; mine more than Michael's. But, Zara and Robert had lived better lives than we had, lives to aspire to. They had led lives I aspired to have, both then, and now; the reasons behind their choices were inspirational. The best way to live a life. The ideal. The model. It is what they wanted for their daughter, and Michael and I wanted it for her, too.

So, the day for lunch and bowling arrived, and I was consumed with trepidation. The issue with making a mistake in what you say, is that it causes you to be overly cautious in the immediate aftermath. Gone are the opportunities to speak with value, even if necessary, because of apprehension.

An English spring is a sight to behold, I am sure you agree. Green trees and fields, plants and flowers bursting gardens into life at every glance; the cherry blossoms falling from the trees leaving a soft, pink blanket, covering the tarmac of humanity, reminds us of how small we are; blustery mornings and evenings cause delight as nature's confetti cascades down. After hurriedly running the vacuum cleaner around the house, mopping the kitchen floor much more swiftly than usual, and putting all the laundry through on quick washes so nothing untoward could be seen by fresh eyes, I popped quickly to the supermarket for something more interesting than the typical, mundane, Saturday lunch. The sights of spring cheered me so much I found I was smiling to myself. A dash to the back of the supermarket, deli and bakery sections are never near the front, and a quick trip through the chiller aisle and lunch was sorted. All that was left to do was to prepare it; Tara was pleased to help with this, upon my return to the house, but wanted to get it done quickly, so she had time to perfect her hair. Some things never change.

Lunch was nothing short of awkward to begin with. A Mediterranean collection of food lay the foundation for a buffet full of glancing. Michael and I glanced at each other, Tara and

Henry glanced at each other. From the corner of my eye, I saw Michael glancing at Tara, and I glanced at Henry. Henry, however, did not glance at either Michael or I, that I saw. He was, perhaps, too nervous to do so and did not want to meet either of our eyes. It was either that reason, or that he was just too involved with Tara to want to look anywhere else; probably the former, rather than the latter, though, I decided. Michael did the sensible thing and asked about Henry's school life, what he had chosen for his options and what he aimed to do when he left school, which career he wanted to pursue. Unfortunately, timing had never been Michael's strong point, and he asked this question just as Henry had put a slice of bruschetta into his mouth; this resulted in a bit of a coughing fit and a red face for Henry. Awkwardness now turned to embarrassment for him. I almost, almost, felt some sympathy for him.

He told us he wanted to work in Political Law. My tilted head caught sight of Michael's raised eyebrow. It seemed we were both impressed. I asked Henry what made him want to work in that sector; for the first time that day he looked me in the face and told me that he wanted to help people, that most of his family worked in the same area, or similar, and he wanted to keep up the family tradition. Perhaps, then, there was more to the boy than I had been willing to admit. Michael asked questions about which university Henry wanted to go to; the replies were a mixture of logistical, logical and aspirational choices. I was pleased he had begun to consider the details of his career, especially being only the same age as Tara. Michael asked how Henry knew so much; Tara interjected that the school had provided a careers morning for the pupils, before they chose their options. Schools do so much that parents do not realise; it is especially beneficial for those children whose parents do not support them as they should. We all know the sort; those who have children without thinking about the work required to raise them, the people who have children and put them in front of the television, those who do not take the time to read to their

210

children, to take them to places, to widen their experiences and broaden their minds. Michael and I, whilst not being biological parents ourselves, had taken our responsibilities towards Tara's development very seriously: we had made sure she read books, fiction and non-fiction; we had taken her to the theatre and not relied solely on the cinema; we had made sure she had been to zoos and wildlife parks, farms with a petting zoo when she was younger, and talked to her about how food was made, and the environment; we had made sure she understood about volunteering to help with her community, for a while she went to The Red Cross and learned how to do First Aid in case she was ever in a position which called for it. But, so many parents did not do that, back then, nor now, and so many children grow up to be less than well-informed adults, and the pressure falls onto schools; thankfully, Henry seemed to not only make the most of the opportunities provided by school, but the ones his family provided for him, also. He told us his parents both worked hard, but dedicated weekends off for him and his elder brother, with whom he seemed very close; he told us they shared hobbies. Michael was pleased to discover they both liked rugby, and played for the school. I was pleased Henry enjoyed music, he proudly informed us he was learning to play the guitar, as was becoming so fashionable with younger people back then.

Whilst the conversation was flowing, I began to tidy away the lunch plates, as Michael stored the left-over food inside the refrigerator. In the reflection of the cabinets, I saw Tara nodding to a worried-looking Henry; she was trying to tell him everything was going well. Suddenly, Michael announced he was going to fetch his trainers from upstairs, and that after he had done that, we would all be going bowling. I must admit, I was relieved when the bowling alley changed the rules and allowed people to wear their own, sensible shoes instead of the shared shoes with awful patterns and worse laces they provided. They were always so uncomfortable, and felt like wearing flippers.

The car journey was filled with teenage chatter, almost alien to my ears with all the modern phrases and sayings that I had not quite been able to keep up with, and the rapid movement of hands away from one another each time my head turned to glance towards the back seat. Michael drove us to the bowling quite quickly, navigating around the Saturday afternoon traffic by taking some of the shortcuts down side streets. He was always held true to the motto that wherever there is a will, there is a way. As he turned left, down one of the smaller streets, he caught my eye; I moved my eyes quickly towards the children in the back seats of the car, then back to his eyes, raising my right eyebrow slightly with a slight smile on my face. I could see the chuckle in his eyes; he had clearly seen the same thing I had through his rear-view mirror and found it amusing. After he slotted the gear stick into fourth, he reached across and rested his hand on top of mine. It reassured me.

The bangs, clashes and clangs of the bowling alley could be heard from the car park as we exited the car. The whirring and buzzing of arcade game machines also spilled out of the set of double doors at the front of the building, followed by the squeals of some small children, perhaps around the age of seven, were playing a game of running in and out of the door, ignoring the chastising of a rather frazzled looking father who, through no fault of his own, was also a player of the game as he tried to grasp each of their arms to prevent them from disturbing other people entering and leaving the building. Michael and I shared a knowing glance and small chuckle; we were both glad Tara was an only child, and we had never had to do things like that when she was young, and that we were long past the infuriating behaviour stage of parenting. We were also glad that we would never have to do that again. As we walked through the doors, only just avoiding the − at that point − crying children, the smells of hotdogs, deep fried chips, shoe leather and shoe cleaner combined with floor wax and alcohol from the bar at the back of the large room encircled me.

Michael quickly paid, and we settled into our booth. Henry took charge of entering the names into the computer, putting Tara's first. It was an interesting gesture of what I thought was a teenage version of chivalry. Michael's name went last, with Henry before mine. I stood, watching Tara trying to choose an appropriate weighted ball, wondering where the time had gone. It seemed like only yesterday she was born, and I had gone to the hospital to go and meet her. Michael stood behind me, rested his chin on my shoulder and wrapped his arms around my waist. I ran my fingers over his forearm, hoping that this gesture of his meant that our relationship would survive.

Tara seemed to enjoy the bowling; she was focused on trying to achieve as many strikes as she could. Henry seemed to spend most of his time gazing at Tara, his eyes barely moving from her. The time in between their turns was spent next to one another; when the first game reached the half way point, Henry became bold and brave enough to put his arm around Tara's shoulders. Stifling a smile, Michael took his turn, earning a strike and requesting a cheer and a high-five from each of us. Occasionally, it really is possible to roll one's eyes out loud.

We ordered drinks to off-set the warm air within the alley; Michael chose an alcoholic beverage, leaving me with a soft drink so that I would be able to drive us all back home. Whilst Michael knew he would be under the legal limit, he was very strict with driving safety - for obvious reasons. After the trial, neither of us were willing to risk even a sip of mind-altering, judgement impairing, alcohol. Despite not having any alcohol, I still was not able to aim straight down the lane towards the pins, and kept veering off to the gutters. Michael called upon an assistant to raise the sides of the gutters, to keep my aim on the straight and narrow. It helped; my scores were slightly better, but still not good enough to come anywhere above third over the course of the three games we played. At the end of the afternoon, Henry and Tara were openly holding hands as they walked towards the car. I linked my arm through Michael's, as we made our way over the pot-holed car park. The downside of a frigid winter is the appalling state of the roads.

Driving to Henry's house involved a lot of confusion; I still struggle, occasionally, to follow verbal directions if somebody is not in the adjacent seat. It is extremely challenging to ascertain somebody's meaning when they say the words "over there" if you cannot see in which direction they are pointing. Henry's house, detached with an integral garage and a driveway alongside a spacious front garden filled with flowers and neatly mowed grass, was in a nice, quiet avenue, lined with cherry blossom trees. I commented to him how picturesque it was; he replied graciously, offering an agreement, adding that his mother had always wanted to live there. I could certainly see why; a lovely, quiet place where children could be taught to ride their bicycles, play hide-and-seek behind the trees, and visit the nearby park and feed the ducks of a Saturday morning. Henry's upbringing must have been so tranquil; I worried how that might affect Tara, if she were ever to compare their early lives. I wondered how much of Tara's life Henry knew; I did not remember his name being mentioned from the years at her primary school, and so I wondered if he knew all she had survived.

Before Henry exited the car to return to his home, he thanked us for lunch and the afternoon, leant over and kissed Tara quickly on the lips. He held her hand whilst he did so, and held on to it until he was too far away to hold on any longer, his arm trailing behind him towards hers, her arm mirroring the action. He told Tara to text him when she had arrived home because he wanted to know that she was safe. I tried to stifle a chuckle.

First loves can be so grandiose.

And, on top of all the gestures and intimate teenage moments I had witnessed that day, I had no doubt that, in their own way, Henry and Tara loved each other.

Chapter 33 – Birds, Bees and Blushing

In addition to Anne, every other weekend, Henry became an almost permanent feature in our home, to the extent that I included extra food each week as part of my purchases from the butchers, the green-grocers and the supermarket, to accommodate his expanding hunger. Teenage boys eat like horses. I was glad I was not a permanent mother to one. He even had a favourite armchair in the lounge and a favourite seat at the dining table, accompanied by a favourite drinking glass for his refreshments between meals.

He was, of course, no real trouble or inconvenience, and his manners remained impeccable. He was a credit to his parents, and Tara and he did genuinely study of an evening on the weekdays he visited and stayed for supper. He seemed to be building a bond with Michael, stereotypically over sport; nevertheless, Michael had nothing but good things to say about him of an evening after coming home after returning Henry to his. Henry even helped with tasks and jobs around the house; he helped Michael replace the garden shed one weekend, mowed the lawn and helped us replace one of the upstairs radiators. He was becoming quite the handyman around the house. Tara, much to my dismay, did not take much interest in learning how to maintain a house; she seemed to have as little inclination towards DIY as I did. I had hoped that the feminist movement, which was sweeping the globe at the time, may influence her in a proportionate way, that she may learn to be independent enough to be able to take care of herself, should she ever need to. She did not, however, wish to partake and spent more of her time in the kitchen, baking and cooking, than she did joining in with her Uncle Michael and her boyfriend as they pottered about her house, fixing things. Once, when I broached the subject with her, she promptly and precociously, informed me that she had a telephone and a laptop, and a copy of the *Yellow Pages* in the hallway, on the stand underneath the land line telephone, and was able to search for plumbers, electricians, and so forth, on it, and that when she was a doctor, she would be saving money by paying somebody else to do the work, rather than take time away from her job and losing the hourly rate of pay she may be on in the future. As you can see, I could not fault her logic; she was correct. Sometimes, teenagers know entirely too much!

Just over six months after the day Michael and I met Henry, the time came whereupon I felt I simply had to have a talk with Tara, that I could delay it no longer. I had tried to talk to her about things on a few, separate occasions, but cowardice had always consumed me and won the battle. Although she had long known about the mechanics of the facts of life, and she had been taught good, Catholic values at school, I wanted to reiterate the benefits of abstaining from physical intimacy before marriage. Whilst I appreciate that in the modern world, at the time of Tara's youth, the pressure to be intimate with another person was far greater than any guidance from the ideal model of the way to live one's life; the normality of physical intimacy seemed to be everywhere: television shows, the lives of modern day pop stars, all over the Internet and in the media. The older I became, the more I abhorred the moral values of the modern day, the more distant I seemed from my teenage self. I was not relishing the conversation I would have to have with Tara, yet I knew it was necessary.

Michael, being the rock of my life that he was, had offered to discuss matters with Tara himself. I flatly refused his offer, much to his relief. It is a mother's job to talk to her daughter about things of that nature. He had, however, offered to go through with me what I might say, a dry run, if you will. I tried being solely factual; I even quoted the law of the time as I practised. That was not the way to discuss the subject. Michael was bored, and I felt awkward. Stifled. I could feel my lungs becoming laboured, and my throat tightening and becoming as dry as the Sahara as I tried to force out the disjointed, unfamiliar words. If I were ever to give another mother any advice, it would be this: never practise this speech before you speak to your children. You will spend far too much time, whilst trying to converse, thinking about what you should be saying that you will lose your focus and be unable to speak effectively and without embarrassment.

So, one Saturday morning after a rather busy week at work, Tara and I went shopping; a girly day out to the local shopping centre to find swimming costumes, sandals and dresses, an entire summer wardrobe, for our upcoming family holiday: a fortnight to Antigua. I admit, I was desperately in need of a holiday, a break from everything in the house, and at work. I had been collapsing into bed each night, consumed by exhaustion, unable to even begin my treasured nightly reading. Falling out of good habits is a drawback of adulthood; a dangerous slope into complacency, one which I was desperate to avoid by making the most of a good, long, hot, holiday. Clothes shops have a certain smell: a mixture of material and expensive, top-of-the-range furniture polish, combined with the faux leather of handbags and the latest style of shoes. I am certain it is a combination designed to encourage the spending of copious amounts of money, as though the smell offers some comfort as you part with your hard-earned cash, or prevents you from using your mental mathematic skills to keep track of how much of it you have spent. As we made our way through the narrow gaps between display racks, searching for appropriate clothing, we chatted about the best holidays we had had. Tara asked me about the best holiday I had had when I was young; the cautionary meaning in the tone of her voice was clear, she wanted to know what my favourite holiday had been before the accident had happened.

We moved into the dressing rooms each with an armful of clothes – not all of them for the holiday, naturally - as we entered neighbouring curtained cubicles, I told her about the holidays that her mother and I had been on together, and all the adventures we went on. Why do we raise our voices if we are talking through a curtain? The barrier is not thick enough to stop sound, and yet, we still routinely do it. In a forceful volume, I told Tara about Greece, and Canada, and went into detail about all the things we had seen in Wales when we visited. She seemed to hang onto every detail and asked probing questions almost incessantly. It surprised me, she had never asked questions before; rather, she had always waited for details. Although, looking back, perhaps I had offered details to her before she had had chance to think of questions to ask for herself. Was that the right thing to do? Was that the best way to parent a child? Perhaps not. I take comfort, now, in realising that every parent makes mistakes; the key to good parenting is to be proactive and analyse what you do before you do it, to avoid as many mistakes being made as possible. I wish I had come to this realisation a little sooner than I did; and, whilst I am certain Tara's development was not too damaged because I did not entirely know what I was doing, I do lament at how much further she could have gone in life had I merely thought about how to parent before I had attempted to do it. The drawbacks of tragedy are too numerous to fathom for one enveloped by it, I suppose.

Eventually, after trying on what felt like more than a million outfits each, and after critiquing our reflections in the alcove of mirrors, we made our way out of the claustrophobic, musty, dressing rooms, with our choices of purchases to be de-tagged, bagged and paid for; but, before I knew which words were leaving my brain and escaping through my mouth, I was giving Tara details about my holidays with Will. The young girl behind the counter, who could not have been many years older than Tara, interrupted with her wishes of going to the same destination for her summer holidays, one year. It was not until she had stopped my train of thought that I realised what I was saying. I did not mean to, and I wish I had been able to bite my tongue and engage my brain before I had spoken my rambling, wandering, thoughts aloud. Before I really knew what was happening, I was offering up details of the Maldives. I had told her about: the white sands of Finolhu, and the beautiful hotel we had stayed in; the depth of the blue in the ocean and how warm the water was; the scuba diving we had done; and, the local delicacies we had sampled. I had even told her about Will's food poisoning scare, one year, and how the aeroplane journey home was long, tense, and simply dreadful. This conversation continued, without the cashier, as Tara and I moved to our favourite patisserie and ordered a double white-chocolate chip muffin, a large, indulgent, piece of Belgian chocolate cheesecake, an iced tea for Tara and a caramel latte supreme for me. As I briefly paused for breath to return my debit card to my purse and my purse to my handbag, Tara, nonchalantly, asked me if I missed Will. The question knocked the air out of my lungs with the force of a sledgehammer.

Have you ever had something happen to you which makes you completely understand the phrase, 'knocked for six'; a moment when something is so totally unexpected makes you react in a primitive way? The heavy, intrusive smell of burning coffee beans and steamed milk attacked my sense of smell, resulting in a light-headedness which smothered me. I could not catch my breath. The world seemed to spin in the wrong direction as I shakily made my way to the nearest unoccupied, clean, table. How could I answer that question? The mere mention of his name filled my mind with the image of his perfect face, and my heart with the memories of my perfect happiness and perfect life. What could I possibly say for the best? If I were to reply in the affirmative, what implications would that have? Would she tell Michael? Despite the passing time, I was not entirely convinced he had come to terms with my adultery, nor was I sure I was in receipt of his whole-hearted forgiveness; every now and then there would be an edge to his voice in a slightly sarcastic comment he would make, a slightly curt tone which made me wonder whether it still weighed heavily on his mind – especially as sarcasm was so out-of-character for him. However, I did wonder whether I should be in a situation where I must live in fear of what a teenager may say to her uncle. If I said no, what would happen then? Would Tara think any less of my relationship with Will? Would she grow up not realising what I had sacrificed to be her adoptive mother? Would she think that adults did not have to give up anything to do the right thing for others and be a caring human being? Did I want her to have to think of these things at all?

Trying, yet failing, to seek steadiness from a deep breath, I told her that I did, indeed, miss Will. My throat felt like a dam, closing and trying to capture the words as they tried to escape my mouth. As a result, the words were much croakier than I intended, and I was aware that I sounded awfully upset. I was, of course, anguished at the memory of *my everything* and the pain of missing him resurfacing; yet, I did not wish Tara to hear the emotion in my voice. There comes, I suppose, a point in all parents' lives where they realise that they cannot protect their child from everything in the world, any more, and that the child must be allowed to be exposed to aspects of the cruelty of life in order to afford them an opportunity to learn how to deal with unfairness, before they become an adult rendered incapable of mature reactions to feelings. This seemed to be the time in my parenting journey.

In a gesture which displayed to me the core of her kind heart, she stretched her arm out and rested her hand upon mine. Perhaps this was because she was beginning to understand what love might be like, and how important it is to a person's life; perhaps it was because she was not accustomed to seeing her Aunt Mimi upset, I had always tried to hide as many of my negative emotions from her as possible so that she would have a stable female role model in me. Her kindness and compassion were admirable for someone of her age, and were exactly what I had hoped would be instilled in her as I tried my best, along with Michael, to parent her and raise her to be a productive, considerate, member of society.

With trepidation, gentleness, and nervousness, I told Tara that adult relationships are a complexity not all are prepared for when undertaking them. I told her that I had wanted to talk to her about relationships for some time. I told her that I felt we needed to discuss ideas about intimacy and love, and what role they played in a relationship. I told her that I understood the pressures of society, and that hormones make teenagers deaf to morals and ideal ways of living one's life. I told her that both her Uncle Michael and I fell short of the mark when it came to adhering to a Catholic way of life in our teenage years. In a puzzled tone, she asked me what I meant; it was then that I realised she did not know that Michael and I had been a couple before Will and I had had our lives together. I was so confused – had we not told her? Had we never even alluded to it? Had her mother and father never mentioned it? I realised that even if they had, she perhaps would not remember because of her young age when they died. Delicately, I summarised what had once been. It seems she thought that Michael and I had been friends, and friends with her parents, but not an item. And so, I told her that, to me, it was a mistake to be intimate with Michael before marriage – that we had not had the same restraint as her parents had, and that it was far more romantic for her parents to be each other's first, last, and only loves, rather than have done what I did by ignoring my instinct and my conscience at the time. I told her that if I had my time again, I would not make the same mistake. She asked me, with a curious tone, why I thought it was a mistake; I had no choice but to tell her that I regretted being involved with Michael, and that if I could have waited for my true love to be my first, last, and only, I would have. I gently, quietly, told her that, at the time, I was not entirely sure that Michael was the one I was fated to be with, that I had a niggling feeling in the back of my mind that our souls did not match perfectly; I told her that I had had some reservations, and that being intimate with

222

him when I was her age was something about which I felt greatly uncomfortable. I told her that I thought that I had been far too young to be intimate with anybody, even if I had been in a relationship with Will, that at such a young age nobody should be engaging in activities like that, that the law was there for a reason. I told her that there could have been significant implications for her Uncle Michael's future career had anyone made a complaint against him, and that, really, we should have known better. Tara, fixated on the ideal of true love, destiny and fate, enquired how I knew that it was right with Will, and so I had to explain, or try to convey in my shallow words, what I had felt when I had looked into his eyes, how my heart had stopped, how I had seen my future with him unfurl before me. I told her that when it is the real thing, one just knows. She seemed to consider what I had said for a long while. The silence allowed me to take a sip of my delicious caramel latte supreme, before it became too cold to be nice any longer. She countered with a question: would I still have given up my life with Will to marry Michael so that we could adopt her?

Without hesitation I gave her the answer.

I moved on, after a short silence, to telling her that in an adult relationship withholding physical intimacy and building anticipation can be a wonderful thing. Delayed gratification, after all, is what we have all been trained for since we were young, is it not? You cannot eat your sweet until after you have finished your main course, you can have your reward after you have passed your exams with good grades, you get your wages after you have completed the work, you get the holiday after you have saved up for it. From the frown on her face, I knew she understood and was carefully considering the ideas I was putting forward. It is, of course, a difficult concept for any hormonally charged person, even more so for a teenager. I did not want Tara to make the same mistakes I had. Then, in what I now realise was a tad of manipulation, I told her with great conviction that if

Henry was any kind of gentleman, he'd wait until after they were married to be intimate. At this point, of course, Tara could imagine no other person as her future husband; and I hoped that she would be able to avoid having her heart broken as mine had been. I hoped that she and Henry would be each other's only loves, as well as first, and that she would be able to live the long and happy married life her parents did not get to fully experience.

The conversation moved towards more practical aspects, which I shall not bore you with now, of course, although I am certain you can imagine what topics were included. Tara did, as all young women do, want to know about the pain of physical intimacy. Naturally, I gave her the honest answer. It would be pointless to sugar-coat something like that, only for her to discover the truth at an awkward moment. There were other questions about mechanics which I tried to answer in as little detail as possible; there are certain lines which a mother and daughter relationship should not cross. Things such as that, I decided, should be left to her friends.

That evening, after we had justified our purchases to Michael via a traditional fashion show in the lounge, Tara turned into bed early. I think she had a lot to think over and was drained after the day's events. As I sat next to Michael on the sofa, leaning my head against his shoulder and tucking my feet underneath myself, I confided in him about the talk that I had had with Tara. Reaching to the mahogany side table to pour us both a large glass of Malbec, he seemed relieved that he would not have to participate in any sort of discussion regarding the matter. If you are wondering, then the answer is yes – I did omit the details and discussion of Will. Michael did not need to know about that. When I told him some of the topics Tara had asked about, his face turned tomato red. It must be uncomfortable for a father, or an uncle, to consider that his daughter thinks about subjects like that. It must be easier to believe the illusion of an idyllic, innocent daughter, who was still their princess and sweet little girl. Poor Michael was so embarrassed by the thought that the red wine he was sipping caught in his throat, almost choking him. In fact, I am almost sure there were some things involved in the chat I had had with Tara of which he was not aware, thus embarrassing him even further when he gained the knowledge.

Upon reflection, he told me, he was certain that children should have both parents involved in their lives; he could not fathom how single fathers ever cope with having a daughter. I, in turn, mused that single mothers must have difficulties with sons. Michael was glad we were in the roles together, at that moment more than any he had been for a while. As was I. I was pleased to be able to reflect, and be reassured I had, at least, done a better job of talking to Tara about the birds and the bees than Michael would have done if he had been alone in the role.

Perhaps we were not doing too bad a job, after all.

I was hopeful that we would have a peaceful holiday.

Chapter 34– Empty Nest

Tara, Henry and Anne spent a large portion of the next four years commandeering the dining room table, or the breakfast bar. There seemed to be more room, or snacks, available at Tara's house in comparison with the others' homes. Of an evening, Michael and I were often relegated to the lounge, watching television or reading. Our conversations lessened; with Tara becoming increasingly more independent, we had less to discuss. Over the years, we had lost touch with a lot of friends, we had stopped pursuing our own interests, gradually, because of the pressures and responsibilities of raising a child for which we had not been prepared.

Despite being married, loneliness enveloped us.

The children worked hard, studying for their GCSEs. After their results day, where Tara and Anne did very well, they enjoyed a summer holiday to Cornwall. Henry did not want to go, because he was disappointed with his results – despite them being good enough to get onto the A-Level courses he wanted – but was persuaded by Michael to join the girls for a summer of fun. We had purchased a new mobile telephone for Tara's birthday, a sleek black screen with a sparkly pink case to protect it from scratches and breakages; she had Internet access on it and all sorts of new-fangled things. We had no worries that she would be able to contact us, should she need to. Showing my age, I was becoming decreasingly familiar with the new technology, so readily available in the pockets of, seemingly, every under twenty-five-year-old, all of whom seemed to immediately, instinctively understand every application made available.

They spent two weeks in a rented cottage, near Penarvon Cove. I was just as anxious about that trip as I had been with the skiing trip a few years earlier. I had heard several scary stories about the tide sweeping people away; I know I was not the only parent worried about this, as Anne's mother had made her promise she would not go into the sea any further than waist height. Henry's parents made sure that he had half a suitcase full of sunscreen, having a tendency to burn rather quickly. We waved them off at the train station, preferring that rather than a coach to send them half the length of the country away. They had enough money to last them for a month, and I had no doubt that they would return with very little of it. All three had been told where the local walk-in centre was for a doctor if they should require medical help, and they had been made deliberately aware of where the nearest hospital was – just in case. I had packed a case full of non-perishable food for them; it weighed a lot and so I had said that Henry must be in charge of carrying it. Stereotypically sexist? Perhaps. But there is something to be said for the biological advantage of a male's muscles and larger fingers, when considering the need to carry large, heavy items.

Henry and Anne had had to use some of their savings from after-school jobs they had to pay for their holiday. Tara, however – I have to admit, was slightly more spoiled. Her holiday was paid for by Michael and I. We thought about making her work for some of the money towards the trip, but we decided that she should be made to use her savings for spending money instead. Why did we conclude this? Sympathy, I suppose. Even so long after the accident, we still thought that she had been through too much in her life for anything making it more of a challenge to be justifiable. Please do not misunderstand me, we made sure she kept her room tidy, and cleaned the house as part of her daily chores, but we did not want her working on anything other than her future if she did not have to. It was also, we thought, the least we could do after we had been living in her house for so long.

The three teenagers came back from the holiday sun-kissed, recharged and raring to tackle their A-Levels. I did not see a difference in Tara and Henry's relationship, and I hoped that

227

they had stayed in their respective rooms during their time away, and had been able to resist any urges which plagued them. I will openly admit to you, I was relieved.

Their two years of A-Levels passed quite rapidly, when I was their age my time seemed to drag like a ball and chain the size of a house attached to my leg, slowing every step I took, yet because I had aged, Tara's time seemed to pass within a heartbeat. Tara so frequently complained of neck-ache because of studying so much that we had to pay for several physiotherapy sessions for her to have some semblance of normal movement. Michael made it his mission to disturb her studying with each hour and a half which passed, to make her walk around the house for fifteen minutes, to drink something, and to eat something, and to have human contact. He seemed desperate to find himself a new role within her life, all his text messages to me revolved around Tara, most of our conversations revolved around her - they had for a long time, but during that time there seemed to be an urgency in Michael's tone which had not been present, before. He was struggling to adjust; the job of the parent evolves with the child, and before becoming irrelevant, parents must ensure they forge new roles for themselves in their child's life. His world, really did, revolve around Tara. I cannot deny feeling the same way; I spent a large portion of my evening times sitting at the table with Tara, reading her text books. Studying her, as well. I learned more than I thought was possible about science; I did not do this because I wanted to be able to help her, but because I wanted to understand what she was learning and what about it she found fascinating. I wanted to be able to keep up with the conversations she and I would no doubt have over dinner as she progressed through university towards becoming a doctor. I had always taken a keen interest in her school work, but the detailed A-Level material in the science subjects she was taking, was so illuminating. I even looked at her class material; the way the teachers made the material accessible, yet challenging, astounded me. There were a few weeks at the end of their first year where Henry and Tara barely saw each other; each too focused on revising for their mock exams so that they could pass the year and move onto Year 13. It was a testament to how strong their relationship was that they could spend so much time apart - when it was the opposite of the norm for them and their generation, it seemed - and minimise the texting and video calling so they could focus on their studies much more.

When they passed their mock exams, we took Henry and Tara out for a celebratory meal at a lovely restaurant in a nearby village. The décor inside allowed for an upmarket, yet friendly and relaxed ambience; it was perfect for a small celebration such as ours. It also had a fabulous selection of desserts; one of the criteria on which our family judged any restaurant. Michael and I wanted to spend as much quality time making happy memories with Tara as we could before we lost her completely. Tara had invited Anne, but she had had plans with her family and so could not attend. We three went on a summer holiday with Henry and his family, not long afterwards, to Rome with a few day trips to other parts of Italy. Michael had hired a people carrier, seven-seater car and did most of the driving, he seemed to enjoy it, thoroughly. The lovebirds sat in the back two seats, in the boot of the car, as we told them that we were much too old to navigate the rear seats to clamber back there. They seemed more than happy to have a barrier between them and the two sets of parents. Henry's parents chatted happily with us about all manner of things, recounting embarrassing stories we had not yet heard from Henry's youth. In all honesty, I am uncertain whether Henry heard the conversations due to being so far away. This was, perhaps, for the best; I am positive he would not have liked to have heard the story about the paddling pool and his missing trunks from when he was five years old, recounted to the parents of his girlfriend. Or his girlfriend for that matter. We visited Vatican City, taking thousands of photographs to document the experience. We all went to Mass in Latin; it was a beautiful celebration. The churches in Italy are stunningly beautiful, and the smell is incredible – rich incense and the incredible smell of melting candle wax and flame. Of course, each church has its own sense of beauty, and its own value, but the ones we visited in Italy stole away my breath. On more than one occasion I had to reach for Michael's arm to steady myself as I absorbed each glorious, colourful, sight. Each time I did, I saw him enthralled, also. Once I had finally worked out how to send photographs via email on my mobile telephone, I attached them all to an email to Tara's secret email address. At that time, it was less than a year until Tara's eighteenth birthday, whereupon Michael and I would give her the email address and password. I wanted to ensure that she knew that it was not a passing phase, that we maintained our efforts in immortalising her childhood and our love for her. Whilst I did wonder if this had been rendered futile, what with the rise of social media and Tara having her own page on which to share such images, I did want to ensure she saw the images I had taken, without her knowledge. All parents have them, the ones we take of our children looking especially angelic, special, or precious, which we wish to preserve to prove to others all the good we see in them truly is visible – if only they would look closely enough.

When we returned home, Tara's life was full of university open days, studying and application forms, and driving lessons. Tara was unaware that there was money in a trust fund for a car for her, and for university fees, paid for by her parents' life insurance policy. She had taken on a part time job, waiting on tables, at a local restaurant. She did not like the job much, but was pleased with the money. Michael and I were glad she was learning about the value of money for herself, yet we worried terribly about her stress levels; but, continuing a life-long trend for Tara, she coped remarkably well. She told us numerous times, in quite a condescending tone, when we fretted during dinner conversations, that she was fine, and that she knew she was working towards her future and we should remember all the people she was going to be able to help when she was a doctor. Even at almost eighteen, she was still a precocious child.

Have you ever tried ignoring your child's not-so-subtle hints about wanting their own car? It is equal in difficulty to ignoring their Christmas list desires. Apparently, my chat with Tara a couple of years earlier about delayed gratification had not transferred to transportation. It was such a covert operation that Michael and I set upon, trying to appear nonchalant and dismissive, or circumventive whenever Tara mentioned anything about her transport needs. Both of us were swiftly running out of subjects to which to change the conversation. We had even resorted to making a list of topics we could divert to before we went to sleep at night. It had replaced any ideas of intimacy we may have had; we had not indulged for years. Not since I had spent the afternoon with Will. I understood why, as did my husband, yet it was never mentioned, aloud. Michael, however, had found a lovely little car for Tara and it was this which formed the majority of our conversations in our bedroom. It was a reasonable price, and so we had released some funds to purchase it and matched that amount with some of our own – a gift from both sets of parents; we had arranged her car insurance and road tax, and a neighbour Michael was friendly with had agreed to store it in his garage for us until she passed her driving test. I did not know the man that well, in fact, I did not know many people at that time. I seemed to have lost a lot of my previous life because of becoming a mother. My world revolved around Tara; the last thing I had done purely for myself was the selfish afternoon with Will. I must wonder, now, whether that was at all a healthy way for me to live my life. Is it good for any mother? What kind of example does that set for one's child?

When the day of Tara's test arrived, I waved her off from the driveway as her instructor, Josh, collected her for one last lesson so she could practise. I implored Tara to text me as soon as possible with the result of her examination. I am sure she thought this was because I was being nosey, but it was because I could then tell Michael whether, or not, to fetch her car, and to get out the giant pink bow I had purchased for the occasion, and was hiding in a suitcase at the top of my wardrobe. The two hours it took to receive the message took an eternity; but the news was positive. She had passed, and we set ourselves into action.

The look of joy on her face when she walked into the driveway of her house was everything I had hoped it would be; Josh had stopped the car just short of the house when he returned Tara home, he knew what we were planning, and so did not want to ruin the chance for us to take photographs to document the moment. I had decided to be brave and record her reaction, hoping to keep my hand steady. Her saucer-wide eyes glistened with happy tears as it dawned on her that the car parked next to each of ours was hers. Squealing with delight she clasped her hands to her mouth, jumped up and down and ran to Michael with her arms wide. He returned her hug with a look of pride and relief on his face, he had done a superb job of selecting a car she liked. He handed over the keys, and she hopped into the car with the speed of an Olympic athlete.

Her eyes were darting too quickly around the car to notice the card we had left, resting behind her steering wheel in front of the, very trendy, speedometer. Eventually, after looking for a place to plug in her new-fangled, does everything but the dishes, MP3 player, she settled enough to notice the vanilla coloured envelope. She opened it without the care I would have liked to have seen, a true sign of ageing, and pulled out the card too hurriedly. The design on the front, a car and a smiling cartoon girl, was ignored. She turned the page and stopped to read the note.

Tara,
Take care of this car, it is a gift from
your mummy, daddy, Aunt Mimi and
Uncle Michael.

We all love you.

Be careful, drive well.

Tears spilled from her eyes. She held her hand to her heart. She clambered out of the car, wrapped her arms around both of us, her head in between ours, and whispered a thank you. Michael and I hugged her hard; we knew that thank you was for more than the car.

We saw increasingly less of her in the following few weeks; as all new young drivers, Tara was eager to get out and about and show off her new car, and find her freedom. It was good for her to get some real life, solo, driving experience, and she spent a lot of time with Anne in the car. They were going to different universities, so wanted to spend as much time with each other as they could.

On her eighteenth birthday, we had a celebration. All Tara's family, including adoptive, arrived at the house bearing gifts. A lot gave money, to help with the running of a car and in preparation for university. Some gave jewellery, others gave vouchers for books she would no doubt be needing for her studies. All gave their time, hugs and love. There were photographs taken, shared on social media, and laughed over. Her friends were also invited, Henry did not let go of Tara's hand for most of the day and Anne was never far away. There were a couple of other friends Tara invited, both from school and from church. It was lovely to see everyone eating and drinking, enjoying one another's company.

Michael and I had bought Tara a locket which we had had engraved with her name on the front, and the words, 'You are loved' on the reverse. It had in it, four compartments in which photographs could be placed. When she opened the blue velvet box, seeing the platinum heart shape she gasped, clearly impressed with the present. When Michael whispered to her to look inside, she carefully released the clasp. We had placed in it, a photograph of Zara, Robert, Michael and me in each of the spaces. This way, all her parents would be kept in her heart, always. With her forever, wherever she went.

Before she retired to bed, after a long day of celebration and laughter, I gave Michael a knowing look. He nodded in reply, and I went into our bedroom to retrieve the details we needed. In my material memories box, in the lower drawer of my dressing table, above the crumpled note from Will, was a small envelope inside which were the log-in details for Tara's email address. I retrieved it, resisting the urge to re-read the note for the five hundredth time. I did not want to be upset that day, and so I left it in its place. By the time I had returned everything to its proper place in my dressing table and descended the stairs, Michael had switched on the laptop computer and typed in the address for the email site Tara needed. She seemed very confused, naturally, until we told her what we had been doing during all the years we had been her parents. Michael had sent some photographs of the day to the email address from his mobile telephone, so Tara would have complete memories until the day she became an adult. I advised her not to overwhelm herself reading all the emails in one night, and that she should read them in chronological order. Yes, if you are wondering, it was not an entirely selfless instruction. No, I did not want her to read the email I had sent her a few years earlier, no, I especially did not want her to read it in front of Michael.

We allowed Tara to have her privacy, and we retired to bed. I heard her ascend, shortly behind us, having read one or two of the earliest emails and decided that was enough for one night. Tapping on the door, she poked her head through the gap which was there and asked if she could come in. She sat on the edge of the bed, fiddling with the edge of the duvet. She told us that she had had a wonderful day, and that she would never forget it. She told us that she could not believe how amazing her birthday present was and, as she held it in her clenched fist, she would never take it off. She told us that she had been especially lucky to have two sets of parents who loved her, and that she thought the email account was an incredible thing that she could not wait to read. Michael warned her, reiterating my earlier sentiments, that taking her time might be a better idea, and that if she tried to read it all at once she may be overwhelmed. She sat in pensive thought for a second, before agreeing, hugging us both and wishing us a goodnight.

Six months later, after another party to celebrate her magnificent top marks in her A-Level exams, whereupon she was showered with more gifts from family and friends, we were back at the car, packing it up full of clothes and shoes, and books and DVDs, and food and washing powder, photographs and stationery as we prepared to lose her to university. One of the hardest things to do as a parent is to let the child leave. The rational part of your mind urges you to believe you have done a good enough job, that they will be fine on their own and be able to survive, that you have taught them everything they needed to know before this point. Your heart, however, wants to wrap them up in cotton wool and keep them at home forever.

The heart cannot always be victorious in battle.

And so, we followed her, in our car, to her university, reminding each other all the way there about the things we needed to do and say for Tara once we arrived. We helped carry her bags into the hall where her room was, and unpack her belongings into the tiny cupboard which was provided. It was a sterile, basic environment, with only generic curtains adding any semblance of colour. The bed looked like it was made of pine, and the mattress, at least, looked as clean as the rest of the room. There was a strong smell of disinfectant, the building obviously had cleaning staff. Tara was lucky enough to have an En-Suite shower room in the corner of her bedroom, behind her front door. When Michael and I went to university we all had to share a communal shower room and facilities with the people on our respective floors. When we tried to mention this to her, Tara waved our comments away before we could complete them, telling us that we were too old and that we should not recount tales of university life from another millennium. When she put it that way, a shared look between Michael and I indicated that we did, indeed, feel old. To add life to her room, we pinned her photographs up onto the cork board, making it already half full of memories she wanted to keep close during her first year. In her second and third years, she planned to move out of halls and rent a house with friends she hoped to make. We spent the day with Tara, imparting what we thought was wisdom and advice whilst dining at one of the places to eat nearby. We spent a fortune in the local supermarket, trying to stock up her refrigerator shelf and cupboard in the shared kitchen. Healthy food really is an expensive business nowadays, I suppose one should make more of an effort to grow one's own. However, I made sure she had fruits and vegetables to eat, I was determined she would not be a typical student when it came to a diet of junk food. I left her enough money for a month's worth of grocery shopping, and a little extra for emergencies. I knew she would find a job to help top up her minimal student loan money, and she had some money from her parents, for university, but she wanted to work for her own benefit, too. I made her promise me she would eat at least one healthy meal per day. You read articles about the importance of nutrients and vitamins and a well-balanced diet; Tara had been brought up to only have sweets and chocolates occasionally, and in moderation. I hoped she would have the self-discipline to continue the minimal consumption of unhealthy food.

And so, when she was settled in, and after there had been hugs a-plenty all around, Michael and I said a tearful goodbye to the little girl who had been the focus of our lives for so many years, and walked reluctantly towards the car. A rite-of-passage had taken place for both Tara and Michael and I. We drove, in silence, back home, unlocking a dark house which had grown tenfold in the previous ten hours, and was as silent as the grave. Michael filled the kettle with water, replaced it onto the stand, and went about making a cup of herbal tea for us both. I, suffering a different kind of misery, wandered upstairs, into Tara's room. There I saw the remnants of her young life, strewn over the floor and her bed. I picked up a jumper which she had not taken with her, deciding that something pink with an animal on the front of it was not university worthy. I held it to my face, inhaling what was left of her in the house.

If I am to be honest with you, I thought I would cry more than I did. But there was only a single tear which descended my cheek to be absorbed by the soft, fluffy jumper I tightly held. I suppose I was too shocked, numb, by the events of the day. It was the latest in a culmination of draining days in my life.

My beautiful baby girl had left. Started her own adventure, her own future.

And Michael and I were left alone together with empty hearts.

In an empty nest.

Chapter 35 – Space

I am certain that every parent who has lost an only child to university becomes lost. How could they not? The little person, around which their lives had revolved for so many years, does not need the parent in the same way, any longer. The parent then, if they have no other children to nurture, is at a loss; what is to be done with all this free time they suddenly find thrust upon them?

Nothing.

I suppose, you could argue, that Michael and I suffered more because we were so wholly unprepared for parenthood, and a life together, and had had to make so many adjustments so rapidly to alter our lives to care for the baby. We had left behind almost everything except our families; gone was the time spent on hobbies, with friends, alongside any remnants of our social lives.

We spent the first week wandering around the house after work in confusion. Both of us almost speaking, yet stopping ourselves at the last second. The silence was deafening. We found that we had quickly run out of things to say to one another after musing about what Tara was doing that day, what she was learning or the friends she was making. The house felt dramatically emptier because we had had three teenagers in it most of the time during the last four years. Now, all of them had gone their separate ways and we were left with nothing but memories. Michael suggested updating the house, decorating and the like, but we soon realised that we could not do anything, really, without Tara's opinion. The house was, after all, hers.

Michael threw himself into maintaining the house, tidying the gardens and re-painting anything he could find which had not been done in the last five years. The garden fences took him a while, which he seemed happy with, but after he had completed the tasks he seemed as lost as before. For me, I took to cleaning out the wardrobes of anything we had not used for twelve months, and donating to charity as much as we could. Michael suggested asking at church to see if there was anything we could contribute to, and so we did. Father Philip pointed us towards the noticeboard to see if there was anything we wished to help with that piqued our interest.

I joined the church book club; I had always loved to read. Michael joined the walking club to boost his fitness levels. He had long since given up rugby, and so felt he should walk more so he could avoid becoming a shape totally unlike that of a man. It took him out of the house for two or three evenings a week. Unfortunately, our groups did not fall on the same days, so we spent a lot of our time away from one another, only spending perhaps an hour each night eating, loading and unloading the dishwasher and preparing for bed. It was as though we were alien to one another.

There was just too much space between us.

The telephone calls to, and from, Tara diminished as time passed and she became more comfortable and settled at university. She had made lots of new friends, seen lots of Henry and had found herself a job working in one of the bars on campus. Michael made sure to ask her during every telephone call if she was attending Mass. She told us that she had found a church within walking distance, and attended every Sunday evening. We offered to drive to her one weekend to come with her, and she agreed for one of the Sundays in Advent. I asked about her workload, a lot, and whether she was eating well. After each of

239

these telephone calls, Michael and I discussed each sentence she had said, analysing her tone and whether we thought she was overwhelmed or coping, enjoying university or missed us too much.

Before long, the telephone calls occurred no more frequently than once every ten days, and we became lost in our own emptiness.

Briefly, there was respite, during the reading weeks when Tara returned home, and during holidays when she remained for more than four days. These weeks were filled with activity, we took her to dinner, out shopping, and spent time spoiling her as much as we could. Michael made Tara spend a day going through the house with a fine toothed comb, asking her what she wanted changing in the house, and if she wanted anything decorating or improving. When she replied in the negative, I saw his heart sink. He was desperate for something to do. Whoever knew that adulthood was so enveloped with boredom?

We were overjoyed with excitement when the end of Tara's first year arrived. Thrilled to have her back at home, I spent a long time planning which meals to make for her, and what films to watch on the new television system that allowed us to download things via the Internet.

That year we did not have a summer holiday, as we usually did, preferring to keep Tara at home and spend leisure time with her. I cannot be the only parent to want to have their child back at home and not steal them away for a holiday after the first year of university, can I? During the second week of the holidays, after spending the first with his own family, Henry became the almost-permanent feature in the house he had been before they both went off for their studies. Anne, too, in time, returned. It was glorious to have a house full of voices again. Michael had a spring in his step which he had not had during Tara's time away,

240

especially returning from his walking club one evening when Henry had asked to accompany him.

As Tara had retired to bed early that night, and Anne and Henry had said their goodbyes, Michael looked at me from across the other side of the lounge, a wry smile dancing around his lips. Puzzled, I asked him what on earth was going on. In a swift movement he traversed from one sofa to the one I was sitting upon, and moved his face next to mine, his lips next to my ear and whispered the secret.

Gasping, I felt Michael's hand clasp over my mouth to stop me squealing, which he knew was inevitable. I turned my face to look at him, his hand glued to my mouth, my eyes wide. When my face smiled below his palm, Michael released his grasp. I realised it was the first time in months that we had had any sort of physical contact other than a courtesy kiss on the cheek for hellos and goodbyes when arriving and leaving the house. I asked Michael when it would happen, and he informed me it would be that weekend at the restaurant in which we were planning to dine. Without thinking, I launched forward, wrapping my arms around Michael's neck. It had been a long time since I had been elated.

That night, I struggled to sleep as much as a small child on Christmas Eve. Michael giggled at me numerous times, finding my excitement amusing despite it preventing his sleep as much as mine. In my mind, I was mentally dressing for the occasion, to ensure that I appeared sufficiently sophisticated enough in the inevitable photographs. I wondered how I could encourage Tara to wear something more suitable for such an occasion, rather than her jeans and t-shirt combination which seemed to suit her student lifestyle. There was still something very old fashioned about my attitude, however, for special occasions I still champion dressing appropriately, to maintain good standards. I suppose it must be a generational ideology.

Have you ever tried to be both subtle and influential concurrently? It is a difficult task to undertake. I suggested a shopping trip to Tara the next day; reluctantly, she agreed, seeming confused by my overt enthusiasm. We trawled the sales in the local shopping centre; I made her try on at least six floaty, classically lined, pastel coloured, summer dresses before Tara asked what all the fuss was about and why I was going to such lengths to find a perfect dress for her. It was so difficult to resist telling her why I was insisting she have a lovely dress purchased for her. From what Michael had told me about his conversation with Henry, this was going to be a surprise for Tara, they had not discussed it in any great seriousness.

And so, when Saturday arrived, I awoke with the birds and began to ensure the house was clean and tidy, I'm not sure why, and that everything was ready before going to the restaurant that night. Not that there was anything to get ready, but I busied myself around the house wiping surfaces and putting numerous, quite unnecessary, loads of laundry into the washing machine. I vacuumed the lounge and hallway three times, much to the bemusement of Michael who was told, sternly, not to wear anything but slippers inside the house. Not that he ever did, but on that occasion, he ensured he pointed out his slippers each time we passed each other. If it had been any other day, I may have scowled at him for being condescending, yet that morning I felt I could not spare the time nor energy to scold him. I did think, at one point, that I heard him whisper something about my being neurotic, but I chose to ignore this, not wanting to ruin the day with banter and a play fight. It was nice to finally have something to talk with Michael about, since we had been so silent in the recent months. I realised I had missed him.

I had wondered, mid-week, if we should order a congratulations cake from the local bakery and send it to the restaurant on the Saturday morning. When I mentioned the notion to Michael, he scolded me for being too intrusive; what if Henry had planned something of which we were not aware? Would it not be considered overbearing and unwarranted? And what if, God forbid, it was not needed? I reluctantly conceded that he may have a valid point. And so, I had to be content with the opportunity to take photographs, whilst Michael promised he would video record the event on his mobile telephone.

Tara was aware of our plans to dine out, of course, but she had not realised Henry would not be visiting earlier that day, about which she was extremely disappointed. He had told her that he needed to spend some time with his family, but that they would all join us at the restaurant later. I had spent a long time helping Tara curl her hair. It reminded me of all the times I used to spend, when she was a young girl, helping her style her hair. In that moment, she was still my little girl, getting ready for a party with her friends when she was around the age of nine. Such strong memories invaded my mind, nostalgia overwhelmed me for a second. By the time her hair was curly, Tara had completed applying her makeup. She looked both grown up and young an innocent at the same time. I hugged her tightly to me, desperate to keep my little girl for a while longer. I told her she looked beautiful. Confused, she thanked me, and went to put on the dress we had purchased for the occasion.

I dressed quickly, myself, putting my hair up in a messy bun which was the trend of the time, back then. Looking back now, it was not an appropriate style for any woman, never mind one my age! Old photographs can sometimes be mortifying; how anyone ever found a partner in the nineteen-eighties is beyond me. Between the mullets and the perms, I am constantly amazed anyone was able to find someone to whom they were attracted. When everybody looks the same, I suppose all that is left are attributes of personality and qualities of character to consider.

The restaurant was busy. The clattering of metal against crockery drifted through the air racing the hubbub of mixed voices towards our ears as we entered. The host seated us at our reserved table for ten and handed out menus. The young waitress, who had not been working there long for we had never seen her before, came to take our drinks order. We ordered a few bottles of wine for the table, and asked for some iced lemon water to cool us down. One of the pure joys in life is being able to peruse a menu and being spoiled for choice. I could not keep still whilst waiting for our starter course, I think I devoured three bread sticks before the bottles of wine had been opened. Michael frowned at me, then raised his eyebrows and rolled his eyes. I could tell he was having second thoughts about letting me in on the secret.

The starter arrived, and was delicious, followed soon after by the main course; a delicious, mouth-watering, pork medallion wrapped in apple stuffing served on a bed of Hassel-back potatoes with a selection of vegetables. It was sublime, but I could not focus on appreciating it as much as I should have because I was too distracted by excitement. Tara excused herself to visit the ladies, and when she came back there was an old, red, velvet box awaiting her on the table. As she sat down, it caught her eye and she froze. Henry got up from his seat, walked around the table and knelt beside her. Michael was already recording the goings-on, and I was trying to discretely take photographs on my mobile telephone.

Henry told Tara about all his favourite qualities of hers, detailing examples from their relationship which he held dear to his heart. He told her that he loved each part of her, even the bad, and he told her that he would forever love her. He asked her to grow old with him and as he picked up the old box from the table, he opened it and turned it to face her, Henry asked Tara to spend her life with him and be his wife. Tara's eyes travelled from Henry's down to the box where they met her mother's engagement ring. Her gasp was so loud it could be heard by each member of our party. So that was what Michael had been so happy about! The swine had kept it from me, but I could not feel angry with him. My happy heart swelled and glowed at the prospect of her parents being always with her, that her father's wish for a tradition to begin with him and his bride was being realised. I wondered if it was Michael's suggestion that the children use Robert and Zara's rings, or if Henry had asked permission. It was the second most romantic proposal to which I had ever been a witness; the first on that list, for me, was when Robert asked Zara to marry him. Tara said yes, quietly, and after her mother's engagement ring, hers now, was nestled into its new home on her finger, she reached for Henry's face to kiss him. They embraced tightly for a long time, her shoulders' shaking giving away the tears which escaped her eyes and landing on Henry's shoulder, whilst every member of our party cheered and applauded. Neighbouring tables joined in, having observed Henry's actions, adding to the joviality of the occasion. The manager of the restaurant delivered a complimentary bottle of champagne to our table, and a waitress followed closely behind carrying a tray of ten champagne flutes. Henry's father popped the cork and began pouring the tray of drinks. Henry and Michael shook hands, Henry's mother hugged Tara before I could envelop her for a hug of my own. I whispered in her ear how happy we were for her, and how I was certain she would have a lifetime of happiness. Michael kissed her forehead adding his own congratulations. I hugged Henry, whispering a warning in his ear, as I am sure Michael had done when he gave his permission for Tara's hand to be given. I was quite assured in my choice of words; if he hurt Tara he would have to answer to me.

Before I knew it, amidst the whirlwind of ideas about wedding venues and colour schemes, Tara had re-packed and was back at university.

Leaving Michael and I alone together, again.

Chapter 36 – The Wedding Planner

Have you ever planned a wedding? If you have planned your own, you will understand that planning a wedding fills your life with stress. Have you ever helped to plan somebody else's? If you have, you will understand why I incorporated a daily check for grey hairs into my morning schedule. There are different types of stress in life, of course: some fun which challenge you and allow you to grow; some break you completely and ensure you are never quite the same after the experiences you are forced to endure – that which does not kill you does not always make you stronger; and, there are some which seem unavoidable but are a daily part of life. And then, there is trying to organise a wedding for somebody else, about whose opinions, of course, one can never be one hundred percent assured. Planning one's own wedding is easier, every decision is made before ordering and bookings are completed.

Tara had never been much of a dreamer, nor someone who expected to marry when she was older. She was far more scientifically inclined to waste time on daydreaming about white dresses and flowers and a happily ever after with a Prince Charming type in her life. When she was younger, I was grateful for this, glad that she was focused on her studies and progressing well through her education. However, since she became engaged, I had become increasingly frustrated that the subject of her marriage had never really been discussed; I was deprived of details from which to help her organise the event. It was especially difficult communicating through sporadic telephone calls, voicemail messages and texting several conversations concurrently. Crossed wires and confused meanings hampered any significant, constructive, progress for several weeks.

Weddings used to be so much simpler, back in the good-old-days. You would select a suitably affordable dress, choose some flowers, ask sisters or close friends to be bridesmaids and dress them in something horrendous and get married in a small ceremony, followed by a small reception. When Tara got married traditions were much different. Instead of one Hen Night to celebrate a last night of freedom with one's female friends, Hen Weeks abroad had become a fashion. Save the Date cards were a new concept to me, also. Although the date had not been set, Tara was adamant that she and Henry should be married before graduation; she wanted her degrees to have his surname, rather than her own. Michael and I had pondered, during one of our few discussions whether to suggest keeping her surname, as the legacy of her parents, but Zara and Robert would have wanted Tara to have been married and to keep with tradition, so we did not raise the topic with her. She was an adult, free to make her own decisions and, if the notion had not entered her mind, we should not task ourselves with putting it there.

There was no real urgency in the planning of the wedding for a significant part of the second year of university for Tara and Henry. When their second summer holiday arrived, a year into their engagement, Tara began to frantically try to organise more from the to-do list. Tara and Henry had decided on a date around Easter to be married. Tradition dictates that the bride marries in her family's parish, and so Henry and Tara went to discuss their marriage with Father Philip and undertake *pre-Cana*. Father Philip was, Tara reported, overjoyed that he would perform the marriage Mass, and nostalgic about all the times Tara and her family had been before him in the Church. So much of our lives were entwined with the Church. The consistency of the same priest involved in all our lives for the previous two decades was steadying. Reassuring. Comforting.

Midway through her summer break, Tara sleepily descended the stairs one morning and curled up next to me on the sofa. Resting her head on my shoulder, she nonchalantly asked me if I was busy the following Saturday, and if I was free, would I go wedding dress shopping with her? I had been awaiting the moment she would ask me; naturally, I agreed. One of the most special days in a mother's existence is the day she helps choose a gown for her daughter's wedding. However, I did not want Tara to purchase a new dress, and so I instructed Michael to make a trip to the loft.

When Tara had a brunch date with Anne a few days later, Michael and I made our move. He ascended the ladders, despite his dislike of dust and dark spaces, and pulled the string to illuminate the loft. I, carefully, followed him up. Lofts have their own distinct smell, which seems to be the same no matter the house one resides above. A heavy, thick air surrounds you as you push upwards, the musty smell of memories makes your mind reminisce, and the smell of aged dust affirms the life in the house below. The cosiness of a loft always made me smile; yet I always lamented the lack of space created by the hatch. It would have been a perfect place to situate a person-swallowing arm chair, a lovely hidey-hole to read, or to listen in peace to favourite radio station programmes, or podcasts which were becoming increasingly popular to download onto one's MP3 player. As it was, there were only two rudimentary short stools in the loft on which Michael and I could perch as we manoeuvred the contents around to find the precious item which had been vacuum packed and stowed away in an old, red, battered suitcase, over two decades ago.

Inevitably, as I am sure you will attest in your own experience, we spent far too long examining everything which obstructed our retrieval of our desired item. There were a couple of boxes of

Tara's old toys which we had saved; the rest we had donated to charity or to the local hospital. There was a pile of old photograph albums, mostly of Robert's family on his father's side, all the cousins and aunts and uncles smiling with details underneath them of the time and date on which each photograph was taken, and the names of all those pictured. I made a mental note to retrieve them later, and add them to the other collections of family photographs, downstairs. There was a junk box, filled with old wires, machines which no longer bore any relevance to modern life, and a few tools which had long since passed their best. For some bizarre reason, there was also a tin of kitchen paint which had not been opened. None of which could Michael be persuaded to dispose; he cited that they should all be kept, "just in case". To think, men criticise women for not removing little-used shoes from our collections!

Finally, after forty-five minutes of procrastination and reminiscing, we uncovered the vacuum-packed rectangle of white material we sought. Emotion washed through me, spilling out in the form of tears. I felt Michael's arms around me as I sobbed; Zara had looked so lovely in the dress, and I missed her so very much. Each time there was a physical reminder that she and Robert were no longer here, grief attacked in the same, painful way. It was so unfair; I should not be playing the role of mother to Tara; it should be Zara who was going wedding dress shopping and colour matching name cards to the bridesmaid's dresses. Life is cruel.

In the familiar, gentle, way that he had, Michael reminded me that we had a job to do before Tara returned. I nodded, wiping the hot tears from my cheeks, and moved towards the ladder. I descended and waited for Michael to pass down the parcel to me. When we had locked the loft, we went into our bedroom and undid the vacuum pack. I unfurled the material within. The dress looked as perfect now as it did the day Zara wore it to marry Robert. The material between my fingers was silky and light, perfect for Tara's spring wedding. If what I wished came to fruition, this would become part of Tara's something old to wear on her wedding day.

I re-packed the dress, and left the bedroom with it in my arms, walking swiftly downstairs. Quickly kissing Michael goodbye, I grabbed the car keys from the bowl on the cabinet in the hallway, I drove to the nearest dry cleaners and asked for a twenty-four hour spruce up of the dress; it had been dry cleaned thoroughly before being packed away, yet I wanted to ensure it was extra fresh for Tara to try on. Returning home before Tara, I searched for the telephone number of the bridal boutique in town on the Internet search engine on my mobile telephone and made a quick call, explaining the situation and asking whether they could do any alterations if necessary. They readily agreed, and confirmed an appointment for Tara on the Saturday.

When the day arrived, I took three extra handbag sized packs of tissues with me to the boutique. Tara was full of chatter, ideas about styles of dress she might like, length of train and so forth. She was determined to wear white, telling me that she was entitled to do so. I was pleased to see that she had inherited her parents' strength of character. Some characteristics may well be genetic, rather than environmental. The bridal boutique smelt of vanilla and citrus. The carpet was so thick our shoes sank into it with each step. The smell of material drifted through the air as we brushed past the gowns hanging against the walls. The terracotta coloured furniture splashed colour in an otherwise white and cream room. There was a collage of brides on the rear wall, previous customers the assistant informed us, no doubt a bid to heighten the reputation of the boutique.

We sat with the assistant, who asked some questions about the venue, and Henry. The manager of the boutique came to say hello, also, giving me a knowing look when she realised who we were. I had dropped off Zara's dress the day before, allowing it to hang ready for Tara to try on during her appointment. Tara gave some vague answers to the kind of dress she wanted; she had not made up her mind because she was not certain which silhouette would suit her best. The manager smiled and assured Tara that she was sure she would leave with a suitable dress. Inside my head, I prayed that from her lips to God's ears that would be true.

Tara should have, traditionally, gone into the dressing room on her own. I could not, however, resist accompanying her there. The thick, heavy, white door's brass handle was pressed, and behind on the hanging rail on the rear wall hung Zara's dress. At first, with everything being a new experience, Tara's vision did not register the gown. And then, a sudden gasp reached my ears and I knew that she had noticed. She asked me in a broken voice if it was her mother's dress and I nodded, tears already in my eyes in a mixture of every emotion possible. She hugged me as tightly as she had when she was a tiny child, crying as she did. It was at that moment I realised this was a complete surprise; not once had she ever considered her mother's dress could be her own, also. I held her head in my hand, squeezing her tightly and running my thumb over her hair; her face pressed into my shoulder I heard her muffled declaration, "Aunt Mimi, I love you."

"I love you more."

She looked perfect. A vision of bridal beauty, and exactly like her mother. The resemblance was uncanny; it was as though I had been transported back a quarter of a century and I was looking into the face of my best friend once more. I told her she was beautiful, stunning, and that she looked radiant. I told her she looked so much like her mother, and that Zara and Robert would be so proud of her at that moment. I told her that they were looking down from heaven and smiling upon her; at that moment, I knew it to be true. I informed her that the dress was her something old, that garters were traditionally blue, and that she could borrow earrings from me if she would like to. She asked me what, then, would be her something new? It was then that we went shopping in the boutique for a veil, which, I informed her, her favourite aunt and uncle would be buying for her. Whilst Zara's dress was lovely, a classic style which held true through the decades, its veil was extremely dated. I could not allow Tara to wear it for fear the fashion police would arrest me on child cruelty charges.

At home that night, in bed, I held my husband in my arms for the first time in months. I told him how amazing Tara had looked, and how she was the spit and image of her mother. I told him he was going to struggle to prevent himself from crying when he walked her up the nave of the church to give her away at her wedding. He nodded, already knowing that to be true, no matter what she wore or looked like. To him, she could have worn a t-shirt and jeans to her wedding and still been the most beautiful girl on the face of the earth.

Nothing in the universe could match his love for the baby. Not even me.

We fell asleep in each other's arms, our hearts full of love for our daughter.

Chapter 37 – Happily ever after?

The next few months passed in a blur; Tara returned to university but came home for our last Christmas as a family of three. It was lovely, cosy, filled with food, lots of love, and lots of television. Mass was attended, gifts were exchanged, photographs were taken, and a lovely balance between being with us and Henry and his family happened through Tara's conscientiousness. We had brought her up to be a caring, loving and generous young woman. Of this, we were so very proud. Final preparations for the wedding were made, and I did everything I could to help relieve some of the stress and workload away from Tara and Henry. The house resembled something from an assault course, with boxes and piles of papers dotted around both the lounge and the dining rooms; invitations, invoices and order forms, receipts, seating charts and copies of the Order of Service, on embossed cream card stood in cardboard boxes along the skirting boards of the hallway. Henry's parents were also helping, and his mother and I were conversing on the telephone at least once a day. By the time St. Valentine's Day arrived, everything apart from a final fitting for Tara's wedding dress was completed. There was nothing left to do but wait.

It was not until one cold March day, when we were huddled on the sofa in the lounge watching an old film, a black and white romantic musical which involved a lot of top hats and dancing, that Michael told me that we needed to talk. Confused, I moved my body weight, from its most comfortable position, so that I was facing him. I remarked that his tone sounded serious and he confirmed that what he had to say was, indeed, worthy of careful consideration. Michael took his time broaching the subject, spending a lot of time fiddling with the crease above the knee of his trousers, staring at his fingers as he did so, but eventually he observed that in all the productivity of the wedding, we had failed to consider where we would live after Henry and Tara were married and graduated from university. He told me he had purchased boxes in preparation for moving, and that they were occupying the rear section of the garage, and that we needed to start packing our things imminently. I spent a while, it could have been a few minutes – it could have been an hour, mulling over what he had said. Taken aback – especially with his proactivity in the acquisition of boxes - I realised that he was, of course, as usual, correct. How had I not seen this looming over us? Was I willingly ignoring it, or had the thought just not occurred to me? The house we had spent so long living in, even called home for a while, was not ours. The mortgage had been paid off with the life insurance of our best friends, the title deed bequeathed to Tara, with us as her trustees until she was of an age to be able to cope on her own. Whilst she had long been that, we had remained in the property until she had completed university. Better somebody living in it whilst she was away, than it be empty and in danger of being pillaged by criminals. But, after graduation, two months after her wedding, Tara would need to return to a marital home of her own, with no adoptive parents in residence to infringe upon marital privacy, nor cramp their newlywed style.

So, what should we do? Michael, quickly, ran through some options he had clearly been considering for a long while; we had a large nest egg created from the money of both our houses' sales, years earlier. We could use that money to buy a house of a similar size, in the neighbourhood, for ourselves, to remain close to Tara and Henry – especially if they were to have children shortly after the wedding. I did not think this likely, as Tara was extremely career focused, but I did not know a Catholic couple who had not had children almost immediately after marriage. Michael also suggested that we could buy a property abroad and move somewhere warm and sunny, taking our career skills with us. We could buy a small house, work fewer hours and semi-retire and enjoy life. He also suggested buying a small house and investing some money in stocks and shares to provide a comfortable buffer for our retirement in what were becoming increasingly worrying financial times. In every scenario he presented, we were together for the rest of our lives.

I told him that we had some time to decide, and that I would think about what I wanted to do. If I am completely honest with you, I had not thought for a second about life after being Tara's mother, or her wedding. I did not see any sort of future for us, because I, simply, had not looked for one. I was at a loss for thoughts, for potential paths to walk. I was blind to my own future, having been so concerned with only Tara's for so long. My silence on the matter must have been deafening for Michael and, whilst I could usually discuss anything with him, I struggled to find the words to convey how focused I had been and how little I had thought about the long-term, life-after-Tara, scenario for us both. It must have seemed to him that I had neglected our marriage.

I am sure I do not have to tell you about the little voice in the back of my mind, nor its whisperings.

That night we slept on separate sides of the bed; the distance between us filled by our future.

When the week of her wedding arrived, Tara was so much a bundle of nerves and anticipation she struggled to stay still, or sleep. Michael and I tried to encourage her to calm herself, to rest, but our sentiments fell upon deaf ears. Children never listen. Tara was, of course, at home all week. She had been lucky with lectures and had more time away from university than others; she would have a week to return home, and then she would go back to university, after she and Henry returned from their honeymoon. The week before her wedding was spent with Michael and I sadly packing our belongings into boxes and making last minute wedding arrangements; double checking the guest list, the reception song list for the party after the meal, and rehearsing makeup and hair also took place. Tara had opted for a simple, elegant hair style, a half-up curled look which would remain a classic style and would not seem dated in her wedding photographs. Her makeup, too, would be simple, understated; she was so beautiful, she needed only a little to draw attention to her delicate features. We visited the local salon and had our nails done, acrylic extensions in neutral colours. Pampering oneself is such an indulgence when one considers the issues in the rest of the world, but there is just something so nice about making oneself look more polished.

The night before her wedding finally arrived. After we returned from Mass, Tara having gone to confession first, Michael made himself scarce, going to bed early but not before wrapping his arms around her and holding her close to him for a long hug, kissing her forehead and wishing his sweet girl goodnight, saying God bless and wishing her sweet dreams for the last time. Tara and I then made final arrangements for the morning. The flowers were to be delivered at 9am, sharp. Tara's friends would be arriving an hour earlier at the same time as the stylist, the cars would be collecting the bridesmaids and I at half past ten, Tara and Michael would follow ten minutes afterwards. We had made last minute telephone calls to the venue to ensure everything was arranged and organised, and double checked with the photographer that he would arrive at the same time as the flowers; the new trend being to have photographs taken to document the bridal party getting ready for the wedding, not merely the ceremony and the reception. He informed us that his assistant would be with Henry, taking similar photographs of the groom's party. Tara giggled at the prospect of Henry's friends in photographs alongside him; she had a hunch none of them could be trusted to take the day as seriously as she would have liked.

When all the telephone calls were finally made, and email confirmations read, I went into the kitchen to make a last-minute snack, something starchy in preparation for the undoubted copious alcohol intake in the next twenty-four hours. We watched a girly film and I insisted she have an early night, citing that she would need her rest and her strength for the next day. Unlike mine, her wedding would be a traditional affair, with a large reception and plenty of guests and well-wishers to converse with and thank for their attendance. I followed her upstairs and into her bedroom, and for the last time in her life tucked the covers over her shoulders, under her chin, swept her hair from her face and behind her ear, said a bedtime prayer with her, and leant forward and kissed her forehead goodnight. Just before I switched off the light as I left the room, I saw Zara's dress, Tara's dress now, hanging over the side of her wardrobe. It really was the most beautiful gown.

I missed my best friend.

I wished with everything I had, with tears in my eyes, that I had not had to be the one to tuck the baby in, that night.

Life is so cruel.

The next morning was a frenzy of activity. Tara's friends arrived earlier than they had planned, full of excitement and noise which was far too much for my ageing brain to cope with at seven o'clock. They bounded up the stairs, almost running Michael over as he made his way to the bathroom for a shower before the ladies occupied the house, and awoke Tara with squealing and repetitively singing the chorus of 'Get me to the Church on Time' at her. It was nice to see some traditions still lived on in the modern era.

Everything passed by in a blur, and I spent most of the morning fanning my face and swallowing hard, trying desperately not to ruin the makeup the stylist had so delicately applied to my face. Waterproof mascara is not all it is purported to be. This was especially challenging when I helped Tara with her veil; I had added the clip that Zara had used on her wedding day, another family heir loom for her to now receive and pass on when it was the next generation's turn. I had to tell Tara how it was part of her something old alongside her dress; that it had been passed down through several generations of her mother's family, and that her beloved mummy would be with her that day, would be watching over her, and would be prouder than any other mother to see the woman she had become. I told her I loved her, and we shared an awkward hug, trying desperately neither to crease dresses nor ruin any makeup.

When, finally, everybody was ready, and all the photographs had been taken, all the flowers distributed, it was time to leave. The bridesmaids and I hurried into the first car. Michael, who looked so handsome and dashing in his suit, and Tara followed us to the church, and we waited outside for her. She emerged from the car more beautiful than she had ever been before; it was as though the beauty of every previous day was amalgamated into that one moment. She was perfection. Michael offered Tara his arm and they ascended the steps and moved into the entryway of the church.

Father Philip greeted us with an uneasy look on his face. When Michael asked what was wrong, he informed us that Henry was not yet inside the church, that they were caught in traffic because of an earlier accident on one of the main roads. Henry had telephoned Father Philip so that Tara would not be left wondering what was happening. The police, Henry had told him, were working hard to divert everyone, but the roads were narrow and were not designed for large quantities of traffic. I glanced at Michael, we shared a knowing look and decided not to ask if it was a fatal car accident. No need to upset Tara any more than she already was. Father Philip kindly allowed us to use the sitting room of his house, attached to the church, to wait until Henry arrived. The bridesmaids volunteered to wait and to retrieve us when Henry was in front of the altar. Michael said he would stay with them, and greet the guests to fill the time. Tara and I were left alone.

When someone has something on their mind, yet they struggle to articulate what troubles them, they have a specific walk. A pacing, rather. They are weighed down by their troubles and the thoughts which consume their mind. Tara paced over the dull carpet of the sitting room, the train of her dress following her in circles. She reminded me so much of her father at that moment; she had the same posture he had had when he was pacing before asking me to choose an engagement ring for her beloved mother. For a while, I assumed she was worried about Henry, and her wedding, and dealing with a racing mind challenged by thousands of terrible images. In a croaky voice, when I asked her what on earth was wrong, she told me that the previous evening she had read the email I had sent after I had committed adultery.

I froze.

My spine froze, I felt the piercing cold spread from my heart backwards, to my spine, upwards to my brain, downwards to my hips, legs and feet, outwards towards my arms and everywhere in between. Stunned, I was a statue.

I was the exact opposite of everything I needed to be on that particular day, of everything I was duty-bound to be. I was not meeting the standards of motherhood I should have been. In

259

that moment, I had failed. Failed Michael, failed Will, failed Tara. Failed Zara and Robert.

At no point had I ever expected to hear this on her wedding day. I was so shocked I could not think. I knew this day would arrive, of course, at some point, and I had dreaded it since the day I sent the email. Since the day I succumbed to weakness. Since the day I cheated. But of all the days in the year, in her life, for her to have read that email, the eve of her wedding was the absolute worst. Why? Why did she have to read it that night? How had she got through them all so quickly? Despair threatened everything. Eventually, my legs thawed slightly, I sank down onto the sofa which was next to her under the weight of the enormity of the situation, and tried to calmly ask her what her thoughts were. I did not dare look at her, worried that she would have tears of shock and upset ruining her makeup, spoiling her beautiful face with red splotches of hurt. I was hesitant to admit that they may also be of anger. She told me that she did not know what to think. She told me that she was questioning everything she had ever known in her life. A natural reaction, I suppose. Did I regret writing the email? Perhaps then, for a second, the answer was yes.

Eventually I summoned the strength to take in the judgement on her face; I asked her if she had read all the words, she silently nodded in reply. I asked her if she believed me when I had said that I had not set out to cheat, that day. The words of the email were etched into my brain, I remembered them with ease as though I had written them only minutes before. Pinching her lips and furrowing her brow she, again, nodded silently. I asked her if she understood why it had happened. As soon as the words escaped my mouth, again my brain not engaging itself in rational thought before my body acted, I realised that was wholly the wrong question. I prayed she did not think that I wanted her to feel any guilt.

Deflecting the question, she asked me why I had married her Uncle Michael. Without allowing me a second to reply, she told me that she thought we were so happy, that she had wanted a marriage like ours. So, we had been able to keep up the pretence for all these years, after all! The words she whispered were accusatory in tone, almost as though discovering what I had done years before had demolished the sanctity, illusion, and aspirational ideals of marriage for her. She was seeking reassurance, in a way, that she was marrying for love and not because she thought she ought to because she had been in a relationship with Henry for so many years. A single question lit up my mind in fluorescent letters: had I ruined everything for her?

I realised that these thoughts, this situation, this conversation, would never have happened without the occurrence of a car accident.

And then she asked me if I had had second thoughts about marrying Michael, and I had no choice but to be honest with her and finally treat her, like the adult she was.

I told her that every bride is consumed by nerves on her wedding day. I told her that I had been no different. That nerves had gripped my body; dread had filled my soul. I told her that my hand shook as I placed it through the arm of my father before we walked up the nave to where her Uncle Michael was waiting for me. I described how my legs were unsteadied in my court shoes as they numbly made their way over the thick, red carpet in the middle of the church, sinking slightly into the fibres with each step. I confessed to her that my chest felt as though it had a dead weight sat upon it, in the middle of my sternum; that my lungs shook with trepidation, despite the deliberate breaths I was trying to take, that my lips parted and trembling as I desperately tried to control the flow of air through them. I told her it is exceptionally difficult to hide panicked breathing when a significant part of you wants to run away from something. I told her I knew I could not. Should not. That I had to do my duty. That I had to provide a stable life for her, ensure she had a high standard of care and love in her life. And so, I told her that this was what spurred me on to take the one hundred steps from the door, just as she would shortly do, past the Holy Water, up the nave and to the man who would become my husband, hoping and praying my resolve would last. I told her that she was marrying for love, not because she had to maintain a standard of care, or do her duty as I had done. I told her that she did not need to feel as I had.

Briefly, her eyebrows moved towards each other, imploring me to continue. I recounted how, as Michael and I stood next to each other before Father Philip, my knuckles tightened around my bouquet of flowers. Hot, moist palms made the material stem of the bouquet difficult to keep steady between my fingers, without betraying the shaking of my hands beneath. I told her I was glad Michael did not reach for my hand because it was holding the flowers; if he had, he would have discovered the regret, doubt and fear which rushed through me. I told her that my head was filled with words reminding me that I was doing this for her. I told her I took a moment to steel myself, and that in that moment I felt determined not to feel negatively anymore. I told her that this is, inevitably, what all brides must do on their wedding day.

She asked me if, at any point, I had wanted to stop the wedding; she wanted to know which part of the Mass I had found most difficult. I asked her which part she thought it had been, and she was correct in her answer; the part which mentioned forsaking all others. I think it was only then that she was truly aware of the sacrifice I had made, what I had given up for her. In her knitted brow was displayed the thoughts and imaginings of whether she would be able to give up Henry. I could almost see different scenarios behind her eyes, each one creating tears as she realised that she could not live without him; there was nothing in her life which was bigger than their relationship, larger than her happiness, no reason to sacrifice it. It was then she understood how much hurt she had caused me when she, a decade earlier, had told me I was not even her real mother.

I rushed over to her, handkerchief at the ready, ready to dab away the tears for fear she ruin the makeup which had taken two hours to complete. I told her that she should not cry. I told her that I would start crying if she did. I told her that she was worth it. That her life was much more important than mine, that she was the next generation and that the code of our humanity is faithful service to that unwritten commandment that says, "We shall give our children better than we ourselves had." That she would pass this on to her children when she made me a grandmother.

I held her in my arms, and it was almost the same feeling as the first time I met her; she was an additional centre for my universe to orbit. She was everything I had put my energies into over the last almost twenty years and I could not have been prouder of her at that moment. She was becoming a woman that day, creating a life and a family of her own, journeying to the future with the other half of her heart; her own soulmate to walk side-by-side with her through their life together. I prayed she would have the happiness I did not.

In a last bid to calm her nerves, and her mind, I told her what I knew to be true: there is nothing more important in your life than the people you choose to be part of it.

She nodded, knowing that she had chosen correctly.

Five minutes later, as I held her in my arms trying not to crease her gown, from the corner of my eye, through the window of the sitting room, I saw Michael walking towards the house. Henry had arrived and was waiting to become Tara's husband.

I walked back to the church on my own, trying to dab my face to remove any trace of tears. Michael was waiting with Tara, I knew he would be saying some last, fatherly, loving words to her: he would tell her how proud he was of her, I was sure; I knew he would tell her how much he loved her, and how Robert would be so proud of his little girl; I was certain he would tell her how beautiful she was, and how that if she ever needed him, he would always be there; and, I was absolutely positive, that he would tell her that if Henry did anything to hurt her, he would have to answer to her Uncle Michael.

I walked into the church, pressed my fingers into the Holy water and crossed myself. The church was bustling with whispers and the guests greeting one another; friends and family making introductions, hugging and kissing of cheeks occurring wherever I glanced. There was an atmosphere of happiness and joy in the air, one which I had not experienced in quite some time. I waved to a few people just as I caught a glimpse of a nervous, but happy, looking Henry at the head of the church. He looked so handsome in his morning suit. I would be proud to call him my son-in-law.

I glanced around, trying to take in all the flowers and decorations of the church. It looked so lovely, just like a movie. And then, as though in one final act of punishment, fate trod on my happiness once more. At the back of the church, in the very last pew, he sat. The one person who could ruin the day, the one person who could cause my rage and hatred to return: James Brimley.

I could feel my eyes piercing through him, anger consuming my face. I rushed towards the back of the church to shout at him to get out, to question how dare he be here on this day? To physically remove him from the church if I had to. Just before I got there, Father Philip stepped in front of me, and placed two firm hands on my shoulders, preventing me from exacting my revenge and causing a scene at my daughter's wedding. I wished Michael was there. Michael would have supported my actions;

Michael would have felt the same way I did. No. That was not true. I wished Will was there, we should have been at this wedding together, as a married couple with our own children in tow, at the front of the church with Zara standing in her place as mother of the bride and Robert walking his little girl towards her new husband.

Father Philip whispered in my ear that vengeance is not Catholic, and that I should hear James out before I did something I would later regret.

Father Philip clearly knew something I did not.

He ushered me towards the back of the church, outside the doors in the narthex. James Brimley followed us.

James began, stuttering over his words, by telling me he was sorry for upsetting me and that he meant no harm. He looked so much older than the last time I had seen him, so much more fragile. It was only then that I realised he was leaning on a walking stick. His hand shook as he tried to steady himself. I believed him. I truly did. It did not make me like his presence there any more than before, but I believed he was not there to cause trouble. He told me, in a shaky voice which had clearly seen happier years, that he was ashamed of his granddaughter, that she was still in prison for all the atrocities she had committed whilst she was serving her original time, and that he had cut all ties with her. I do not need to tell you what I felt at learning she did not have any freedom. I am certain you understand. The tone of his voice betrayed him; he felt guilty for not doing more for her, for not being there for her, for still caring about her after all she had done. He said that he wanted to see that Tara was happy, and that she had been able to have a good life despite what his granddaughter had done to her family. He told me, wiping his brow with his handkerchief, that he had pondered whether, or not, to buy a gift, or write a card, but did not know how much

Tara had known about her parent's accident. I asked him, after being able to calm down slightly, what he was planning to do for the rest of the day. He replied that his intentions were to stay for the wedding, to pray for her happiness, and then he would leave and go back to his home.

Looking at Father Philip, I knew he wanted me to make the right decision, to do the right thing. Father Philip could not ask any of his parishioners to leave the church, everyone was welcome, after all. Could I get past my rage? My anger? Could I be mature enough to realise that James' life was separate than that of his granddaughter's? Swallowing my pride, anger, feelings I suppose, I sighed and told him that nobody could ever have too many prayers said for them, and that he was welcome to stay for the wedding, but that the reception was full and I did not think it was appropriate to try to tell Tara who he was, on her wedding day of all days.

He nodded, with what looked like gratitude on his face and a weight lifted from his shoulders. I realised, in that moment, that it was not just Zara and Robert's life which had been stolen on that autumn day all those years ago; James had suffered irreparable damage, also.

Vengeance is not Catholic. But forgiveness is.

Father Philip smiled as I walked James back to his place at the back of the church. I placed my hand on his and smiled a half smile, before walking up the side of the church, up the aisle, and to my place just before Michael appeared at the back of the nave, Tara on his arm looking perfectly beautiful and the music began.

So did my tears.

I was happy, for the first time in years.

~~~~~

"By the power vested in me, I now pronounce you husband and wife."

With these words from the mouth of Father Philip at the altar at the head of the church, an echoing coming from the high, hollow ceiling, a rush of emotion runs through me. Pride, happiness, joy, love and a feeling of overwhelming contentment expands from my heart through my veins to every, last nerve ending I possess in my body. If it were possible for me to glow with this sense of wonderment, I would be as bright as the sun on a cloudless day. And yet, at this very same moment, a feeling of sadness, despair and anguish flows through me. My emotions are threatening to spill out of me in the form of tears, conspiring to ruin the moment, the day, and reveal my anguish. A smile spreads over my face, and indeed within my heart, but a small, yet loud, part of me howls in dismay for the people who are missing; unable to witness this moment of happiness, the start of this journey.

Would Tara and Henry live happily ever after?

I, truly, hoped so.

Chapter 38 - Aftermath

The wedding was beautiful. The reception was wonderful. Everyone in attendance enjoyed themselves. I did not see James Brimley after we had left the church. He must have left before the procession down the nave. Perhaps during the signing of the registers.

We have danced all night and now my feet hurt. Michael has twirled me around the dancefloor until I thought I was going to collapse. My sides hurt from all the fun, frivolity and laughter. Not long ago, I realised how much I truly do love him: my rock through all these years. My friend. All the food has been eaten, or put into doggy bags for guests to take home, including slices of the wedding cake. The top layer, of course, will go back home for the freezer; hopefully it will be needed in the not-too-distant-future for a Baptism.

We have all waved Tara and Henry off on their honeymoon, Henry's gift to his new wife. But before she left, Tara hugged both Michael and I one last time; squeezing us with as much strength as she could muster so that we know how much she loves and appreciates us. She whispered something into my ear, but I could not quite make it out through the ambient sound of the party and everyone else's well-wishes. It sounded as though she said something about making a telephone call, but about what I could not hear. Perhaps she was talking about the cab company to arrange a taxi home for Michael and I, since we were both on the tipsy side of sober. She told me she loved me, thanked me for everything, and that she was happy and hoped I was, too. I merely nodded, in a bit of a daze and unable to really tell her I loved her too in any great detail, for fear of bursting out into a flood of tears, again, and happily waved her off.

The bridesmaids have taken all the gifts back to the house. We have said goodbye to all the guests, the last one to leave was very tipsy and struggled to get into the back of the taxi which had been called for him - one of Henry's friends, I think. I have not told Michael about James, there is no need to trouble him with details like that today. Michael does not need to know about that. After all, there has been no harm done.

I sigh, weary after the long day.

Silence falls between Michael and I, and I am looking out into the darkness of the evening, and I realise what Tara said to me.

Crystal blue eyes meet mine, and my heart stops in my chest, just for a second. I am frozen to the spot I stand on. Dressed in a sharply cut suit for the occasion, looking as beautiful as ever, my *everything* appears about twenty-five feet in front of me, at the edge of the car park. If I reach my hand out, can I touch him? Can I place my hand over his heart? Can I hold his face in my hands? Can I press my lips to his and tell him I love him? Is he really here? Is he real?

When my heart starts beating again, it once more beats for him.

Michael has not seen him; he turns to face me, breaking the connection between Will and I with his chocolate brown eyes, full of love and compassion, and asks, "What's next?"

And so now I stand here, a crossroads before me. I must move out of the house which has been my home for so many years before Tara and Henry arrive back from their honeymoon. Most of my boxes are already packed; there is not much to show of my life as her mother. So, do I move to be with Michael? Do I go it alone? Or do I walk towards my *everything* and try to recover my life with him?

What would you do if you were in my position, faced with this choice?

I take a deep breath, squeeze my lips together, nod my head once, and move my feet forward.

I have made up my mind.

About the Author

Louise Hazeldine was born in England in 1982. She graduated from Staffordshire University with a 2:1 BA(Hons) English degree, in 2012.

If you wish to follow Louise Hazeldine, you can do so @LouiseHazeldine on Twitter and Instagram. You can also follow her on Facebook at www.facebook.com/LouiseHazeldineAuthor/

You can also visit her website www.louisehazeldine.co.uk for updates, her blog, and much more.